Constitutionalists

The McGowan Collection Series:

Book 10

Col. Lee Martin

Terry S. Byrnes, CPPB
Contributing Editor
I.E.R. Media

That which does not kill me is a tactical error on your part.

- *Bruce McGowan*

The McGowan Collection
Series Website:

https://colonelleemartinbooks.com

All Rights Reserved
Copyright © 2024

Edited and Produced by:
I.E.R. Media
Printed in the United States of America

ISBN: 979-8-9897104-4-7 (pbk)
 979-8-9897104-5-4 (ebk)

Because of the dynamic nature of the Internet, any Web addresses or links contained in this book may have changed since publication and may no longer be valid. This is a work of fiction. All of the characters, names, incidents, organizations, and dialogue in this novel are either the products of the author's imagination or are used fictitiously.

Table of Contents

Chapter One 1

Chapter Two 14

Chapter Three 27

Chapter Four 38

Chapter Five 49

Chapter Six 60

Chapter Seven 69

Chapter Eight 75

Chapter Nine 87

Chapter Ten 97

Chapter Eleven 107

Chapter Twelve 117

Chapter Thirteen 126

Chapter Fourteen 134

Chapter Fifteen 148

Chapter Sixteen 160

Chapter Seventeen 166

Chapter Eighteen 173

Chapter Nineteen 183

Chapter Twenty 194

Chapter Twenty-One 200

Chapter Twenty-Two 209

Chapter Twenty-Three 217
Chapter Twenty-Four 226
Chapter Twenty-Five 234
Chapter Twenty-Six 241
Chapter Twenty-Seven 249
Chapter Twenty-Eight 262
Chapter Twenty-Nine 269
Chapter Thirty 276
Chapter Thirty-One 283
Chapter Thirty-Two 291
Chapter Thirty-Three 301
Chapter Thirty-Four 308
Chapter Thirty-Five 318
Chapter Thirty-Six 330
Chapter Thirty-Seven 341
Chapter Thirty-Eight 350

Chapter One

I hadn't taken my baby out for a drive for weeks. I've kept her under wraps now for twenty years, ever since my ex-wife, Darlene, relinquished her to me in gratitude for saving our daughter's life. Darlene had gotten possession of her in our divorce and had held her hostage all that time I was away from home, taking down bad guys, terrorist elements, and other threats to our lives, liberties, and pursuits of happiness. But then, after my ex had pursued her happiness, remarried, and mellowed out for a few years, she released my beautiful, British-Racing-Green Austin-Healey 3000 with saddle leather interior and wide, toothy grille. It was the one thing in my life besides my lovely second wife and my daughter, Caroline, that has meant the world to me. Everything else I could lose and declare good riddance.

Few other things in this world are so glorious as a West Virginia fall. Century-old maples, full of blood-red leaves, ash, and hickory, showcasing their leaves of yellow-gold and purple leaf sourwood against a forest of evergreen cypress; such beauty will often compel me to stop along the highway and click off a volley of pix on my Nikon. There is that hint of woodsmoke, never pungent enough to spoil the fresh, crisp autumn air. And then there are those long shadows created by towering pines that stretch across emerald-green meadows and bone-white fences, making for a picture-postcard day.

Col. Lee Martin

That day, as I stood beside my Healey, taking in deep breaths of the light, intoxicating breeze, playing on my car radio, were some of my favorite ballads from the '60s... Etta James' At Last, Andy Williams' Moon River, and The Vogues' Turn Around, Look at Me. Nice. The music added a sweet ambiance to my view. A view like what I remember seeing in movies such as The Sound of Music, Far and Away, and Under the Tuscan Sun. From where I was perched on a high pull-off area, I began sweeping my eyes over the panoramic Greenbrier Valley. Below me lay large, white farmhouses and red barns, bales of rolled hay, and smatterings of Black Angus, Gelbvieh, and Herefords. One of those farmhouses belonged to my family. My brother Joey still lived there with his wife.

Being so far away from the hustle, noise, and chaos of a big city, I was enjoying a wonderful life there in Greenbrier County, West Virginia. I was no longer chasing down rake-hellish miscreants, nor was I at the beck and call of federal law enforcement. I was retired. Been retired for ten years. The only person I answered to was the lovely Adriana McGowan, my wife of nineteen years. I was enjoying a wonderful life, and all was right with the world. The only thing that would spoil a day like I was having would be a sudden thunderstorm. I'd then have to drive back home with my top up.

But when I'd arrive home, Adriana would not be there. She was again in Florida at her parents' house. Her mother had fallen, and as many of the elderly are prone to do, she broke her hip. I was going to be bacheloring for a couple of weeks. Not much would change. I'd still be tending to chores around the house, inside and out, meeting three of my buds at the local golf course on Friday morning and taking our new pup, Lionel, out for a run and his daily constitutional. I named him after my boss

The Constitutionalists

who commanded the counterterrorist division where I spent a dozen years after my career with the FBI.

I'd be on the road for about two hours if my GPS was accurate. The suspension on my 52-year-old Healy was as tight as I remember it being when I bought it. Although it didn't handle like modern-day sports cars, it still ate up the curves and hills like it was glued to the road. Of course, the skill of its driver had a lot to do with it. The engine groaned a bit on the steep grades but settled down to hum on the straightaways like it was singing a sweet song. Having upgraded its sound system with a CD player, I chose to shut off the radio, considering its reception was failing. I then put on something classical…Requiem.

As I mentioned that two-hour drive, I was on my way upstate to Harrison County where I had heard from a mutual friend that one of my Zulu team partners, now retired like me, was running a country store that also supplied hunters and fishers of the mountain streams with ammo, bait and camping equipment. I couldn't imagine multilingual, highly cultured Kurt Albrecht going from Brooks Brothers suits to bib overalls and plaid shirts. But maybe he just owned the place and had a couple of good, ol' mountain boys running it. As he did not know I was on my way up to see him, chances are he might not even be there.

I stopped about halfway up at a roadside store for a ham sandwich and Coca-Cola where I also found a good bit of local color, meaning good country people, and then pulled back onto the road. My spiffy sports car captured a lot of curious looks from the likes of farmers, miners and retired codgers driving rugged-looking pickups for the most part. I took it not many people in the backcountry of "West-by Gawd" Virginia, ever

Col. Lee Martin

saw an Austin-Healey or anything that resembled one. Nor had they seen very many dudes like me wearing a tweed, Gatsby flat cap. But when a guy is driving a classic Austin Healey, he has to look the part.

Just after eleven-thirty, I spotted Kurt's store on the left side of the road. The sign on the roof that read Kurt's Store was my clue I had the right place. Pulling off the road, I parked the green hornet among what appeared to be a dozen pickups…Fords, Dodges, Chevys, and an ancient International. No foreign makes. Mountain boys don't buy Toyotas and Nissans. However, I was determined I wouldn't be intimidated when I pulled my British gem in between two jacked-up American-made beasts.

Upon exiting the Healey, I immediately caught sight of two good ol' boys having late morning Budweisers, wearing soiled work jackets, ball caps that read John Deere and Red Man, and packing automatics on their hips. As they eyed me like I was from another world, I did toss my flat cap onto the passenger seat. When I then took off my light Greg Norman jacket and laid it on the seat, I exposed the fact that I was also carrying…as I always did…my Springfield Armory XDM. It was not an intent on my part to let them know I could be ready for a gunfight if necessary; I was only informing them that although I might look like a city-slicking pansy, I wasn't. As I walked by them toward the door, they both nodded howdy, and I returned the gesture.

The moment I stepped through the door I was hit with a dozen smells and odors…stink bait lying in the open air, stale spilled beer, cigarette and cigar smoke, leather goods and ramps cooking on a camp stove of sorts to name a few. However, the smell that drew me to the counter was coffee. I needed a cup. I thought about ordering something, like a soy latte, caramel macchiato, or frappe to get a laugh out of the gaggle of rough-looking mountain boys just standing around, but I thought I'd probably get beat up once I went back out to the parking lot. So, in my gruffest voice, I said, "Coffee...black."

"Comin' right up," was the response from the husky woman behind the counter with the smoker's voice, hairy arms and lip full of Skoal. Not the face of somebody you want to turn over in the morning and see first thing. After she had poured the nectar, which resembled used motor oil, she added,

"H'aint seen you in here before. Passin' through?"

"Just out for a long drive. From Greenbrier County."

"Gawd's country, people say. But to me, this is what Gawd had in mind for Almost Heaven."

"Yeah. I can see that. Like the John Denver song."

"Who's that?"

"You know...the singer-song writer...*County Roads, Take Me Home...*"

"I know the damn song...just don't know where it came from."

"I thought everybody knew...never mind." I wasn't going to go any farther with it. She'd think I thought she was an uninformed moron, and she'd be right. But she was also wearing a gun...a .357.

Col. Lee Martin

The coffee was strong, as I expected, but good. As I stood looking around, I saw that every eye in the place was on me. Curious, even suspicious eyes. It was a bit unnerving, to say the least. I thought maybe I recognized a few of the faces from the movie Deliverance or maybe from that reality show actually set in that part of the state called Appalachian Outlaws. It was about Ginseng hunters. The face I didn't see was that of Kurt Albrecht. The last time I saw him was maybe ten years back when he took over Team Yankee, the companion counterterrorist team to my Team Zulu. He didn't look anything like these long-haired, bearded types.

But just when I was about to ask one of them if he was around, I felt a hand on my shoulder. I think I actually jumped.

"Aut viam inveniam aut faciam." I then relaxed and translated it back to him to English.

"I will either find a way or make one." It was Kurt. He had quoted our team motto.

"Hello, Scorpion," he said.

"What the hell are you doing up here?"

"I can ask you the same thing, Raven." Scorpion and Raven were our code names in the state department's respective counterterrorist teams. I hardly recognized him. Short-cropped beard and dressed in a denim shirt with jeans to match, he looked 25 years older. His blonde hair had partially turned white and was now down over the collar of his shirt.

The eyes were the same, however, still unwavering and piercing.

"Well, I didn't fall off the world, if that's what you're insinuating. I was tired of the federal law enforcement game and came up here thinking I just wanted to hunt and fish. No more hunting terrorists. The four-legged types don't shoot back."

"But I always thought you enjoyed "the challenge and the kill" part of our game. At least that's how you phrased it."

Kurt looked down at the wooden floor and shook his head. "I'm different now, Bruce. I guess you could say I changed both my politics and my way of thinking. Then I had a bit of a run-in with the new division chief and retired from the state department. However, regardless of what's happening with this new administration, I'm still a patriot."

"But what planted you here?"

"Me. I had to get away from the phony suits in Washington, D.C. I couldn't take the lies and liberalism that began festering like a sore. Actually, the sores have been there for years and guys like me never opened our eyes. As I remember, you were openly critical of what was happening as well."

"Yeah, but I didn't separate myself from civilization, Kurt. As you remember, I was newlywed, and my wife was a big part of my decision to retire. I no longer had to "play the game" in the Washington environment. I rarely even watch the news. It turns my stomach."

Col. Lee Martin

"And that's the reason I'm out here."

"But how has your wife adjusted to it?"

"Karen?" He looked back down at the floor. "She died about five years ago. She didn't like it here very much, even though I built her a nice house with all the modern conveniences. She wasn't near any malls or nice restaurants, and I saw her go downhill. She became really sick, and the doctors didn't know why she was deteriorating. It was not long after she passed, I realized that it was likely her depression that wore her down. Her heart just stopped one day."

He then looked up at me with tears glistening in his eyes. "I as much killed her, Bruce."

I shook my head. "You didn't talk about it with her?"

"I tried. She didn't want to disappoint me. Said she loved me and would live with me anywhere and under any conditions. I believed her, but I should have seen that she was just appeasing me. It was the worst decision I had ever made coming here…asking her to stay with me."

"And you're still here."

"And I'm not leaving. I bought this store just before she died; it was my salvation. It's a place a lot of good-hearted people like you see standing here enjoy coming to. I stock it with goods they like and need for their way of life that they can't get in a regular store. Look around. Much of this you won't find at Kroger, Home Depot or even Bass Pro. These people are my family now. We never had kids and I never cultivated friendships anywhere else like I have here in Harrison County."

I nodded but didn't reply.

"So, how did you find me, Bruce?"

"You remember Kenny Darby, who was one of the analysts in the counterterrorist division? When he retired, he settled in my area. He goes to our church. We were talking one day at the A&P grocery, and he told me about you."

"Yeah, he mentioned that. He comes up every once in a while, to fish our streams. I've gone trout fishing with him a few times. And so you came up here today to look me up."

"My wife Adriana is out of state for a couple of weeks to tend to her mother. It was a beautiful fall morning and I decided to take a drive through the upstate. You had, for some reason, been on my mind, and I just decided to drive up."

"Glad you did, old man. I see you're still packing."

"As is everybody in your store."

"It's a different world, Bruce. You know that. I don't have to worry about getting mugged, car-jacked, or even killed way out here, but one never knows when the city filth will come up here to make trouble. And as you can see, if the government comes here and tries to take guns and other property from these good people, these woods will be lit up with spent ammo. There are more weapons and militia types in West Virginia alone than in several Army divisions."

"I have no doubt some of those good people you are talking about are right here in this room."

"The FBI has turned into an evil, liberal, racist organization, Bruce. I know you are retired Bureau, and I hope you're not taking offense, but we both know it's not the same honorable federal law organization it once was."

I didn't comment. Neither did I nod in agreement. The Bureau had been good to me and I still had a lot of friends in the organization.

"Why don't you come up here and hang out with us this weekend? You're not that far away."

"Who's us? These guys here?"

"And others. Tell you what, Bruce. We've had a population growth of coyotes recently, especially in the farm area of the county. They've been raiding chicken coops and even calves. Farmers have killed a few but haven't made a dent in the number. How about since your wife is out of town, you coming back next week and spend a couple days at my cabin. Bring some long-range firepower."

"You know, I'd actually like to do that. It's been a good while since I was out in the woods."

"There are two or three guys I'm sure would like to go out with us. I sold my house a couple of years back and now live in the cabin. It's large enough to bunk a half dozen fellows. Sometimes I have meetings there."

"What kind of meetings?"

"Kind of like lodge meetings. Close knit group, we are."

"Lodge, huh? Like the Elks or Lions?"

"Not exactly, but you'll find out. Maybe you'd like to join us?"

"I live over two hours away, Kurt. I wouldn't be attending too many meetings."

"Well, anyway, you might find you have a lot of things in common. What day can you be here?"

"Today's Wednesday. How about the day after tomorrow? I could spend two or three days. My wife Adriana just left a couple days ago and won't be back for a while."

"Friday is good, then."

I looked again at a large flag on the wall behind the counter. It was black, which has always been the color preferred by anarchists. In its center was a white sword against the background of a golden griffon. Below it were the words "Audemus Jura Nostra Defendere. Nihil Obstat." He saw me studying the flag.

"My Latin is a little rusty," I said. I can pick out a couple of words, but…"

"It says: We dare defend our rights. Nothing stands in our way."

"Which is about…"

"It's a mountain code, Bruce. These guys are a proud Mountaineer bunch. We're our own people up here…not to be messed with."

I looked around the room at the faces…rugged, bearded, fierce. "I can believe it."

Albrecht then placed his hand on my shoulder. "Well, Irma is giving me a signal. Guess I'd better get back to my job in running this place."

"Irma's your coffee maker?"

"Yeah. Good people she is."

"Someone I wouldn't want to meet in a dark alley."

Kurt laughed. "She can handle herself…and that's a .357 magnum she's packing."

"I'll need to be getting along as well, Kurt. Great seeing you after all this time. And I look forward to Friday."

He nodded, smiled, and turned heel.

The Constitutionalists

As I headed toward the door, the eyes were back on me. The men had stood talking and drinking the entire time I was in the store. I didn't see any of them leave. The thing was, this was a weekday and I wondered why they weren't at work. Did they even have jobs? I knew unemployment was rather high in that part of the state. Maybe they were part of it.

On the way back down the mountain road into what I would call civilization, I kept the radio off to mull over everything that I saw around the store and heard from Kurt. The stone faces and searing eyes of the men were still in my brain, and so were some of the things that Kurt had said. Where was this 'lodge' he talked about and why was there a flag with Latin words that likely none of the men in that store understood? There was that reference to the number of guns that could fend off Army divisions. I had questions and will hopefully be learning the answers.

Okay, I must confess. My trek upstate to Kurt's Store was not just a leisurely drive on a nice fall day to see an old friend. Even though I'm no longer in government, I was there on government business.

Chapter Two

It is said that age is just a number. I would agree with that unless you're talking 95 or so. I'm in my late sixties, a jogger, and at 6 feet tall and 170 pounds, in as good a shape as I've ever been. I've been mistaken for a 50-something-year-old at times. Yes, I have my share of physical maladies, but I don't dwell on them. Still, I relish the fact that I'm retired. Adriana and I no longer even have a B&B business. Wolf Laurel is merely our residence. We're still living comfortably on the cool million I was paid by our government for killing The Viper a few years ago. He was the number one terrorist in the world after the takedown of bin Laden. Actually, I didn't pull the trigger on the Viper. My friend, sniper extraordinaire Atticus Steed, took off the top of his head with a 7.62 round at over a thousand meters.

Even though I was called back into action several times as a contractor after I retired from the State Department counterterrorist unit, I have kept promising my wife and partner I will no longer be going after terrorist threats…regardless of the fact I was and still would be the best in the business if I chose to stay in the game. I don't do things behind Adriana's back. So, even though she would be out of town for a spell, would I do it if I received a call to 'make something happen' while she was gone? I have to plead the 5th on that.

Allow me to go back a few days. Two days before my morning drive to Kurt's Store, National Security Advisor Ben Marshall

The Constitutionalists

called me. About three years before, Ben had replaced my old friend, Preston Johns, who had been in that position throughout two different administrations. Ben had had a similar career as mine, except he was ATF before he became a counterterrorist asset for the Department of Homeland Security. However, I had crossed paths with him on a few cases and although we were not what one would call friends, we had been close collaborators.

"Bruce got something we'd like you to do."

Quickly, I replied, "No. Won't happen."

"Uh, what do you mean 'won't happen.' You haven't heard what it is."

"Why me? You have assets."

"Hear me out. We just need…"

"No. Go to someone else with your need."

"Come on, Bruce. Give me a chance here."

"Alright, I'm being rude. What?"

"You have an old friend and co-worker living not too far away. You, of course, remember Kurt Albrecht."

"Yes. Why are you mentioning him?"

"We think he's gone rogue."

Col. Lee Martin

"He's retired. How can you go rogue when you no longer work for the government?"

"As you must realize, those retired who had a secret, top secret, and especially sensitive compartmented information clearances are charged with maintaining their confidentiality and silence post-service on classified matters as well as maintaining their allegiance and public trust. You people had the highest level of clearance."

"So, has he sold classified information to the enemy?"

"No. He could actually *be* the enemy."

"What? What are you talking about?"

"We suspect that he is the leader of a subversive militia having anarchist plans to either attack government agencies and constituents at their locations or, worse, attempt an overthrow of the government itself. Albrecht is just the man with the knowledge, skills, and abilities to train and lead elements in attacks on government resources, especially those that are lesser secured or understaffed."

Couldn't be, I thought. Not Kurt. I remembered him as a super patriot…trustworthy, dependable, mission-oriented.

"Are you sure about your information, Ben? I was pretty damn close to Albrecht."

"That's why I'm calling you. Domestic intel sources from the nearby NCIC location in Clarksville and a mole we planted in that organization, who by the way was found face-down in a local creek, have provided credible information. There is supposedly an armed militia of over 300 men and woman somewhere in those hills in a three-county area."

"And so what do you want me to do…go put Albrecht down?"

"Not exactly. We thought since you're living a couple of hours from his location, you could get reacquainted with him for old times' sake and nose around to see if you can pick up on anything. He owns a store under his name. Go reconnect and spend some time with him."

"I know about the store. Also heard about Kurt's retirement venture from a mutual friend. And my remuneration?"

"As a contractor, you'll make five grand a day."

"How many days?"

"You should gain enough knowledge and be able to report back within five days."

"Up to 25 grand then."

"You think you nosing around is worth more?"

"It's enough…unless I'm found out and get zapped."

"In that case, then it's definitely enough. Dead men don't spend money."

"Funny. So, why don't you have the Bureau on this?"

"First, you know him and can gain his trust. Nobody I know in the Bureau of Counterintelligence is as cool and coy as you. Those boys are too regimented and Joe Friday-like. They'd be found out in two minutes. Just get inside for a few days; watch and listen; try finding out who they are and if you can verify what our intel provided. Let Albrecht see that you're sympathetic…that the government is NOT for the people and must be taken down…stuff like that. The more you convince him you're on his side, the more you'll learn. Do and say whatever you need in order to gain his trust."

"In other words be a mole."

"You have the savvy to do this, Bruce. Do your country a service just one more time. Make it happen."

"So, what you're saying is you want me to join their organization."

"Not in so many words. You're a creative guy. Find a way to spend some time with your old friend and get inside his head. If your findings reinforce what intel we already have, I will be speaking with the Bureau's director, and he'll send in his SWAT element."

"It had better be a force larger than a SWAT element, and they'd have to hit these guys when they're congregated in something like a force-wide meeting or training exercise."

"And maybe you can find out when that will be."

I let out a sigh. "Give me a day to think about it. This won't be an easy task."

"How about half a day? Call me this evening."

"Alright. I'll also be thinking if you're paying me enough."

"God and country, Bruce."

"Right. Talk later, Ben."

And so, after our phone call, I did begin thinking about it. Maybe I'd first go on a casual recon. Wednesday might be a good day. If I saw enough in my initial contact to consider Albrecht and his mountain goons a genuine threat, I'd come up with an infiltration plan. I figured I had a few days to devise one.

That same day, following an early afternoon jog from Wolf Laurel through the Greenbrier countryside and back, I settled into my easy chair with a Coors Light to think. Lionel jumped up on my lap and buried his nose into the chair's puffy arm. He was tired, not yet being all that used to my jogging pace. His little beagle legs had run as fast as they could, but I had spared him that afternoon from over-exertion by cutting my usual runtime in half. As he got older and more programmed to both my pace and distance, he'd stay with me. As I got older, I might then have trouble keeping up with him.

So, how would I carry off this infiltration? If I found that Kurt was the leader of a 300-man right wing extremist force, I'd first be gaining his trust… convincing him how tired I also was of the liberal politicians now in control of the legislature. And how lame was this new president? Mr. Tax and Spend. An inept, self-serving, and indecisive leader. How he had practically ignored the veterans and police, placing more emphasis on programs that fostered early criminal release and those that benefitted illegal immigrants. It would be easy for me to feign supporting the mission of this so-called mountain militia since I myself had been critical of our current liberal government. Would Kurt believe me if I agreed that anarchy and revolution was what the people needed? Maybe another civil war? Apparently, I had to gather my intel within five days or less. How would I do that? How would I be able to put myself inside? And how long would it actually take to gain the information I needed? Five days might not be long enough.

Later that same evening before I talked to Marshall again, I called to check on Adriana.

"Hey, Love. How are things in Florida?"

"Mom's still in the hospital but will go to a rehab center tomorrow for physical therapy. She'll be there a week and then a therapist will come to the house three times a week thereafter to work with her. She's in good spirits, though, and so happy I came down to do for her. And how is my husband?"

"Living the good life, my dear. Just Lionel and me."

"How can you be living the good life without me?"

"Hmmm. You got me on that one. Let's just say I'm doing the best I can on my own. Lionel and I went for a run earlier and I heated up one of the meals you left me. The meatloaf and mashed potatoes dinner was dee-lish."

"You're not feeding him any table food, are you?"

"No. Just the Puppy Chow."

"And just make sure when you open the door he doesn't run out. Beagles are known to take off on adventures and never come back. And be sure he's on a leash when you go for a run."

"Yes, Mother."

"Oh, stop that. If I were your mother, I would have done a better job raising you." She then laughed.

"We're doing fine here. My face is always wet because the little guy can't control his licker."

She laughed. "I've thought about you boys all day long today."

"Used to be you just thought about me."

"Are you jealous there's another love in my life?"

My turn to laugh. "He began whining as soon as you left the house. But don't worry; I'm taking good care of him. But enough about Lionel. Now talk about me…how you love me and can't live without me."

"Oh, you know that's the case. You are staying out of trouble, aren't you? You haven't accepted any missions from the government, have you?"

Col. Lee Martin

I had to smile. Was she a psychic? Did she somehow know I had been talking with the National Security Advisor who wanted me to do some Sneaky-Pete work? And how many times had I done work for the government since I retired?

> "Don't you worry about that, darlin.' My days of danger are long behind me."
>
> "Except when we were on vacation in Paris. I'm not soon forgetting that one."
>
> "And you know that wasn't my fault. An old nemesis came out of the woodwork like the roach he was, and set all that up."
>
> "I know, I know. But next vacation I plan."

We talked for another ten or so minutes about nothing, punctuating the conversation with some lovey-dovey junk and then said goodnight.

A minute later I made that second call.

> "Okay, Mr. Marshall, I'll go see Kurt Albrecht. I'm considering it a recon for now. If there's an opportunity to spend some time nosing around later, I'll make it happen."
>
> "Thanks, Bruce. When are you going up there?"
>
> "I think Wednesday, two days from now."
>
> "Good. I'll look forward to your preliminary."

That was my initial conversation about Albrecht.

And so it was that Wednesday afternoon following my trek upstate to Kurt's place, I called Marshall again and told him my plan.

"Coyote hunting, huh?"

"Will get in a little target practice with my .308 at the same time seizing any opportunity to learn more about this alleged insurgent group."

"Not alleged, Bruce. We know they're out there; we just don't know what their plans are…and when Albrecht will carry them out."

"Well, Albrecht and company are not going be all that transparent with someone like me, especially in as little as three to five days. Kurt knows me and that I am historically loyal to the government. He knows I wouldn't actively sign on with any plans to attack government resources…or in any way be supportive of an insurgency."

"Maybe not; but I know you're resourceful and have a very convincing personality. Although a lot of your own missions were considered clandestine even to people like me, your name and reputation got out there. You have uncanny abilities and insights for uncovering and assessing threats. You're the first person my predecessor told me about. Preston Johns said you have the very nose that can sniff out terrorist threats like nobody else."

"A nose that got bloodied a few times. However, you can stop with all the accolades. I said I would give this a shot. I just don't know how much I can learn. These people are close-knit and tightlipped. Many are likely former military and have fought for this country. I doubt they will so quickly turn heel and fight against it. There has to be some reluctance to do so within the organization."

"And those would be the very people who might loosen their lips."

"I'll be up in that country only three days. What time I'm not on a hunt for coyotes I'll be bunking with a half dozen guys in Albrecht's cabin. There'll be ample opportunities for dialogue, I'm sure. I don't know at this point whether any of these people are part of any subversive organization. But if they are, will they be so free to talk about it? Again, it's only Albrecht who knows me. I'd think he would keep them from letting anything slip."

"But he might see an opportunity to try recruiting you."

"He knows I live down in the valley over two hours away. I wouldn't be much good to him."

"Do you remember me mentioning there were several counties involved in his organization? Greenbrier has a small element in his militia, we think fifteen or twenty men. If Albrecht tries to bring you in, he might suggest you join up with them."

"All speculation at this point. I'll be back sometime Monday and will give you a report. One other thing…on the wall at Kurt's Store was a large flag with a Latin inscription. It was black, which represents anarchy, with a sword and griffon in its center. Have you seen anything like that?"

"Yes. The sword would represent strength and might. You probably saw that the griffon had the head, wings and talons of an eagle and the body of a lion. It's the symbol of valor, military courage and leadership. I suspect you'll see that same flag other places. It would be the banner they'd carry into battle."

"Battle? You think they'll plan a battle?"

"Maybe. But we're damn sure they're planning some kind of covert activity against a government element or facility. That's one piece of intel our mole provided before they killed him. We just don't know where or when."

"Okay, Ben. I'm set. Anything else?"

"Just watch your back. I'm not asking you to go there just to end up face down in a creek. This is a dangerous bunch and if Albrecht gets the slightest hint you're there because we sent you there…"

"You forget who you're talking with, my friend."

"Yeah."

"We'll talk again Monday."

Col. Lee Martin

"Good luck, Bruce."

Chapter Three

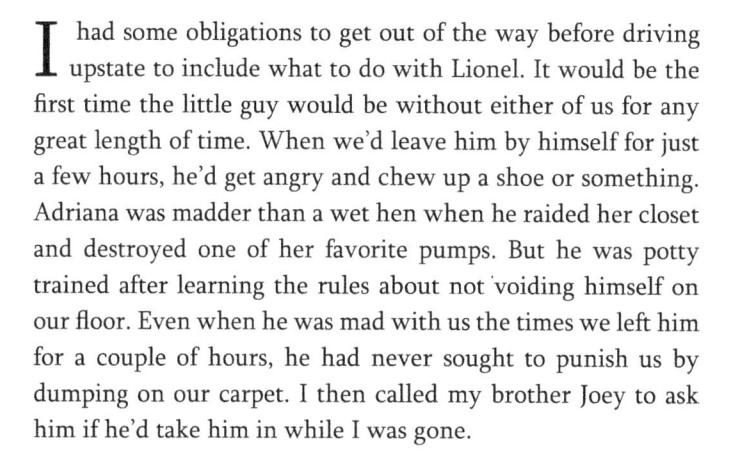

I had some obligations to get out of the way before driving upstate to include what to do with Lionel. It would be the first time the little guy would be without either of us for any great length of time. When we'd leave him by himself for just a few hours, he'd get angry and chew up a shoe or something. Adriana was madder than a wet hen when he raided her closet and destroyed one of her favorite pumps. But he was potty trained after learning the rules about not voiding himself on our floor. Even when he was mad with us the times we left him for a couple of hours, he had never sought to punish us by dumping on our carpet. I then called my brother Joey to ask him if he'd take him in while I was gone.

"Yeah, sure thing," he said. Joey and Lionel were pals. Actually, Joey had started coming around more often after we rescued the mutt from the pound. All my brother had to do was wheel into the driveway, and Lionel's wagging tail went into action. Then, when Joey came through the door, Lionel practically jumped into his arms. So, I wasn't going to be worried about my boy. I'd be more worried that Joey or his wife would take their eyes off him and then have to spend the better part of the day looking for him somewhere on their fifteen acres of farmland. But my brother knew to keep him inside and to put a leash on him when he took him out for his constitutional.

On Thursday evening, I loaded up the rear of my Suburban with what camping gear I had, canteens, binoculars, a couple of cans of Vienna sausages, peanut butter crackers, a box of protein bars, my Ranger knife, Starlight scope, my Remington 700 .308 sniper rifle complete with three boxes of 7.62 rounds. All the essentials of a hunter. I'd don my boonie hat, camp vest, and XDM on Friday morning with a .45 ACP 13-round magazine. My Sig 9 mil would be strapped to my right boot.

That evening, I called Adriana and told her about my camping and varmint-hunting plans with an old acquaintance, and she was happy I was going to get out and do something. But then, being concerned about the other love of her life, she asked what I was going to do with Lionel. She was happy to learn he would be on vacation with Joey, not in a kennel.

That same Thursday evening before I turned in, I performed a bit of internet research on survival, militia, and even domestic terrorist groups. I had in my cabinet of confidential material the list of such known individuals and groups from my previous counterterrorism work life, but the information of course was woefully obsolete. Some of the groups were still out there but over the past ten or so years, I was sure a good many others had sprung up. I could not find anything resembling Kurt's organization in my files, at least any group up in the woods at that location. However, I did have some information about a short-lived anti-government group in the same area called the Mountaineer Militia which sprang up in the 1990s. It was subsequently shut down in 1998 by the FBI.

Ben Marshall had not told me much about Kurt's people, but I had the impression in talking with Kurt that it had not been in place more than a few years, which meant it probably was organized after my retirement. Nonetheless, what I would find on the internet would likely not include organizations that the government had kept away from public knowledge for various reasons. I had investigated several foreign terrorist elements, a couple that my team and I had brought down in covert operations, one specifically the Islamic Jamaal al-Fuqra element training over in Virginia, which my friend Atticus Steed, and I had wiped out.

However, Albrecht's militia, although likely just as concerning, given its probable mission, was different. It was made up of Americans. These home-grown threats always made me think of what our country was experiencing 150 years ago…Americans fighting Americans…the Blue and the Grey. Like the Confederates, these back-woods warriors were fed up with the government and were planning on becoming violent to do something about it. So, what would I learn? Or would Kurt and his people try to keep me from learning anything?

Nonetheless, I had the feeling Kurt was intending to bring me in. He knew my history and could use a resource like me. I also had those skills, knowledge, and abilities to help train and lead those poor, dumb bastards, many of whom could only shoot and otherwise do what they were told. He just had to find out if I could be discipled. Was I also fed up with the government, and did I have the gonads to do something about it? The only thing he really had to do to find out, however, was if I was too loyal to the government and if I could be trusted. If I learned too much and made it known to him that I was against any plans to sabotage government resources, subsequently taking evidence to the Department of Justice, I may not be heard from again.

Around eleven that evening, my eyes grew weary, so I shut down both my computer and my brain. Five-thirty AM would come early.

I dropped Lionel off at Joey's just after 7:15. As eager as the pooch was to see him, I began wondering if he liked his uncle better than he liked me. When I'd be away just a few hours or for much of the day, he never ran and jumped into my arms. He just wagged his tail a little, licked me on the hand, and looked at me with his puppy dog eyes that said, 'Where's my dinner?"

"I'll be back on Monday, Joey. You guys have fun."

My mortician brother then asked, "Do you mind if I take Lionel to the funeral home with me?"

"And freak him out?"

"You're the only guy I know who gets freaked out with dead people. What I know about the things you used to do is you were around them a lot."

"I just made them that way. I didn't put needles in them, drain their blood, and pump in formaldehyde. That's creepy."

"Uh, huh. What I do has run in three of our generations. I can't believe you don't have the stomach for it. It should be in your DNA. But, hey, Lionel will be alright. I promise not to take him into the embalming room."

"I appreciate that. Well, I guess I need to light out. Ready to do some varmint hunting."

"Of the animal kind, I take it."

I smiled. "*This* time, Brother. See you Monday."

My Suburban, which I call The Beast, didn't straighten out the curves like my Healey. In comparison, it was like driving a bus, leaning, swaying, and groaning on the hills; still, it was comfortable and, for more than six years, dependable. And it had a great sound system. There's something about listening to classical music while taking in the colorful fall beauty of the West Virginia hills. Like watching one of those films with changing landscapes set to lilting music in doctors' waiting rooms.

It took two hours and fifteen minutes to get to the point where Kurt's Store came into view on the left side of the road. Again, it was nothing but pickup trucks, CJ5s and Harleys jammed tightly into parking spaces. I did spy a 70s model Olds Delta 88 with duct tape holding together its rusted out fenders. It was the first time I had seen a sedan with a gun rack on the rear window parcel shelf. I was still amazed at how many men were not working somewhere at ten-thirty on a weekday morning.

I finally found a place to park off the right side of the building beneath a large poplar and brought the beast to a stop. A couple of men in flannel shirts and orange hunting caps walking toward the front door briefly turned their heads in my direction, giving little thought to me. They would have if I was driving my spiffy green sports car and wearing my flat cap. As I was wearing jeans, my tactical vest, and the camo boogie hat all of which was accessorized with my Springfield Armory XDM .45 on my right hip, I pretty much fit in with the throng of good ol' boys. However, being a stranger in them thar parts, I garnered some looks when I stepped inside. It for some reason reminded me of some western movie scene where a strange-

Col. Lee Martin

looking gunslinger walked through the swinging saloon door. But I wasn't set on challenging anybody to a gunfight.

The store was one huge room with shelves of groceries, jars of pickled eggs and pigs' feet, smokes and chewing tobacco on one side, bins of outdoor clothing on the order of duds from L.L. Bean or Backcountry on the other, and a bar toward the back of the room. There was a door behind the bar that probably led to Kurt's office. Bartender Irma was setting up the mountain boys with bottled and draft beer. There was hardly a spot I could find where I could belly up to the bar if I chose to do so. I figured some of these guys were actually sucking down their mid-morning breakfast. A fog of cigarette smoke hung in the air except where it was moved around by one of two ceiling fans. If that wasn't enough for my lungs and stomach to digest, the place stank with the lovely aroma of bait in open containers. In further checking out the place, my eyes once again found the black banner with the bayonet and griffon on the wall behind the bar, and also at least three cameras…not that Kurt's would ever be in any danger of getting held up. There were enough guns in that room to take out a small army. There were other, smaller, recognizable flags that hung on the walls, such as the Stars and Stripes, a Confederate battle flag, one with a snake that had inscribed Don't Tread on Me, and the West Virginia state flag. A vintage shotgun, probably dating back a hundred years, hung over the huge country fireplace above the mantle where sat two kerosene lanterns. All in all, a true picture of nineteenth and twentieth-century backwoods America.

I was not there for a beer nor to stock up on Copenhagen, but I did get Lionel a chew toy, a pack of gum, and some beef jerky. It's my version of Mail Pouch. In checking all the heads in the place, I didn't see Kurt's. As he was expecting me, I thought maybe he'd be out mingling with the roughnecks. After about five minutes, I took my purchases to the end of the bar where Irma, after finishing pouring out a draft for someone, came to ring me up.

"You were in here the other day, cutie. Couldn't stay away from me, huh?" She grinned and I think I counted four teeth.

"Uh, yeah, that's it, Irma. But there's someone else I need to see as well."

"Kurt, right? I understand you boys is friends. Saw you talkin' to him back a couple of days ago. I'll go get him."

She turned heel and disappeared through the door behind her. A moment later, she returned and asked,

"Your name's McGowan?"

"That's me."

"Then he said you can go on back."

"Thanks, Irma."

"When you're done with him, you can come back and talk to me, lover."

I smiled and nodded. To be polite, I rapped twice on the door. Kurt answered, "Come in, Bruce."

Col. Lee Martin

I found him sitting at a desk off the left side wall with a stack of papers in his hand. He peered over the rim of a set of readers.

"You did come back."

"You know me. Did you think I wouldn't?"

"I wasn't sure. Thought I may have scared you off."

"I've always said that's the one thing that's better to keep than to give…one's word."

"I do remember what a philosopher you were. Smart, witty, but hard-core when necessary. You only get one out of three with this bunch out there." I allowed the comment to gloss over.

"So, what are the plans this weekend?"

"You always did get to the crux of matters quickly. Well, allow me to fill you in with our itinerary. I thought we'd go down the road to the Cottonwood Cafe for a good, home-cooked lunch. We can do some chatting, then I'll introduce you to three of my friends who'll go hit the field with us this afternoon. You won't believe the number of coyotes out there, especially when it starts getting dark. What did you bring with you?"

"I take it you mean in the form of firepower."

"Knowing you, it's going to be the latest and the best."

"Do you want the full nomenclature? Remington 700 SPS .308, tactical-blued sniper rifle with SLX illuminated Griffin X scope, MIL Reticle…"

"Okay, I got it. You probably have an arsenal at home as well."

"Unfortunately, accumulating dust and cobwebs. I've been looking for an opportunity like this to take something down."

"Well, I believe you'll have some good opportunities out there. It'll give us a chance to catch up, talk about the old days and maybe something else I have on my mind."

I knew what it was that was on his mind as he had alluded to it in our last conversation. I was going to be receptive.

We left the store just after 11:30 to get into the popular Cottonwood Cafe before the people came from out of the small surrounding towns and down from the hills to catch the Friday, all-day catfish fry. I wasn't much on catfish and instead went for the country-fried steak, mashed potatoes, and green beans. It was a little heavy for lunch, but Kurt said we probably wouldn't be able to get dinner being so far out in the boonies. I'd have my jerky.

The lunch table was a good place for us to talk about the days of old and people we knew, leaving out specifics about missions, killing bad guys and such. Kurt also chose not to get into anything heavy about who he was now, as the leader of the home-grown militia, or whatever he was calling his organization, even though I suspected all ears that could be listening belonged to anti-government sympathizers themselves. Even the little old ladies in their beehive, blue-tinted hairdos and 1950s-style dresses and their be-speckled husbands wearing white shirts and low-quarter military-looking black shoes with white socks. Our lunch companions looked as country-conservative as anybody I had ever seen. Being anti-government, however, was not being anti-American, especially in good ol' West by Gawd Virginia. Still, Kurt's recruiting conversation was for another time and another place. Kurt sprang for lunch for which I thanked him. Once the bill was paid, he shook hands with a few of the customers he knew. I took it that he had become quite an icon in the area the short time he had lived there in the county. I figured a few of those hands either belonged to people in his organization or they were both moral and financial supporters. When we returned south the two miles to the store, Kurt's three companions were in the parking lot waiting. As soon as we exited his heavy-duty F-350, we walked to where they were standing by their pickups.

"Bruce McGowan meet three loyal friends and associates...John Murphy, Elijah Collier and Bear Bronson...actually, it's Darwin Bronson, but as you can see from his size, Bear fits him better."

"Yeah," Bronson gruffly added. "Never make the mistake by callin' me by my given name." As he was six-six, three hundred pounds plus and sporting a full, coal-black beard, I wouldn't think of it. When we shook hands, however, it was like he had merely laid a slab of flabby meat in my hand. I had expected him to crush my fingers. Murphy was clean-shaven, unlike most of the mountaineers inside, thirty or so, lean and well-hewn and reminded me of perhaps a special-ops warrior recently separated from the service, maybe a Ranger or SEAL. When he shook my hand, he only nodded; but his was a firm grip. Collier, white-haired, 55 or 60 and wearing a dingy-yellowed white shirt and jeans, sported a short-cropped white beard for some reason resembling some back-woods, Pentecostal preacher. I don't know why he gave me that impression; maybe it was the way he said, "Welcome, brother. Good ta meetcha" in his folksy brogue. Kurt then said, "Well, now that the introductions are out of the way, you all can follow me out to Timberlake Pass."

"What's there?" I asked.

"A conservation area that joins several farms. We'll rendezvous at Lew Johnson's well, spread out into the tree line and wait. Might be twenty minutes or maybe nightfall before they come out. Old man Johnson says they hit his cows last night. He lost two calves. It's a full moon tonight, and even if you have your starlight scopes with you, they may not serve you well. You got cellphones, so before we leave here exchange numbers. Whether we are able to make a dent in the population or not, we'll meet back at my cabin. Bruce, I'll give you the coordinates. I'd say 2300 would be a good time to wrap it up. Okay, if no questions, good hunting, boys. And Bruce, you'll follow me out of here. You and I will initially set up in one place where I'll give you more coordinating instructions."

"Fine. Lead on, McDuff."

Chapter Four

As I stayed on Kurt's tail for eight or so miles, he made several turns down county roads and onto rugged trails. If I was to follow verbal directions and not his rear bumper, there was no way I'd be able to tell where I was at any time. I was good with a map, but I was also sure those backwoods roads and firebreaks were not on them. If at any point he and I were separated somehow, thank goodness I had GPS.

Kurt pulled off the road at a branch of what was called Bridle Creek, crossed it, and took a right onto the Johnson Farm, where it opened into some beautiful grazing land. I spotted a half dozen cows immediately. Farther into the meadow there were a dozen more plus three or four calves. Maybe three hundred yards up a small grade sat an ancient, weather-beaten barn. Kurt then dismounted and strode toward the well he had mentioned. Moments later, two trucks pulled up behind us. One had two heads. The two of them had truck pooled. From the looks of things, I figured for much of the afternoon we'd be on our own in the field looking for anything that moved in the woods, the meadows, and beyond.

After all of us rendezvoused at the well house, a man I took to be Lew Johnson joined us.

"Afternoon, Kurt. Sure, do thank ya for comin' up here with these boys and knockin' off a few of them varmints. I can't afford to lose any more beef."

"Glad to help, Lew. A couple of us will be out here till later this evening and then start out again in the morning.

"Again, much obliged. Guess I'll see you fellas next week at the exercise, eh?"

I saw Kurt narrow his eyes and then look at me. Johnson caught on quickly. I was the strange face in the group who didn't need to hear about any planned exercise.

"Oh, I didn't realize there's somebody with you I don't know," Johnson quickly added.

"Lew, meet Bruce McGowan. A friend from another life." Except even back then, we were not exactly friends.

"Pleased to meetcha, Bruce."

"Bruce is from down in Greenbrier County. We met for the first time in years the other day and I asked him to come up here to help on the hunt."

"Well then, thanks for joinin' in."

"Glad to do it," I said.

"I've been meaning to do some target practice. Why not on coyotes?"

I could tell Kurt wanted to end the conversation and begin setting up.

Col. Lee Martin

"Well, guys, we need to get moving." He handed us each a walkie-talkie.

"Bruce, I want you and me to take a position up ahead. See that giant oak jutting out? We'll start there and look for both coyote tracks and shit. We'll position for a while and then move farther west toward that grove of pines. Bear, you and John set up somewhere near the chicken coop. Coyotes like a little chicken dinner for a change in menu. And Elijah, how about you perching on Lew's back porch? You have very good visibility of the barn and several hundred yards of the pastureland. We will then have a complete viewpoint and range of fire anywhere there is livestock."

I thought it was a decent tactical plan. I didn't know whether Kurt wanted us to stay together so we could talk; however, a good hunter knows he has to remain quiet and still. Even a whisper can be picked up. When he gave the signal for everyone to move into position, he told me he and I would be in separate locations several yards apart near the big oak. He pointed out that just one hunter would have difficulty covering a panorama of the vast meadow which spanned about 220 degrees. He wanted to perch on a high bank on the right side of the oak as I was to set up about forty yards on the other side where I'd cut the semi-circle in half. Our fields of fire would then better overlap. And so, any of the talking he wanted to do wouldn't happen until later…probably at his cabin. One thing I've grown to realize over the years…a person's brain is the loudest when he, or she, is alone. When I'm driving longer distances, while part of my mind is still on the road, the majority of it is allowing a multitude of thoughts, some fleeting, others entering, becoming entangled, until my brain is flooded. The same occurs when I am sitting watching, waiting, anticipating something appearing on the horizon until it's in a position where I can zoom in on it with my scope. Leading up to that moment, the thoughts that will run through my brain during those long hours, can be about anything or nothing. A thought pops in, usually beyond my control; I may or may not digest it; then I move on to something else. But one thing for sure…when all around me is deathly quiet, any thought seems to have a voice, sometimes almost screaming inside my brain. Moving nothing but my eyes, I am so still, I can hear myself breathing. But then when I suddenly spot something on the horizon and put a bead on it, the voice dies, just as whatever is in my crosshairs does, be it human or beast.

For two long hours, I thought about everything I had seen and heard to this point about the militia group. Was it nothing more than just a bunch of grown-up boys playing Army back in those woods? Maybe Ben Marshall and the justice department investigating Kurt and his organization had just overreacted. There were militia groups all over the U.S. and many were harmless. Most were just paranoid survivalists. Then I began thinking about Kurt and who he was back in the day when I knew him. I never really worked with him. We were just in different, competing counterterrorist organizations. So, what was it that happened that made him retreat to the hills and launch at least a threat of an insurgency against the government? Other questions: if he was thinking about recruiting me, how would he know I'd join with him? How much would he let me know about his organization? Was his plan just to give me a nibble…let me see what he wanted me to see, then observe how I'd react? Was this weekend just an appetizer, and when I said I'd be interested, would he, little by little, start feeding me the main course?

It was just after four-thirty that afternoon when I spotted one. It was sneaking up on a cow at my eleven o'clock. I kept the crosshairs on its body just behind the front leg muscles. As I squeezed the trigger, my rifle exploded a round, at the same time sending the shock of its recoil hard into my shoulder. I watched the animal drop through the lens of my scope. It had practically slithered through the grass where it had gotten within no less than twenty feet from the cow. The face of my radio then lit up, and I heard Kurt's voice.

"Good shot, Bruce. One down."

My three-hundred-yard shot proved to be the only kill that afternoon; however, as coyotes generally do, they would pack together at what we used to call in the military EENT (Ending Evening Nautical Twilight) and go on the attack. After my kill, we all had a long wait. Texts from Kurt's friends a couple of times informed there were negative sightings from where they were positioned. However, Murphy reported he caught the tail end of a bear through his field glasses, disappearing into a tree line.

Per my watch, it was six-fifteen when my stomach began gurgling and I broke out my bag of jerky. It was the long-chew kind that stayed in my mouth for over twenty minutes. When it was finally down, I chased it with a few swigs of water from my canteen. Except for the one kill, I wasn't finding the wait much fun. However, the purpose of my participating in the coyote ambush was only intended to be one of fact-finding for not only me but Kurt as well. I needed to gain more knowledge about his militia group, and Kurt needed to determine if I were someone whose knowledge and skills would be a boon to the group…that is, if he could trust me. I was sure I'd be under his microscope the remainder of the weekend.

The Constitutionalists

It was then fully twilight as the sun was casting its dying rays on the tops of the trees. The temperature had also cooled considerably, and my light jacket proved beneficial. I was glad I brought it. It wasn't long when we began hearing them. Their wails were eerie, even unearthly. Coupled with the fog that was rising from the meadow that gave the impression of spirits rising into the night air, the howling almost gave me chills. For a reason I couldn't explain, my mind suddenly returned to another place where fifty years before, I might have laid on another ambush site where the NVA and VC tried to rattle the American troops by wailing like banshees. Now, here on friendlier soil, it was these other creepy little blood-thirsty bastards that were calling one another for dinner...for the kill. Being close to Halloween, the whole scenario somehow reminded my of a Washington Irving novel; only instead of reading it, it was unfolding over the landscape before me.

"Be ready, gents," whispered Kurt. They're on the prowl."

It was still barely light enough for me to see them crouching, creeping ever so slowly toward about fifteen cows fifty or so yards away. One of the other men, maybe Bear or Murphy, fired the first shot and I saw one go down. At first, they seemed disorganized, some stopping in their tracks while others began retreating. I fired, knocking down a second, and then I heard Kurt's gun taking out a third. Finally, they began running as a pack away from the cattle with the exception of one who was obviously hungrier than the rest. Just as he sprang for a calf, I nailed him while he was still in the air. His corpse landed not three feet from his prey.

Would they return before the night was over? Kurt thought they might. The blood of their own might bring them back. He radioed us again. "Stay in position, boys. If we don't see them again by midnight, then they know they will be next to fall. They're smart like that. They'll give it up for the night and start again tomorrow. The thing is, they might be on the prowl again at first light."

Bear Bronson then asked, "You want us to stay on watch tonight? The wife ain't expectin' me home till Sunday mornin.' I can catch a couple hours sometime durin' the night and set back up about five."

"If you're good with that, I'd appreciate it. So would Johnson."

"I'll stay also, Kurt," Murphy said.

"Maybe move up into the field there and get a little closer. Bright moon tonight and it'll illuminate that entire pastureland. I got coffee in my thermos and breakfast food in my mermite for the rest of us."

"Well, I need to git back home, fellas," radioed Collier. "My wife's been rather poorly lately."

"I know that, Elijah. You go on. As for Bruce and me, we're going on to the cabin. Got some catching up to do about the old days. We'll be back in the ten range in the morning. Remember, I'll have steaks on the grill tomorrow evening and a fridge full of beer. Good hunting, boys."

I followed Kurt's taillights back across the creek as we retraced our route to the main road. I stayed close to his bumper all the way to his cabin. As the country landscape looks completely

The Constitutionalists

different after dark, I wasn't taking any chance being left stranded in the West Virginia hill country.

It was eight thirty-five when we arrived at the cabin which was about a half mile back in the woods off County Road 25. As soon as his truck pulled down the gravel driveway, his flood lights came on, illuminating an area that extended something like 40 feet from the house. Immediately, I heard dogs barking from inside the cabin eager to be let out once Kurt opened the door. And then when he did, two Dobermans sprang out and made a beeline for my truck. I hadn't yet exited, which was a good thing, as they would probably have torn me to pieces. However, Kurt whistled and they went down on their front paws. Just in case, I rolled my door glass down and called out to him.

"It's okay, they're just greeting you, Bruce. They're used to different people coming here and as long as I'm on the grounds, they'll never attack anyone."

I then grabbed my backpack and rifle and opened my door.

"Okay, Zeus, Apollo, be cool, " I said. And they remained still, although I wondered if they were actually sizing me up like a lamb chop. After I walked by them, they followed me up the small set of steps to the front door.

It was a sprawling cabin, maybe 4,000 square feet, a place he called home since his wife died. The living area was large with a stone fireplace, a kitchen with a dozen walnut cabinets, and what looked to be a score of handmade chairs where I'm sure he entertained at least that many of his lieutenants.

Col. Lee Martin

"Nice, Kurt. Rustic yet in good taste."

"Beyond that door," he pointed, "is a large room of bunk beds that can sleep 25 if need be. My room is on the left. Farther back are two more bedrooms, one of which will be yours. I don't have but one TV which is in my bedroom that also doubles as my home office. I don't watch anything but conservative news whose commentary about the vermin in Washington angers me to no end. But I don't want to go into that right now; I just want to hand you a beer and relax over some conversation. Relax and have a seat. I'll get you something."

"Sounds good to me."

He then went to the refrigerator and pulled out two Bud Lights. Handing one off to me, he asked,

"Is this okay? I also have some Coors."

"It's fine, Kurt."

"I don't have any beer in this house coming out of foreign countries. I don't serve it as well in my store. Everything I own is made in America except probably that TV. It's full of gook-made parts as are all TVs. If it says made in China, Malaysia, India and especially any commie country, I don't own it. I check the origin of everything I buy and stock in the store."

"I'm glad I pulled up today in my GM-made SUV."

"Except just about all the car parts and even the American cars are made in China. I took all the parts and accessories I could find in my Ford out there made in China and replaced them with parts made in this country."

"How about your appliances? Most every one of them is made in China or Korea anymore."

"You see that fridge over there. It's old…and a Whirlpool…thirty years old. My washer and dryer…Maytag. My couch and all these chairs are manufactured out of Burlington, North Carolina."

"You're serious about all this, huh?"

"I'm passionate about living the life of a true, red-blooded American. I'm by no means a bigot, Bruce. I've got Blacks and Hispanics in my organization who feel the same way; and I hate with a passion what's happening in this country."

"You brought up the organization…does it have a name?"

"It does. We are The Constitutionalists. The government knows who we are and has been keeping tabs on us. It even sent in a mole to infiltrate us."

"As I remember, there was a Mountaineer Militia organization close by here that was shut down in the '90s because of its conspiracy to blow up the FBI's CJIS complex outside Clarksville."

Col. Lee Martin

"They were a bunch of domestic terrorists, Bruce. Our organization has no connection to them. And that was going on 30 years ago, anyway. We are people who have had enough. We're an ultraconservative group seeking to right the wrongs that our government continuously imposes on us. We would not be doing that through violent means. No one will die at our hands. Yes, we're armed, but that's only for our protection…not aggression. I suppose you now realize that I did not just invite you to come up here on a varmint hunt. That was just for fun and to help protect several of our neighbors' stock. I wanted to take a little time to educate you as to who we are and to see if you'd consider being a part of our organization. You'd be a tremendous asset and still remain a true patriot to our country as I know you are."

So there it was…the bait. Now I was ready for the hook. Over the next couple of days, he would be putting it out there for me.

Chapter Five

"Tell me, Kurt, how did you get to be a part of this group?"

"I didn't join it, Bruce. I founded it. When I bought the store, I made friends with a good number of people…mostly from the hills, hollows and creeks. I found myself talking to people who were not just disappointed but angry at this fascist government as well as the last couple of administrations who devised the policies and decisions that took money out of the people's pockets and put money in theirs. And then keeping the borders open allowing those illegal immigrants to bring into the country disease, drugs, prostitution, crime, and human trafficking just to mention a few. Furthermore, the government sanctions abortions, supports filling the minds of young children in the educational system with notions they may not be the right gender and to question how their parents are bringing them up. The Christian religion is made out to be nothing but a cult and a crutch that destroys imagination and free will. And then the military's hands are tied when they are at war with a country. In Vietnam, I myself experienced established no-fire zones where I could take fire but not return it. There's rampant crime in our cities that goes unpunished and when criminals are arrested, they're released within 24 hours or not prosecuted at all. Our police are being physically abused, defunded and even murdered where they sit in patrol cars. Need I go on?"

"I hear you, Kurt. But what will an armed bunch of private citizens do to create change in all this besides do what the rest of the population does…get out and vote?"

Kurt pulled from his jacket pocket a cigar and lit it. He then handed me one which I politely refused.

"Bruce, there will be a time when this government will come after our guns. They will come directly into our houses with court orders and take anything that spits out a bullet. We, as a force, are training to defend our rights under the Second Amendment. The average citizen will not be able to defend himself and his family if all means of protection is taken away. Our mission is to train and educate our friends and neighbors on ways to keep this from happening."

"Do you really think the government will come to confiscate all weapons? Are you not being a conspiracy theorist?"

"Get ready, Bruce. They will abolish the Second Amendment and tell us they're placing everyone in their protection. In doing so, we will be free from crime and invasion. This is the same government who is shrinking our police forces and reducing the effectiveness of our military. For God's sake, we have men in the cabinet wearing skirts and pumps. We are in moral and spiritual decay. Where has the American male gone? I have never seen this country in such dire straits. We must be ready as citizens to take over where the police and military's hands are tied. Organizations like ours are this country's last line of defense. No, we have no plans to attack the government, but we do have plans to defend our citizens."

The Constitutionalists

I took the last gulp of my beer, which, because I was so engrossed in what Kurt was telling me, had lost both its taste and temperature.

"Okay, Kurt, I've been all ears. I'm with you on this. I don't disagree with any of it. But what do you want from me?"

"Like I said…I want you to join me in our quest to put his country back together."

"You mentioned you wanted to see the government brought to its knees. And how do you propose that will happen?"

"I need people like you to not only train up our men…and women…for readiness but, be my idea guy; help me come up with plans that turn into operations. We need to have a show of force ready to fight and defend our way of life. If you put yourself back into the eighties and nineties, would you have ever thought the United States would end up looking and being like we are now?"

I shook my head. But then I said, "I don't know how I could help or make a difference, Kurt. I am a mission-oriented dude…a man of action. Short of insurrection, I don't see how this can be done. Is that your ultimate plan…take over government facilities, take out legislative menaces, take down the government itself? That would be criminal, even treasonous."

"We don't plan to destroy anything or cause loss of life. That's where good plans and ideas come in. Make this administration and liberal legislators bleed without becoming violent. Make them lose face, power and position. Restore that power to the people."

I settled back in my chair and gazed thoughtfully at the ceiling.

"I'd like to sleep on it, Kurt. I'd like to give considerable thought as to how I could make a difference. I'm just one man…someone who has always been loyal to the government, even though I have vehemently disagreed with policies and decisions that went against my code. I have to admit I didn't always play by the rules and was accused at times of being a rogue or renegade. But I've never gone against the government. Give me a little time with all this."

"Fair enough, Bruce. I've always respected you as a thoughtful, level-headed guy with solid-gold principles. Most of these guys on our team, like you saw today, are a little rough around the edges. They need someone like you to teach them how to make sound and timely decisions and not go off half-cocked. They are each to the man loyal, respectable and patriotic. But you and I can teach them to be both disciplined and calculating."

I saw that it was now after ten. I was tired and my eyes were burning from cigar smoke.

"If you don't mind, I'd like to go turn in. I often do my best thinking lying in bed."

"Absolutely, Bruce. Your bathroom is across the hall from your room. You'll find clean towels and wash cloths on the racks. I'll have some bacon and eggs on the griddle around

0700 and a pot of hot coffee. I don't have one of those coffee makers with the pods." He smiled.

"They're made in China and Malaysia," I added. "Have a good night, Kurt."

"Yeah. By the way, your kills this evening were spot-on. Very impressive. You're almost as good a shot as these Mountaineers."

After I deposited into the toilet the beer I had drunk, and took a shower, I slid into bed and pulled up the covers. If I stayed awake long enough, I would be thinking about everything we discussed that evening. He had told me just enough about "The Constitutionalists" group for me to be fully ignorant. He told me nothing about how he planned to make the government "bleed" except that no one would get hurt. From what Ben Marshall told me, someone did get hurt…actually dead. It was the government mole who had infiltrated the group. Kurt failed to mention him. As Kurt thought we were chums, certainly having a history as associates in the counterterrorism community, if my motives were discovered, would I also end up face-down in a creek bed or with a bullet in my brain? I had a decision to make: either get inside and report organizational plans back to Marshall or take the 15 grand I'd make over the weekend and go back to my sedentary, uncomplicated life with the lovely Mrs. McGowan. That was another thing; how could I partner with Kurt Albrecht to train and lead his people when I had promised Adriana I would not get involved with the government on any more missions. Speaking of my bride, I tried calling her, finding that there was apparently no cell coverage there in the boonies.

Col. Lee Martin

I was awakened the next morning by something cold and wet against the exposed skin on my back where my tee shirt had ridden up. I turned over quickly and came face-to-face with one of the Doberman Pinchers. It was his nose that nudged me awake.

"So, which one are you…Zeus or Apollo?" They were both spitting images of Higgins' dogs, "The Lads" from Magnum, P.I. Well, I didn't get an answer. However, whichever one it was, he then took off. My watch read 5:45 and it was the smell of bacon and coffee that dragged my body out of bed. After a visit to the bathroom, I shoved on yesterday's cargo pants and a fresh shirt and made my way to the kitchen.

"Good afternoon, action man," was the greeting. He remembered what I said the night before. "Coffee?"

"Please."

"Sleep okay?"

"Yeah. Fine…until."

"Until Groucho stuck his nose in your back."

"Groucho, eh?"

"He's my alarm clock. Does the same thing to me. Chico, however, is better-mannered."

"They are good-natured dogs. I was a little apprehensive when I pulled up last night in my SUV."

"They're all bark and no bite."

"But what happens if you get people out here that might be coming after you?"

"You heard my whistle that settled them down, telling them that you're a friend. I have a different one when I put them on the attack. You don't want to be anywhere in range when they charge. You're going to lose a body part."

"I'll try to stay on their good side."

"Okay, got bacon and toast. How do you like your eggs?"

"Usually scrambled."

"Good. I have a tendency to break the yolk anyway. Got some melon as well."

"Sounds great. Thanks."

Kurt stirred up the eggs and beat them into small pieces as they fried. As he did so, he opened up the expected dialogue.

"You said you'd sleep on it; how about it?"

"How about first answering some questions?"

"Shoot."

"How many in your organization?"

"All together, something over 300.

"Where are they located?"

"Let me first ask you? Are you still working for the state department? Your questions sound like you're fishing."

"I'm retired, Kurt. If I were coming in, I'd want to know as much about the group as possible."

"Maybe it's a little early for that since you haven't committed. But I think there's no harm in telling you about how we're organized. Of the 300, most are headquartered just down the road here on land that is owned by one of our wealthier men. That's where we have meetings and perform maneuvers. There is a unit outside of Elkins near Snowshoe that has over forty volunteers and then there are twenty-five or so down your way who meet over near the fairgrounds in an old warehouse."

"The Greenbrier unit seems fairly small to be effective."

"I'm without firm leadership there. You're close by. Maybe I could use you there to recruit as well as train."

"Considering you're more than two hours away and Elkins even further, that would work for me…that is if I were interested."

"Are you?"

The Constitutionalists

"Still mulling it over. It's a big decision for someone like me."

"Like me, you've always been a man of action. You won't ever think of our group as something like the Elks or Rotary Club. Very soon we will be mobilizing and causing the government some serious consternation. You will want to be a part of that."

"And what do you expect that would entail?"

He laid down his spatula and wiped his hands on a dishtowel. Standing with his hands propped on the table where I sat, he said,

"You'll have to give me something here, Bruce. Something in the way of commitment for me to answer that question."

"It sounds like you have already begun planning something."

"Maybe."

"Let me ask this. Before I do commit, can I attend the next meeting with your group? It will help me get the gist of what you're all about. I hope you can respect that I wouldn't charge into something that might have legal ramifications…not saying there are, of course."

"Of course. That's a fair enough request. I call our 'meetings' exercises. We don't just sit and talk about how bad things are in Washington and how we're all hurting. We

Col. Lee Martin

practice fire and movement, have weapons qualification and educate as to urban warfare just like the military. You talked about having a history as an action man. You'll see action. Look, Bruce, I know what you did not only in the Army but missions you took part in where you took down terrorists, most of it covert activities. We don't take anybody out but we train to do so if threatened by any organization, be it police, justice department or military. We may find ourselves out-numbered but every man and woman is prepared to give his or her life to preserve our freedom. And it's our freedom that's being threatened. On two occasions in our young country, oppressed people were compelled to take up arms. They called the first people revolutionists, and 150 years ago, Confederates. We, my friend, are Constitutionalists. The Constitution is the law and set of codes that are dear to the heart of true Americans. Not so much anymore to those in Washington. Now, that was a long explanation. You know now where I'm coming from and what I must know about you. I know you're a patriot, but so are we. *True* patriots."

I knew I'd have to give Kurt my answer if the weekend continued. If I didn't he'd clam up and all we'd be accomplish on this Saturday would be killing coyotes.

"Alright. It's a huge decision for me, Kurt. I have a wife who has made it clear she doesn't want me involved in anything again where there's a weapon involved…except for a little hunting. However, I have to weigh her wishes against my desire to join The Constitutionalist group. Like I said, I am in agreement with all of your observations about how America is tanking. And yes, I'd like to be a part of an organization that is not afraid to challenge the government about the wrongs it's perpetrating on its people." I took a deep breath. "So, yes. Count me in. I still want to attend one of your exercises, though."

"Then I have good news. This afternoon after we return from a few hours of hunting Wily Coyote, we're not cooking steaks here at my cabin. We have a force-wide exercise that begins at 1500 today and ends Monday morning. We do night fire exercises today, small unit tactics tomorrow after chapel service and night patrolling during hours of limited visibility…just like being in the Army, Special-Ops Captain McGowan. Oops. As we've been talking, I've let your eggs get cold. Do over."

Chapter Six

We left the cabin at 10:10 but before I pulled out, I informed Kurt I tried to call my wife during the night to no avail. "Yeah, we have no cell towers out here and you'll have to wait until we're almost back on the Johnson farm to try getting her."

It took us about twenty minutes to return to the farm. After pulling into the same spot as the day before, I let Kurt join his compadres before I made the calls. Yes, calls. I first quickly called Ben to inform him about my conversations and that I'd be attending a training exercise that afternoon into the next night. I had nothing tangible for him but would call again on Monday when I returned home.

I then called Adriana, telling her about the blood I shed the day before and that we were on our second day of hunting.

"Wonderful," she replied. "Just what I wanted to hear first thing this morning…out shedding blood. You are playing it safe, aren't you?"

"Well, let's see. I've handled guns now for over fifty years and this time, nobody's shooting back at me."

"And you're killing these poor animals why?"

"Because they want to kill cows and if they do that, they might be killing my next steak dinner. How's your mama?"

"Mending, but she's pretty much bedridden. I'm staying busy cooking, washing bed linens and keeping the house clean, which is a constant chore. Dad is no help and doesn't much contribute to my workload around the house. I told him he could at least clear the table after a meal and pick up after himself. He thinks because he had that heart attack, he's not supposed to lift a finger. Unfortunately, all this is prolonging my stay. I want to come home."

"Well, come on. Your mom can get a nurse in to help her and a maid to keep the house going. They have the money. You have a life."

"The older my parents get, the more medical maladies they accumulate. And both have fallen to where the rescue squad and them are on a first name basis. They refuse to leave their big old house and move to a senior environment where there is on-site medical care, meals prepared and people to look in on them. I've been at my wit's end."

"And I feel for you, sweetheart. You are at the point where you have to insist, they move. You can't keep flying down to Florida every time one of them gets sick or injured."

"Yeah, I know. We'll be talking about this when I get home. I miss you."

"Same here. I'm anxious for you to get back here. Keep the faith, babe."

Col. Lee Martin

When we ended our conversation, I stepped out of the beast and traipsed over to where Kurt and the others stood. At their feet lay two more dingoes, blood still oozing from their mouths.

Kurt told me, "Bear and Murph got them at first light. There's another over by the henhouse that Elijah bagged. Leaving their carcasses out here for the buzzards should be a deterrent to the rest of them for a few days. The good thing is, their population has been significantly diminished since yesterday afternoon. They'll be back, but so will we."

"Well, Commander Albrecht, instead of standin' here jawin' like we are," Bronson said, "Let's go git some lunch. We ain't had nothin' to eat since yesterday's lunch."

Commander, eh?

"Sounds good, Bear. How about the Dairy Queen out on 41?"

After wolfing down our burgers with ice cream chasers, we set out for what was called 'the compound.' It was another isolated venue closer in to Clarksburg; however, upon entering the open iron gate where stood a guard in a camouflage jacket with an AR in hand, I saw a well-weathered sign that read 4H Camp. I was then set to wonder if the Constitutionalists shared the camp with the kids or had moved into the compound after the youth organization had left. As it was just before one-thirty, I didn't see that many vehicles in the vast parking lot. We still had an hour and a half until a call-to-order, and if the rally was

The Constitutionalists

to be force-wide, I was curious as to how many of the estimated 300 paramilitary types would be attending.

My question about the compound's history was quickly answered when Kurt said, "In case you were wondering, Bruce, at one time this site belonged to 4H-ers. We have subsequently converted the buildings you see to our purposes and added a couple others for storage and messing. That larger building, which was at one time a youth barracks, has been expanded to accommodate our people, a portion of it to bunk our women."

"How many women are active in the Constitutionalists?"

"Twenty-six. And you will see they are as tough and efficient as the men. There are a few more who only cook our meals."

"Okay, a question I thought about last night…where does your support, financial and otherwise, come from?"

"Not only does every member of our organization and family provide the support, but there are non-member people and businesses around the county who are just as concerned about this country as we are, who provide for us. They realize we are their true protectors…their saviors from the government and its fascist policies. They have the same heart as did the citizens back in 1776."

That was when John Murphy, who had been standing within earshot of our conversation, stepped up and placed his face within eighteen inches of my mine. "McGowan, you ask a lot of questions. Should we be worried about you? Maybe you're here as a government spy."

As I was on the cusp of shoving his face to a respectable distance away with the palm of my hand, Kurt said, "Let's not do this, Murph. I invited Mr. McGowan here. I've known him for years and I have told him to ask all the questions he wants. I believe you will find he is on the verge of joining us."

Murphy continued glaring at me. "You know I'm damn good at sizing people up, my having a history with PSYOPS in Special Forces; I've studied this guy's demeanor and actions and don't trust him. He shows up out of the blue, starts asking his battery of questions from the get-go, and has that look of a government agent."

I broke in. "I was a government agent, Murphy, doing much the same as your boss here, but now I'm retired. That's the one and only time I'm going to respond to your accusations. One thing you need to learn about me, chum; I don't take kindly to people who are bent on "sizing" me up and sticking their noses in where it doesn't belong."

Albrecht threw up his hand. "Whoa, gentlemen. Let's not allow this to escalate. We're all brothers here. And Murph, it's not the first time you've challenged someone new coming into the organization. And you yourself have not been a part of us all that long."

"But I have proved my loyalty many times over. I'm just wondering if this asshole's intent is to join us or spy on us from the inside."

I had to hand it to Mr. PSYOPS; he was right-on with his suspicions about me. And if I was to carry out my mission for Ben Marshall and the 5 grand a day, I'd have to keep my eye on this dude. It was obvious he had his on me.

But then, Kurt asked Murphy to walk with him. When they stepped away, Bear just looked at me and shrugged. I shrugged back which non-verbally said, "What's with this guy?"

Moments later, the two of them returned and Murphy stuck out his hand. "Sorry, McGowan. No disrespect intended."

I nodded. "Apology accepted, Murphy. Maybe I was a little out of line myself."

When I shook his hand, his words appeared to be those of contrition, but his vise-like grip, even more crushing than before, said, "I'll still be watching you."

Kurt then placed his hand on my shoulder. "Let me show you around, Bruce. I'll start with the barracks."

Whoever the contractors were that had refurbished the sleeping quarters had done so very nicely. The bunks were obviously new, handmade, and solid; the wood floor was of good-quality pine; the latrine was equipped with modern toilets, urinals and shower stalls. It wasn't the same place that had housed a bunch of 4H kids probably as early as the 1950s.

I was then led to the mess hall, also redone. A lot of money had gone into the large dining area which set me to wonder where it all came from…certainly not from the community, considering the average income was less than $40,000 annually. The kitchen showcased the latest in commercial cook stoves, two of them, and wall-sized refrigeration. The dining hall itself had been expanded and would comfortably seat a company-sized force. Money was everywhere.

"As you can see, Bruce, a lot has gone into this compound."

Which told me this was not just a run-of-the-mill backwoods militia organization. Kurt and his people had created the beginnings of an alternative, citizen army. How far would he expand it? I wondered if there were paramilitary units in the other 49 states that equaled what I was seeing.

"With the money you have tied up in this compound, is there 24-hour security?"

"We have shifts of security guarding this place," he said. "Most of our members, of course, work, so a number of them rotate shifts when they're off from work to stand guard at the gate with the other fifty percent sleeping. Yes, 24 hours of at least eight, four of which are either stationary, keeping watch, or patrolling the perimeter. We have barbed and concertina wire surrounding the compound."

"Has law enforcement or government entities ever tried to breach the place?"

"When we were first developing our group here, yes. It was thought we were a reincarnation of the Mountaineer Militia. We didn't have a skirmish, but the feds were promptly escorted off the premises. That was maybe five years ago.

Nothing since. Except for the one unfortunate bastard who was escorted face-down into the creek."

"I see you have a large assembly area, kind of like an outdoor amphitheater."

"When the group arrives, they'll be forming up and then seating themselves on the grass there."

"What are those two buildings over there?" I pointed.

"Just where we keep equipment and gear in storage."

"Do I take it they have their own weapons with them when you do maneuvers and such?"

"Their personal weapons stay in their vehicles. We supply the weapons they train with."

"Which are?"

"Mostly AR-15s and older, Vietnam-era M16s. They are stored in our armory when not in use."

"Live rounds?"

"Of course."

"No blanks, eh?"

He smiled. "Why would there be?"

"But isn't there a danger of someone being wounded or even killed in training?"

"That's where our leadership comes into play. Most of our members are prior military and commanded by seasoned leaders who were officers and NCOs. Remember, these people are also hunters and have practiced firearm safety standards over their lifetime. We don't have in our organization a bunch of snot-nosed neophytes who never grew up with weapons. But, these are all good questions and are an indication you're interested in joining us." He then placed his hand on my shoulder. "I'm sharing a good bit of information with you, allowing you to see what non-members will not. I hope you understand that I'm sticking my neck out here in doing that. So please don't disappoint me."

"And how do you think I would do that?"

"By reporting what you find here."

"To whom?"

"To someone in the government who might be investigating us. I'd have to do something I wouldn't want to do."

"Which would be what?"

"You don't want to know."

But I actually did know.

Chapter Seven

At around 1445, a swarm of pickups, motorcycles, and a few cars began pouring in. Kurt and I were still standing off to the side, talking as they passed by, their tires kicking up dust from the dirt road. Kurt either waved, nodded or returned salutes from a few of them. I did see a handful of women coming in with their significant others, a couple, however, by themselves. After they exited their cars, they socialized a bit and then began moving toward the grassy area of the amphitheater. That's when they formed ranks made up of squads and platoons that mirrored military formations. Subordinate leaders took account of who was there, marking off names as they took their positions. I could tell it was old hat to the prior service people. There were no uniform parts worn except most had on either camo pants or ball caps that read Army or Marines. A few read Vietnam Veteran, with miniature pins denoting their service with The First Division, 101st Airborne or MACV. They could easily have been veterans angry with the VA about their treatment or denial of benefits. I took it that everyone was angry about something in the government, else why would they be in the organization?

"Good bunch of people, they are," commented Kurt. "Patriots all."

When everyone had settled down, the subordinate leaders called them to attention. A roll of drums and the first notes of the Star-Spangled Banner piped in from somewhere began blaring through two loud speakers to either side of the four

Col. Lee Martin

platoons. Immediately, everyone in those ranks formed a hand salute. When the last stanza of the orchestral music had ended, the hands dropped down to their sides.

Then it was Elijah Collier who stepped forward to offer an invocation. Caps were removed. I was right about him, the insightful dude that I was.

After calling for the downfall of tyranny and fascism and for the bestowing of blessings on each and every Constitutionalist, he ended his prayer with "in the name of our Lord."

"My turn," Kurt said.

"What should I be doing?" I asked him.

"As you haven't been officially sworn in as yet, just observe. I think you'll find all this rather impressive for a bunch of hillbilly soldiers."

An adjutant of sorts called the formation to attention and Kurt then smartly took his post to their front. After pausing a moment to look out over the troops, he raised his fist and yelled, "libertatem defendimus!" His people raised their fists as well and repeated his words. He shouted once again and their retort was even louder. And then a third time. I didn't remember much Latin, but I was sure the words had to do with the defending of liberty.

Kurt didn't have a little mustache under his nose nor were the ranks extending their open hand high above them, shouting Sieg Heil, but to me it sure as hell felt like a Nazi rally. He then began, "Fellow patriots, citizen soldiers of our great country, welcome back. You, my loyal friends, are the very backbone of this country, the salt of America. You are the people I chose to live and work with in the state I love. I wouldn't think of spending the rest of my life anywhere else. Like me, you love this country and because you do, you chose to be here at this point in time with me defending its liberties, its constitution, and its flag. And you want this country to be dedicated to the principles on which it was founded…freedom of religion, freedom from tyranny and freedom to be who you want."

Cheers began swirling.

"Even since we were last together, this country's diabolical leadership has made us an even greater laughingstock to the world. Our children's and grandchildren's lives are even more so in peril. As we are living in a cesspool of moral decay, our offspring will have it even worse."

The ranks now erupted with boos and groans.

"Ladies and gentlemen, 1984 is alive and well today. Today as every day, we find ourselves at the mercy of not only a damnable and dangerous administration but an incompetent and self-serving bunch of legislative morons." More boos.

As the black flag of the Constitutionalists waved above his head along with the Stars and Stripes of the U.S. flag, Kurt Albrecht continued his speech, covering every failing of the U.S. government, which included the abandoning of our missions and allies in the time of war, a failing to prosecute murderers of the police, gang members and those who kill babies, and levying the heaviest taxation in history onto America's citizens.

Col. Lee Martin

"And so who is left to protect and defend the rights of our people when our own government will not? Who can the weak and impoverished depend upon to come to their rescue? And who will mobilize and rise up to protect America when there is a threat of an invasion by evil nations such as Russia, China and North Korea? It will be concerned citizens such as ourselves who proudly wave their own flags of freedom in every state. We and other militias like us in the 50 states must rally to take this country back. We will devise plans and means to do just that. Those who rose up against tyrannical governments and their intolerable policies, such as the Continental Congress of 1774 and the noble Confederacy of 1860, were called rebels, revolutionists, and anarchists. What will they call us?" He then dramatically lowered his voice and swept his eyes over his troops. "They will call us…America's saviors." A massive cheer once again erupted even louder culminating into a chant.

"Kurt! Kurt! Kurt! …
He smiled and stood with his arms out.

I was watching a man drunk with power. Was he in essence a modern-day cult leader like Jim Jones and David Koresh or a revolutionist such as Fidel Castro? Was he insinuating in his speech he would be orchestrating a coup? An attack on or a takeover of the American government?

Albrecht then returned to where I was standing and put his eyes on mine, seemingly looking for praise and approval. I didn't exactly give it to him as the entire episode turned my stomach. But I did say, "Well, no one can say you don't captivate an audience."

"Thank you," he replied. He obviously took what I said as a compliment.

"What happens from here?"

"An early dinner of steaks and fries, then they draw weapons and hit the range for a night fire exercise. You will see some real shooting. Come with me. I'll introduce you to my second in command and staff."

I followed him to the mess hall where I observed his cooks and support personnel preparing the food. At a table in a corner sat six people, five men and a woman. They stood respectfully when Kurt approached them. "Folks, this is a former acquaintance of mine when I worked for the State Department a few years ago. Bruce McGowan, meet my Chief of Staff, Major Tom Gages; my personnel officer, Doug Parsons; the organization's intel officer, Charlie Schwartz; our operations officer, Carlton Hall; my logistics officer, Brett Donovan; and last but not least, our medical officer Gail Delancy. She is a registered nurse but doubles as our female advocate. Just so you know, although our women are integrated within the ranks, they have separate quarters."

"I see your command and staff is organized the same as an Army unit. You know, I can't remember if you ever told me you served in the military."

His eyes hardened. Apparently, it was a topic he never wanted to come up.

"Yes and no would be the right answer. I was drafted toward the end of the Vietnam War, but while I was in Basic Training, the Army began cutting back on its force and upon graduation from Basic, was placed in the Individual Ready Reserve. A month later I was released and that was it." He seemed embarrassed, gave me a hard look, and took a deep breath.

What I had established in front of his staff was that he was only a private and technically never served. He had made himself a commander of troops without any experience.

"By the way, everyone on our staff has military experience. Chief of Staff Tom Gages retired as a Marine major. He has the most experience and oversees both our weapons qualification and unit tactics."

I nodded and didn't ask any more disconcerting questions that would expose Albrecht's lack of military experience. However, although he never commanded anything or anybody, the fact that he was a retired counterterrorist agent gave him credibility. He had hunted, tracked down and taken the lives of bad guys all over the world. Like me, he was a force to be reckoned with, so I was taking nothing away from him. I was sure his staff and platoon leaders were cognizant of his resume. What was good for his organization was that he had surrounded himself with experience. It allowed him to stand in front of his paramilitary force and look good making speeches, then let his command and staff do the rest.

Chapter Eight

After chow, around 1730, the force readied itself for rifle practice, slipping on clothing that took the evening chill off, then lining up at the armory building to draw weapons. That's where I was most interested. It allowed me to stand at the door and get a good look at both faces and weapons. Most of the rifles were AR-15s, but as Kurt had told me there were vintage M16s that had been stockpiled somewhere post-Vietnam. If they had seen service during the war, I wouldn't fire one round through the bore. They were prone to jamming and in a lot of cases didn't work in a monsoon rain. I was sure there'd be a lot of jams on the firing line that evening. If the Constitutionalists bearing M16s intended to go skirmish with anyone, they should consider taking their own guns to battle.

While watching people go in and out of the armory, I saw a few camo and civilian jackets with patches, some familiar from their prior service experience, but also a patch I hadn't seen before that bore the name Mountaineer Militia. These were older members of the Constitutionalists who served in the paramilitary unit that was taken down by the FBI in the late 90s. As I recall in my days with the Bureau, the Mountaineer leadership had not only conspired to bomb the FBI's Criminal Justice Information Services Division not five miles away in Clarksburg using nitroglycerine and C4 but assassinate West Virginia's Senator Rockefeller and Federal Reserve Chairman Alan Greenspan. Blueprints of the FBI complex had been obtained and sold to an undercover FBI agent who the leadership believed was a member of an international terrorist group. I counted seven people wearing these patches which told me that within the Constitutionalist organization were people who could detrimentally influence what Kurt told me was a group that would neither hurt anyone nor damage or destroy government property.

The firing line was about fifty yards wide and firing positions safely three yards apart. There were targets set up at thirty, fifty, one hundred and two hundred fifty yards down range with a high berm in the background. A sergeant with a bullhorn who appeared to be experienced at controlling firing exercises began giving safety instructions followed by the command, "Commence firing!" When the collective popping sounds began, through my field glasses, I zeroed in on the targets. These people were good…tight shot groups either on or only centimeters from the bull. Every woman I observed was a good shooter. But what would one expect from people who grew up with firearms and became crack-shot hunters? They were West Virginians, by Gawd.

But what I expected to happen did. Several of the M16s began misfiring and jamming. Two NCO types including Mr. PSYOPS, John Murphy, stayed busy up and down the line helping shooters clear their weapons. When the first order of shooters was finished, they, in turn, took positions behind the second order, loading magazines and then handing them off.

At six-thirty, when it was fully dark, the firing line and targets were illuminated. The first and second orders were once again pushed through, this time a night-fire exercise. Again, through heavy lenses, I checked out the targets. The scores weren't nearly as high as I had expected. Shooters firing the M16s were beyond frustrated as they continuously failed when they got hot; moreover, the chambers began filling up with carbon. That made it dangerous to the shooter as well. Kurt Albrecht, standing beside them, merely shook his head.

The night exercise ended around eight, and that's when two hundred seventy-four militiamen and women went through an ammo check and then split up to take their weapons to the mess hall and assembly hall for cleaning.

"Let's go get a nightcap," Kurt said.

"All right," I replied.

I then followed him to his quarters, which were basically a squad leader's room off the end of the barracks. I took his easy chair, and he crashed on his bunk. As I don't drink hard liquor, I had a Bud Light while he poured himself a Scotch.

"You need to get rid of those 16s, Kurt; I think you now know that."

"Yeah. I'm working on it. As you have seen, our organization is made up of mostly good ol' boys, but some educated businesspeople as well. People with money. And they have friends with money who have almost exclusively been our financial support. One insurance executive gave us ninety percent of the money to purchase the ARs. We're constantly soliciting funds from those believing in our cause, but that support is drying up. People are tapped out. I will have to allow some of these folks to practice their live fire exercises with their own weapons; however, we will supply whatever ammo they're using.

Col. Lee Martin

"So, to switch gears, what do you think of our women?" he asked.

"From what I observe, they shoot as good as the men."

"And drink as hard as well. Wait till you see them light up tonight once they get a few beers inside them. What did you think of Gail?"

"The nurse?"

"The everything girl…a looker to boot."

"What's her story? She doesn't look the type that fits in."

"Single, works in the emergency room at the hospital in Clarksburg, former Air Force lieutenant, and extremely dedicated to what we're doing here."

I took a swig of my beer. "And what are you doing here besides training once a month like a National Guard unit?"

"Allow me to tell you something about how I came to lead these people. I'm sure you've been wondering. Being a native of this state and holding a position like yours with the government back then, I knew about the former paramilitary unit that occupied this camp…the Mountaineer Militia. It was taken down by the FBI before the new millennium. This place laid much in ruins for twenty-five years. I retired, settled here with my wife who was from Clarksburg, and then she died. I then bought the store down the road and built my cabin. After becoming friends with many of the people you see here, and at the same time having all I could stand with our government, the very people who once paid me and kept food on my table, I stood on these very grounds with people who helped me put this organization together. They were businesspeople and people like Major Gages, who had the military experience I was looking for, local conservative politicians, and influential people with money. I suggested the founding of a new organization that I would put together and heavily recruit through my store. I felt I had the knowledge, organizational skills, and leadership traits to command the militia and to further the moral and constitutional tenets that our government had long since abandoned. I answer only to a local secret board of directors and one very powerful individual in Washington. And so, old friend, the time is near when we make Washington answer for what they're doing to its own people. And we are the force to make them."

"You have between 250 and 300 men and women, and you think your organization alone can move on Washington, D.C., and, as you say, "bring it to its knees?"

"The Constitutionalists is only one of many units in the Virginias who can mobilize and launch a surprise."

"What kind of surprise? And how?"

"You're not into our organization yet, Bruce. There are things I can't share with you just yet. I will tell you this: there are people, political people, and people with money in Washington, D.C., on the opposite side of this administration who control all of our militia groups in all 50 states, and all they have to do is blow the whistle. We then organize, band together at a strategic, confidential location then flood

Col. Lee Martin

Pennsylvania Ave with our vehicles. It will be sudden and unexpected. The military and police professionals will not be able to react in time because Washington, D.C., will come to a screeching halt."

Our conversation continued for another hour. By a quarter till ten, I noticed that Kurt's speech had become slurred and his bottle of Scotch down to the last few drops. I also noted he was telling me things that had he been sober, he would have been more judicious. I knew somewhere there were tangible plans and names. I looked around the room for a filing cabinet, but there wasn't one. Nor was there a desk. Just a small table. A laptop was on his nightstand. I didn't think he would be foolish enough to put any such plans and names on the computer. If any such information or any conversations about it were on his email account, the government had ways and means to find it. If any plans, in fact, existed, I figured any documents associated with him were either in his store office or one of the buildings in the compound.

But there was one building at the north edge of the compound that he didn't show me. I noticed it was padlocked. I had also noticed that there was an armed guard standing close by the entire day on rotating shifts. Something important was in there. Maybe a stack of documents that would prove that Kurt's organization was something more than just another nuisance militia group to which Ben Marshall had alluded. Could I get in there? Considering there were nearly 300 people in the compound, including the roving guards, I didn't see how. And I didn't have any bolt cutters. So I'd have to sleep on it.

"Where am I bunking these two nights?" I asked him.

The Constitutionalists

"With the men in one of the barracks. I think I set you up in Building Two. Let me see…yeah, that's right. Just go in and grab a bunk." His eyes were now even more bleary, and his words were nearly indiscernible. "But the party's jus' started, ol' friend. Go grab you one of our honeys and have a good night."

I didn't respond but just left him sitting on his rack, fading fast. When he fell back onto his pillow, I slipped away.

After I had stopped by the Suburban in the parking lot to grab my ruck, on my way to the barracks I saw that a large fire, actually a bonfire, had erupted in the center of the compound where scores of people were pulling up chairs to sit around. Several had positioned coolers on the ground beside them containing bottles of beer and ice from the mess hall. It was the party Albrecht mentioned. I didn't intend to participate; however, Nurse Gail Delancy unfolded a lawn chair in a spot beside her and said, "Join us for a while, Mr. McGowan."

"Well, I'm a little…"

"Tired? I expect we all are, but this is a way everybody unwinds. Sit and have a beer with us."

It was a crisp fall night and the fire felt inviting. Maybe talking with one of Albrecht's subordinates might be a good idea. Perhaps I could pick up from someone besides him a valuable tidbit that could prove informative…considering I was being paid to be an informant. "Yeah, why not?" I said. I took the chair she had set up. She handed me a beer.

Her dark hair now unpinned and down on her shoulders, she had a different look entirely. As we hadn't exchanged two words earlier in the mess hall when Kurt introduced her, I wanted to see if this gal was actually as hard-core as he said she was. However, in observing several of his female troops during the day and evening, I could see that Gail Delancy was of different stock. Maybe being a nurse as well as a former Air Force officer had something to do with that. Physically alone, she stood out amongst most of the other women, many of whom were overweight, verbally brash and fairly damn rough around the edges.

She initiated the conversation. "And so, who are you, and what are you doing here, Mr. McGowan?"

"I could ask you the same thing. And please call me Bruce."

"Okay then, Bruce. But you go first."

"I knew your commander back ten or so years ago when we were both working in counterterrorism. I ran into him the other day at his store and after we had talked a while, he asked me to not only come help weed out a pack of coyotes on a farm near here but learn something about your organization. He's trying to recruit me in."

"And are you interested?"

"Let's say I'm intrigued. I needed to see if this organization was comprised of true patriots or just a mob of good ol' boys…and girls…who just want to shoot guns, booze it up and curse the government. And you?"

"I met Kurt one day when he came in to the ER with a snake bite. He was charming, good-looking and had an inviting nature about himself. He told me he commanded a patriotic peoples defense force and asked me to come take a look. I too was intrigued, just having resigned my commission from the reserves and not happy with this execrable government of ours, so I took him up on his offer last year. He needed someone with medical training out here and I needed something to help me unwind from my long hours at the hospital. I liked the message I found here that citizens like us need to band together and to stand up against this socialistic government. And so, are you planning to join us?" She grinned and patted my hand. "You have a charismatic nature about yourself as well and would bring some culture and class into this rag-tag outfit."

I laughed and took a swallow of the beer. "Haven't decided yet. I'm from down in Greenbrier County which is a bit of a drive from here."

She scooted her chair closer into mine until our elbows touched to which I said in my mind, "Uh oh."

We sat without word for a moment and then I caught Gail studying my face, her eyes dancing back and forth like a girl does when she's on the make. "You have kind eyes, Bruce; but they're also cold eyes…steady, piercing, killer eyes."

"I think I'm supposed to resent that last part."

"I didn't mean it to be insulting."

"And I didn't take it to be."

"Well, anyway, you shouldn't be concerned so much about being down in Greenbrier County. It's only one weekend a month, like being in the reserves, and we could get to know each other better."

The bonfire becoming more intense, causing Gail's face to glow even more radiantly than it did naturally. She was perhaps 40, petite, not beautiful, but pretty in that fresh-face, girl next doorway. Her eyes sparkled in the warm light, and I took her as someone who probably shouldn't even be with this rough-necked group…rather somewhere in a bubbly social setting having a margarita with some of her nursing friends.

"I see you're married," she said. "Noticed the ring."

"Yes. Going on twenty years."

"Darn. All the good ones are either married or gay."

"So I take it you are not."

"What gay or married?"

"Take your pick."

"I'm neither," she said. "I was married for four years but gave it up for lent one spring day."

"I won't ask why."

"Let's just say he had a wandering eye and wandered off."

"Oh."

"So, again, are you going to join this little terrorist group?"

"Why do you call it that? Is there any truth to it?"

"I haven't seen any signs of it, although Kurt has alerted us that something big is about to happen. I certainly don't like what's occurring in this lame government of ours, but I don't want us to be involved in any terrorist activities. Demonstrations, show of strength and solidarity, I'm okay with. Kurt promises no killing or destruction of government property and facilities, but I know there's some kind of plan."

"But you don't know what."

"He keeps saying Washington, D.C., will see firsthand who we are and what we are capable of doing. No, I'm not in the know."

We talked into the early morning hours while someone was playing songs on a fiddle that reminded me of the Civil War music in Ken Burns' documentary. It had an Irish flavor to it, sad and mellow, not like something I expected to hear from Deliverance. Nobody had cranked up a banjo and so far, no one had told me I had a purty mouth. However, the lively hoard sitting around the fire drinking their beer and Wild Turkey was not so lively any longer, and as 1:30 and 2:00 were now part of history, little by little, the good ol' boys were abandoning ship.

I then said, "Well, as the fire is now embers and the drink-fest is over, I guess I need to turn in as well."

"Me, too. I enjoyed our chat, Bruce. Are you sure you're married?"

"Happily, Gail."

She laughed. "Don't say you didn't have your chance."

"Have a good sleep. See you later this morning."

She left first and I watched her walk through the woodsmoke that had drifted in the light breeze across the compound. Her gait was poised, even stately, which further told me that she didn't belong there. But then I saw where she was headed…not to the women's barracks but to Kurt's quarters. It was now clear to me why she was part of this organization. But if she expected a night of frenzied sex, she'd be disappointed. Kurt had long since passed out, thanks to Johnnie Walker. I figured Johnnie was the only drink he had that was not made in America.

Chapter Nine

At 0600, some idiot was in the center of the compound blowing reveille. There were sixty bunks on my floor, and a groan coming out of every one of them. I had only had about four beers the night before, but it was enough to put my lights out. Now, four hours later, I was thinking of opening a window and sending a .45 caliber round through somebody's bugle. However, since I was now awake, I decided to beat the other 59 bubbas on my floor to the showers. Most of the men had gone back to sleep anyway sawing logs.

At seven-forty, I sat in the mess hall with my hands wrapped around a hot cup of coffee, taking in the aroma of bacon frying on the griddle. The first face I saw besides those of the cooks and DROs (Dining Room Orderlies) was Kurt's. When he sat down and took off his sunglasses, the whites of his eyes looked like a Texas roadmap.

"Morning, Bruce. Did you take in the party last night?"

"I did…and had a nice conversation with your women's advocate."

"Gail? How do you like her?"

"Very pleasant. You have a good one there. But, to me she looked like a fish out of water in comparison to the other women."

"A very refined and polished lady for sure, Bruce. I guess she told you how we met."

I nodded. "You don't look any worse for wear this morning considering you absorbed a liter of Scotch."

"I don't usually do that. But last night, I felt like I needed to drink."

"I'm surprised you made it up this early."

"I was hoping you'd be here this morning so we could talk before the troops came in."

"You're wanting my answer."

"Yes."

"I think I'd like to join up with the Constitutionalists. The only reservation I have would be that I couldn't make too many trips a year way up here."

"Remember, I proposed that you'd be in charge of the Greenbrier unit with hopes it would be expanding as a result of your leadership and dedication."

"And that would work out better for me."

"We have a healthy representation of Greenbrier boys here this weekend. I can corral them and introduce you sometime today."

"Alright. What else do you have happening?"

"Breakout meetings where assigned platoon sergeants and squad leaders educate their troops on a variety of short subjects such as First Aid, offensive and defensive operations, self-protection, responding to the police and military when engaged, and hand-to-hand combative techniques."

"I'll look forward to observing."

"All that aside, here's the big deal. I would like you in on my briefing of subordinate commanders and staff on something I have planned. You will learn something today that only two or three other people know about. You'd better tell me now if you plan to back out of joining us. As I told you Friday night, if you hear it and then quit on me, there will be consequences. None of my plans can get out."

"I will ask you again: what are the consequences?"

He leaned forward and bore down on me with his eyes. "And my answer is still the same. You don't want to know."

"It sounds like you would have a guy killed."

His laugh was almost maniacal. "I am no longer in the killing business, Bruce. But those who cross me end up paying in ways where people wish they were dead. If you leave right now, there is no consequence. We say goodbye, and there will be no hard feelings, but once you hear my plan, you're in too deep. There's no turning back."

"I don't take threats very well, Kurt, and this sounds like one."

"And I don't take treason very well. That's what it will be if you turn on me. Look, I'm talking to you as a friend here. I know you're a patriot and love this country as much as I do. And because of that, I also know this is probably a hard decision for you. We both have had to keep secrets in the past. We did it for the good of the country. This is for our country as well. That's all I'm going to say. But my last question is…yes or no? If no…then goodbye."

I took a short moment for effect "Yes."

He then pushed his hand across the table, and I shook it.

Of course, the real answer was no. And just like that, my life was once again in danger. Thank you, Ben Marshall.

"Before I sit in, I need an hour or so off campus. I'm still not able to get any reception this far off the grid and need to call my wife. I've never gone a day without talking with her unless I'm out of country. And that's been a while."

"Sure, Bruce. Family is important. And as I hope you have digested, it is for the sake of our families we're all doing this. You should be able to pick up reception about five miles up on 24. You'll have to tell me more about Adriana one day."

"I'll stay for breakfast and the religious service, then leave."

"That all-important meeting is at 1300 in the dayroom outside my quarters."

The Constitutionalists

"Who's going to be in attendance?"

"Eight total. My staff, you and me." He then grabbed me by the shoulders. "Be here, Bruce."

"I won't miss it."

I planned a morning call rather than a late afternoon call so that Kurt wouldn't think I'd heard his plans and then run right out and call someone I was working with to report what I had found out. My timing was calculated. Yes, I'd be calling Ben Marshall along with Adriana, but I also had something I needed to pick up.

When all the bubbas and bubbettes had finished the morning meal, the troops gathered on the grass in the arena for the religious service. The previous night's fiddler, with an accompanying guitar player, had begun playing traditional hymns. Before he began his sermon, Elijah Collier joined in with them, sounding much like Hank Williams singing Let Freedom Ring. He was even in a good voice as a singer. After a long prayer, he began his message. Its content was about the government and Supreme Court taking God and the Bible out of school, that our children would be learning nothing but trash. In place of the traditional subjects, they were learning about sexual intercourse, pro-choice rights of women, that we evolved from animals and fish, and it was a Big Bang and not some invisible man in the sky that created the universe. Just as with Albrecht's rousing speech the day before, Elijah's sermon was endorsed by his congregation with cheers for the good and boos for the bad.

Col. Lee Martin

I thought I had seen every face in the compound the last couple of days, passing through the armory, eating in the chow hall, and on the firing line; however, there was one face I had not seen. In a folding chair off to my right sitting by himself with no other person within thirty feet was a small, mousy-looking man about forty-five with coke-bottle lens glasses. I thought Gail, with her Cover-girl face, looked out of place there in the compound, but this Wally Cox-looking dude definitely did. During Elijah's sermon, his expression never changed. He had not joined in with the cheers and boos. It was obvious he had not been caught up in the message as the others had. So, who was this guy, and when had he slipped in?

When Elijah was done and had given a short invitation to the troops to repent of their sins and receive Jesus, the congregation stood up and began milling around. When I looked back over at the man, the chair was empty. He had vanished as quickly as he had appeared.

At 1105, after I had cranked my Suburban and pulled away from my parking space, the guards opened the gates and allowed me to pass through. If my memory served me well, off of Route 24 on the way to Kurt's Store, I had passed an Ace Hardware. Was that where it was or did I get that wrong? But then, after going about five miles, just as I had begun second-guessing myself, there it was, off the right side of the highway in a small shopping mall. I pulled into the parking lot and unsnapped my phone from its case. I immediately saw I only had one bar. By plugging it into the charging port, the hour or so I was to be away from the compound should give it renewed life. But I did find there was good reception. I got my call into Marshall first.

The Constitutionalists

"Hello, Bruce," he answered. "I started not to answer out here on the third tee, but when I saw it was you, I decided I'd just forego my shot and take a par on the hole."

"Did you cheat in school like that growing up?"

He laughed. "What do you have for me?"

"I committed to join this morning. They call themselves the Constitutionalists."

"I see. There are several militia groups throughout the U.S. with that name, the headquarters being in Northern Virginia."

"I have observed much of their activities, and it appears to be a fairly serious outfit. Albrecht of course is the commander, as he calls himself. The group is organized like an Army unit with a staff and a four-platoon command. This was a full command exercise with the Elkins and Greenbrier units attending. I'm outside the compound now, but as soon as I return, there is an informative meeting scheduled with the leaders where Albrecht will get specific about something big coming up. He let slip in a drunken stupor last night that it will involve Washington, D.C.."

"A bombing or some kind of attack?"

"He vows no one will be injured or killed and no government property will be damaged."

"Interesting."

"There have to be written documents about this somewhere under lock and key in one of two places. I have a plan of my own to locate them."

"Does it involve a bit of covert activity?"

"It does. There's another concern, Ben. He says if I sit in on what he considers secret information and then I back out of joining, there will be severe consequences. He alluded to the fact they could be fatal."

"Sounds like you're looking for more dough."

"I'm looking to stay alive. Remember, there's a group of these people in Greenbrier County and it will take little effort to locate where I live. Albrecht is so serious about it, he may drive down and do it himself."

"I thought you said he and his people were not into killing anybody."

"That's what he says; what is does is another thing."

"When are you going back home?"

"Tomorrow morning."

"Call me about what you get out the meeting as soon as you get home."

"Wilco."

"I'll be looking to hear from you."

I then called Adriana. I suddenly missed her like the devil. Maybe that wasn't a good analogy, but I wanted both of us to be home doing husband-and-wife stuff. It was a fairly short conversation as I caught her at the supermarket. She, too, was anxious to get back home, but given her mother's immobility, she didn't know when that would be.

After my call, I went inside the hardware store directly to the tool department. I saw immediately what I was looking for. As I proceeded to checkout, I ran into a familiar face…Irma, Albrecht's behind-the-counter gal. She also recognized me immediately.

"Hello, handsome. You're back in our area, eh? Can't stay away."

"I'm hanging out with your boss and his people this weekend. He invited me up to observe."

"So, you're at the compound. Whadda-ya think?"

"I think they're a very serious bunch."

"They're needed, you know. The people need them."

"Yeah. You're not out there with them?"

"Honey, I'm too overweight and have a bad hip. I'd just be in the way. I'd go out in the woods on one of their maneuvers, trip, and fall, and they'd have to send a crane to come git me."

I chuckled. "I'm sure there would be things you could do that involved no physical activity."

"Nah. Don't got time for it. I'm fine workin' there at his store."

"Well, I have to get going. Good luck to you, Irma."

"Come see me at the store, good-lookin.' "

Chapter Ten

I was back through the gate well before 1300. I had missed having lunch but after the stack of pancakes I had earlier, I wasn't hungry anyway.

Albrecht had already set up in his building for the meeting. When I arrived, I found he had posted an armed guard on the dayroom door. "It's okay, Butch, he's good to come in." At one o'clock, the eight of us were seated at the long table. Gail looked good in a pair of tight jeans, a black long-sleeve top bearing the Air Force logo, and pinned-up hair.

"Before we start, I want to caution everyone in this room. Some potentially unsettling yet delicate information will be shared here today and I want to be sure what is said in this room stays in this room." He then paused and looked everyone in the eyes. "Am I clear?"

We all nodded.

He then looked at me. "Bruce, please hand me your cellphone."

It was a bit of a surprise but I knew what he was going for. I gave him a bewildered look and repeated, "My cellphone?"

"Please."

I shrugged and then handed it off. He found the phone icon and touched it. He was looking to see who I had called. "Hmm, a call to a 561-area code."

"My wife is in Florida looking after her mother who broke her hip."

He nodded. "Somewhere near West Palm."

"That's right."

He ran his finger over the other numbers. "404, Atlanta."

"My daughter."

"Okay, I'm fine then. It looks clean."

"Sounds like you don't trust me yet, Commander."

"Just a precaution, Bruce. You leave the compound before our meeting and go make a phone call. Had to check."

"I think I'm offended."

"It's just good business, Bruce. Don't be."

He didn't find my call to the 303 Washington area code. I had not only deleted it but all the other calls to and from Ben Marshall as well. Then I erased the delete file. Yeah, I take precautions too.

Albrecht then stood and went to an easel that contained a large flip chart. I could barely make out a series of words and diagrams under the blank top sheet. In checking his watch and fumbling through some papers in his briefcase, he appeared to be either stalling or not ready for his briefing. However, at seven minutes past 1300, the face I had seen in the lawn chair at the Sunday service entered the room.

Kurt smiled. "Professor, welcome."

Albrecht's staff appeared bewildered as they began looking at one another. Had they even seen this guy before?

"Folks, I want you to meet Dr. Mendelssohn, atomic physicist from Berkeley. Before Berkeley, he spent more than eight years at Los Alamos doing research on EMP bombs and then took that research back to his university to create an unconventional, state of the art warhead. You might ask "what is a noted scientist from California doing here with a bunch of rag-tag mountaineers?" He then chuckled. "This, my friends, is where science meets valor. Dr. Mendelssohn has invented a powerful bomb that has to this point never officially been detonated. However, his device has been tested several times over and proved successful. It is we people who will on the 15th of November, a bustling Saturday in Washington, D.C., employ the device." Everyone's eyes widened and mouths fell open. Gail Delancy, who I knew was Kurt Albrecht's bedfellow, looked especially troubled.

But it was I who jumped up. "Whoa, commander. You're talking a weapon of mass destruction here, I presume. You have told us that any move on Washington will not result in casualties or physical demolition."

Albrecht lifted his hand and swept it over the table. "Easy, Bruce. It's not what you think. I will let the professor explain what will happen. No one will die and no buildings will come down. However, the Washington grid and its surrounding cities in Maryland and Virginia will go down. It's a revolutionary device, excuse the pun, that has never before been employed against a government. But it will be against ours."

"So, you're looking to explode an EMP device."

"Please have a seat, Bruce. I can understand your uneasiness." He then turned to Mendelssohn. "Professor, you're on."

Mendelssohn, whose eyes were as cold as an ice box, then stood. In his mealy, almost unmasculine voice, he began. "Gentlemen...and lady...the Electromagnetic Pulse. Once just a theory, but after my successful private testing, now a reality. Allow me to educate you about my bomb. It is in comparison a small bomb based on the M388 that I have created that will be fired from an old weapons delivery device called the M29 Davey Crockett. Commander Albrecht has acquired an M29 which we have already tested by firing a dummy missile into the troposphere. The timing of the detonation is all important and I have calculated the blast to be fifteen seconds post launch. My bomb will automatically detonate at between 25,000 and 30,000 feet over the Washington Mall area.

"What will be the realized effect? The bomb doesn't kill and the only things it either destroys or at least over a greater period of time freezes is everything that runs, operates and drives. In other words the entire power grid, all IT, all vehicles having electronic parts, the Pentagon, the Capitol building, the Congress and the White House…all will shut down. Nothing sent, nothing received, nothing communicated. Commander Albrecht, if you would be so kind, next chart, please.

"An EMP is a burst of electromagnetic energy which can cause electronic disruptions by knocking out power grids, either damaging or destroying all electronics. In this chart, I have penned a graphic showing a high altitude burst and its effects on the electrical grid. Older vehicles which don't have all the electrical parts may survive, but still their batteries might not withstand the sudden electrical burst. This E-bomb is largely built up of high-density metal oxide semiconductor devises where very little energy is required from the blast to irreversibly damage commercial computer equipment such as radio and radar receivers, data processing systems, industrial control applications, electronic flight controls and all the UHF, VHF and low band communications."

Albrecht then added, "Basically, what this will do is knock out all communications in the greater Washington area. However, it is not intended to make America indefensible to attacks by a foreign government. The blast is intended to show the government that its citizens are not only angry but can be punished by its citizens in ways that will inconvenience it and even disable it. As such, the government will be placed under pressure to repair itself and return to its former self. For a lengthy period of time, manufacturing will come to a halt, international trade will cease, and this country will find itself back in the 1800s."

Mendelssohn again. "Commander Albrecht and the people who have financially supported this mission have said they

Col. Lee Martin

want to bring the U.S. government to its knees…for the people in its office to understand how they are sabotaging our way of life. And I have created the weapon to do just that."

I was listening to a mad scientist, such as one we might see in the movies or on TV. And because Albrecht and his financial people had brought him and his weapon in, the man I had once collaborated with to take down terrorists and their regimes was mad as well.

Mendelssohn continued. "Next chart, sir. Normally, a nuclear or non-nuclear EMP device is delivered into the stratosphere by aircraft or long-range missile. My electromagnetic device will be delivered from the back of a two-and-a-half-ton truck. And once detonated over the area previously mentioned, the electromagnetic effect will be realized over the entire Washington grid. Computers, commercial and otherwise, roadway signals, telecommunications equipment, antennas, microwaves, cell towers and military equipment will be the most affected by an EMP. When people, including children, lose their TVs and cellphones, just wait for the fallout. But not to worry, this weapon is non-lethal."

I think we all sat stunned with the exception of Gages. I took it that considering he assisted Albrecht in founding the militia group, he was already in on it. I glanced at Gail who appeared stoic. I'm sure she was thinking of hospitals losing their power and having no ability to back it up.

"Less than a month away, folks," added Albrecht. "Our entire group will be mobilized five days before and asked to drive their personal vehicles to a rallying point in D.C. where we will have a show of force. The people will see first hand our

The Constitutionalists

capability. In taking credit for the EMP incident, I'm sure I'll be arrested and charged with conspiracy, but that's okay. I will have proven that not only are we a force to be reckoned with, but although we would greatly inconvenience the citizens of Washington and throughout three states, we did so to get this abhorrent, appalling government's attention."

I settled back in my chair and took a deep breath. I didn't mean for it to come out so abruptly, but I just couldn't help myself. "Do you realize that indirectly you could cause the death of many people, senior citizens in nursing homes, patients In hospitals who may be critical, cause fatal traffic accidents, aircraft could drop out of the sky. And the militia members who drive their vehicles to D.C. to become part of this spectacle will also be arrested as conspirators. Even if they're not, they won't be able to even start their vehicles to drive back home. Not only that…"

He interrupted. "I won't say there will be no losses, I…"

"You would indirectly kill people to prove a point?"

He glared at me. "Bruce, are you with us here?"

"I'm not sure if even the others at this table are."

"You've all committed to support Constitutionalist plans and operations. Those who won't are on notice; as you have now heard the mission spelled out, there's no backing out. Remember, there are consequences to your decision. So, who stands with me? I want to see a show of hands of those who are with me."

Col. Lee Martin

One by one every hand went up, I figured either out of fear or because they genuinely supported him. Gail was the last one to raise hers. I was surprised she did so. I didn't. "Then we go forward," he said. "But Bruce, when the meeting is over, we need to talk privately."

"Good. I had planned to do so, Commander."

"Well, we have some hip-pocket training going on. The rest of you are directed to go and observe. Remember, we have a night tactical mission in the mock-up village beginning an hour after chow."

As Mendelssohn began folding up his charts, Albrecht's staff stood and filed out of the dayroom. Gail and I exchanged looks on her way out. I surmised she had only agreed to go along with the EMP plan out of fear. Of course it could also have been because she was involved in a relationship with Kurt Albrecht.

When they had all left the room, Albrecht said, "Sit back down, Bruce." When I did, he said, "Why did you buck me, especially in front of my staff? You said you were in and I believed you."

"I was in until you decided to explode a nuclear bomb over Washington."

"A non-nuclear EMP bomb. There's a difference."

"Did you not hear my counter-points?"

He leaned back in his chair and sighed. "Bruce, you and I are cut from the same fiber. We've seen considerable action and have taken down countless terrorists. We're both die-hard patriots who love this country. And I know you're also with me as to the incompetence and audacity of our government. From the president on down, it is despicable, even criminal. Cabinet members, congressmen and women, appointed czars…every leftwing asshole in the government needs to be put out of office. If I wouldn't be found out, I'd send assassins out to nail every one of them."

I'm sure my eyes bore the intensity of two laser beams. "You're out of control, Kurt. You've just told me how dangerous you are."

"You disappoint me, Bruce. I thought you would be with me." He leaned back in his chair and rubbed his forehead.

I knew I was putting myself on thin ice with him. And maybe Ben Marshall as well. The National Security Advisor had asked me to embed myself in the organization and play along with Albrecht in whatever he had planned against the government. I wasn't doing a good job of it. So I swallowed hard and told him what he wanted to hear. I lied. "Okay, Kurt, okay. Yes, I believe in what you're trying to accomplish, but I…I just needed to have my say."

"And I appreciate your candor, Bruce. I know you have compassion and are concerned for those who will be affected. I respect that. So, can I depend on you to support me and the upcoming mission?"

Again, I had to lie. "You can." I reached across the table and he shook my hand.

Col. Lee Martin

"Beautiful. I'm delighted you're with me. You had me worried for a moment. Come on; let's have a cold one to celebrate our partnership."

Chapter Eleven

I begged off on the drink, telling him I needed to go clear my head. But I suggested I might play in the urban mock village and woods with the troops, maybe be an aggressor or something. It would allow me to feel like I was back at Benning in Ranger School…only this time with a company of hillbillies. I wasn't making light of the organization or people from the West Virginia hills, my being one of them; but except for their marksmanship, I didn't know if I'd ever want to go into battle with them. The night exercise would be without weapons, thank God. Albrecht's purpose of the exercise was to observe them in an urban setting if confronted by police and military. If the police became brutal or the National Guard started butt-stroking members of the militia with their M4s, what would the reaction be? I thought I'd play the part of law enforcement giving Constitutionals a bad time. Might be fun. However, I didn't intend to be in the training area all that long. Somewhere around 2100, I would be slipping away to do some of that Sneaky Pete stuff I was telling Marshall about.

Before the night exercise began, I sat with Gail Delancy at the dinner table, talking about what we heard at the briefing. I was careful that no ears were listening, especially those of the commander or his staff. However, as they sat at the command table across the room, Albrecht kept his eyes on us. I hoped he couldn't read lips.

"Apparently, Kurt was not happy with you today, Bruce. He made that pretty clear."

"And what is your opinion about detonating this EMP bomb?"

"I can't deny it shocked me. I thought we'd just be marching on Washington, gaining visibility…protesting, demonstrating, that kind of stuff. I realize it might not make much of an impact, but a bomb…?"

"Exactly. However, I did make amends with Kurt, ultimately telling him I'd support him."

"That's good. I don't know how he would have reacted, if you sat in on today's briefing and then backed out."

"I have an idea."

"Yeah, I think I do too."

"Are you afraid of him, Gail?"

"I think you may have picked up on the fact that we've had a relationship of sorts for a few months, now. For me, it's not all that serious. The only thing I would be afraid of is his reaction if I said I didn't want to see him anymore. I've seen his temper and when he doesn't get what he wants, he can go ballistic."

"Just watch yourself, Gail."

She nodded. "I intend to."

As darkness approached and the troops began preparing for their last exercise of the weekend, I dressed in my black cargo pants, black jacket and Army green ball cap that had embossed on the front a subdued Ranger tab and jump wings. If I was going to play the game, I'd impress the rest of them with a hat that showcased my Army skills from the days of yesteryear. Since nobody that was training that evening was to be armed, I didn't have my XDM on my hip. And without it, I felt a tad naked. However, I had cheated. My small frame Sig 9 mil was strapped to my ankle inside my pant leg.

Each of the large platoons walked single file down a narrow trail just over three hundred meters to where Albrecht and company had erected the mock town that included store fronts simulating a grocery, jewelers and a McDonalds complete with the golden arches. There was also a bank, school and church. Streets were actually composed of concrete. Junked cars sat on the curbs. Obviously, a lot of money had gone into the town's construction but I figured it was just a drop in the bucket compared to the purchase of over 250 AR-15s and of course Mendelssohn's EMP bomb. I was sure he didn't come cheap. Some wealthy people were funding the Constitutionalists big time.

I suggested to Albrecht that my role that evening would be as an aggressor. About 30 minutes after I had positioned myself in the village, that's exactly what I became…but not as part of the exercise. As everyone was or should have been in the village, I backtracked through the woods and made my way to the parking lot where I was careful not to hit the Suburban's key fob button which would have made the chirp sound. Instead, I put in my code on the driver's door, opened it quickly, touched the remote button and lifted the rear hatch. The light in the cargo area had burned out but I easily found what I was looking for. After retrieving the heavy-duty bolt cutters, I closed the hatch, looked around to assure the roving guards were nowhere in proximity, and made my way toward the mystery building.

Slipping back into the tree line which bordered the building, I waited until I saw the guard approach the front and then made my move. I didn't hit him that hard with the bolt cutter, but it was enough of a clubbing to put his lights out. That's when I dragged him and his weapon into the woods at about the same place from which I had sprung.

The oppressive light over the the door had to go. Anyone left in the main compound would easily see me working on the heavy-duty padlock. So I reached up with the bolt cutters and smashed it. As the October moon was bright enough for me to see what I was doing, I placed the cutter around the shackle and squeezed hard, popping it cleanly. When I pulled open the door, stepped inside, and turned on my cellphone flashlight, I experienced a surprise. It was a false room. However, immediately to my front was a flight of stairs going down to an underground level.

My flashlight leading me down the steps, I then found myself in a large basement filled with boxes and crates containing 5.56 and 7.62 ammunition. Opening the lid to another crate, I saw that it was filled with smoke grenades and flares. Yet another crate contained canisters of CS, which is basically tear gas. These would be the usual items a militia unit would carry into the streets to scatter people and disrupt events such as campaign rallies.

But then I saw it. It was crated with the words Compact

Non-nuclear EMP Device, rocket fired with a nomenclature combination of letters and numbers. The crate was about as long as a golf cart. In seeing a crated bomb one other time, I was amazed how such a small device could paralyze a three-county metro area. But maybe it wouldn't. Maybe Mendelssohn was a fraud. If he was, and the electromagnetic effect was not realized, he'd better find a hell of a big rock to crawl under. With my cell light still on, I began taking photos of the crate, specifically the nomenclature. The bomb itself was wrapped in a tarp.

But then suddenly a chill crawled up my spine. Pressed against the back of my head was something cold and hard…the muzzle of a weapon. And then a voice. "If you even flinch, McGowan, I'll blow your head off. Turn around."

My flashlight still on, its gleam illuminated the face of a very big man…Bear Bronson. He was too big to take down. Anyway, he was the one holding the AR-15. He had impressed me by coming down the steps with a degree of stealth that I didn't expect.

"Commander Albrecht is not gonna be happy findin' you here. So git back up them stairs and go face the music. And don't try nuthin.'"

I did as ordered. However, I was holding our only source of light, so when I was halfway up the steps, I flicked it off and sent a blind kick into Bear's chest. That's when I heard him tumbling back down the stairs and the AR clattering along with him. As it was now as dark as the inside of a coal mine, I had to feel my way up the steps. However, I had to hurry toward the door; at such time Bear recovered from his fall, all he had to do was spray rounds up the steps and at least one would find me. But then when I threw open the door to the outside, I was met by another AR-15...*this* one held by Kurt Albrecht.

"Bruce, Bruce. How you disappoint me. You couldn't leave well enough alone. I figured this is what you would be up to. You see, I received a call from good ol' Irma who told me she ran into you at the hardware store. Now just why would you be buying a set of bolt cutters? I thought about it for a good while and then it came to me. The only buildings with padlocks on them were the armory and this one. You saw that there were only racks of ARs in the armory, but you didn't know what was in here. Maybe records and attack plans you would be sharing with the feds? No. They're not down there, Bruce. They're locked away...just not here. And Dr. Mendelssohn has already destroyed his charts and plans. Nothing here, old boy, but a little old bomb. Now before I cause you to disappear, you need to tell me who it is you're working for. The FBI? Homeland Security? Maybe the NSA?"

"Whoever that is, *old boy*, he knows I'm here. So, if I do disappear, as you say, a shitload of bad, government types will descend on this place and take it apart, piece by piece, putting you and your toy soldiers out of the militia business. They'll find out about your EMP plan and you will in turn find yourself very popular in the shower room at the D.C. Federal Detention Center. Careful not to drop the soap."

Albrecht didn't say a word in response but took a couple of steps toward me. The last thing I remember was seeing the butt end of his AR-15 flying straight at my head.

The Constitutionalists

When I had regained consciousness, wherever the hell I was, it was still dark outside the window. I was tied to a chair with ropes, and my hands bound in front of me with duct tape. Two-forty on my watch. Sitting in a chair opposite me was Bear Bronson, cradling his AR. A large bandage was on his forehead where he had taken a nasty fall down some stairs, as I remember. I felt his pain, literally. There was a huge knot on mine. I then saw there was another figure in the dimly lit room standing against a wall. Murphy's eyes were bearing down on me like lasers. No one spoke, so I decided to.

"Hi, guys. I sure hope you're having a better morning than I am. Sorry, about the bump on your head, Bear."

He didn't reply. I assumed he was still pissed at me. I looked over at Murph who was glaring at me. One word to him and he'd probably come over and put another knot on my head. The first thing I had done when I woke up was feel for my ankle gun. They had found it.

I was allowed to sit there in my chair, roped up like a steer, for another twenty minutes without anyone saying a word when Kurt Albrecht came in. I knew he would start on me again, but I didn't want to hear any of it. Still, I had no place to go and was compelled to sit there and listen. He pulled up a chair.

"I had plans to use you, Bruce. I was actually excited about you coming in. You breaking into my building and taking photos of the EMP, of course, let me know the only role you wanted to play was that of an informant. Are you ready now to tell me who sent you?"

"We have nothing to talk about, Kurt."

"You know this is not going to end well for you."

"Or for you."

He laughed. "I beg to disagree, old salt. If anyone asks where you are, you never showed up here. Who's going to say anybody saw you here? There's only one person in this compound who proved he's disloyal and I'm looking at him. I trust everyone else, unquestionably."

"Don't be so sure, Commander. The feds will drag any one of your people out of here and put him or her on the hot seat. Under oath and under the third degree, they'll sing like canaries. As a matter of fact, these two bozos right here would turn on you within five minutes."

Albrecht looked at each one of them, and they slowly shook their heads.

"If you're trying to save your life, McGowan, forget it."

"And so you were not telling the truth when you said no one will die as a result of what you and your would-be soldiers are doing."

"No one except those who betray me. Treason may no longer be punishable by death in this country, but if you commit treason in my command, you may as well bend over and kiss your ass goodbye." He then looked again at each of his men and said, "The time for talking is now over. It's time to die. Gentlemen, escort Mr. McGowan to his destiny. One of you drive his vehicle out to the river and dispose of it along with him. Be ready in case he tries something. I know him and his reputation. He can be a dangerous man." He then stood and, without giving me another look, left the room.

While Murphy untied my ropes, Bronson kept his AR trained on me. It's difficult to try anything when the muzzle of a high-velocity weapon is pointed at one's head.

"Now, move out," the Bear said. "Next stop, the parking lot."

When we arrived at my Suburban, Bronson told me to get into the back seat. Murphy then took out a set of handcuffs, looped them through the passenger assist handle at the roof line, and snapped the cuffs on my wrists. Bear slid behind the wheel, inserted the ignition key they found in my cargo pants, and started the SUV. When he pulled away from the parking lot, Murphy, in his pickup, fell in behind him.

While Bear was driving to our destination, I tried in vain to break the handle away from the roof. It was likely bolted to metal. Bear noticed me struggling and laughed. "Give it up, McGowan. You ain't goin' nowhere."

It was a short ride to a secondary dirt road where within a couple of minutes we came to a stop. The SUV's headlights were now shining onto water. The river.

Murphy, who had pulled in behind us, exited his vehicle and opened my door to unlock the handcuffs. What looked to be my Sig 9 mil was in his hand. Bronson then came around and placed the muzzle of his AR at my head. "Get out," he said.

Col. Lee Martin

I did, slowly. I saw no way I could take down two men with two weapons trained on me.

Bear then said, "Now, down on the ground, face down. This will all be over in a few seconds. Good time to say your prayers."

Well, this is it, Lord, I said to myself. I pray you will accept me into your kingdom. Then I heard the shot. But wait; I wasn't dead. That's when Bear's huge body fell on top of me. I looked up to see Murphy standing over us, the gun now lowered. He had placed a bullet in Bear Bronson's head.

"Wh…what?" I stammered. "I don't understand."

"Special Agent John Murphy, FBI, Mr. McGowan."

Chapter Twelve

Murphy rolled Bronson's body off me and reached out his hand to help me up. I was still in shock, partly because I was once again facing certain death but also because Special Agent John Murphy had revealed himself. I had read him wrong. He was a good actor.

"Thank God, and thank you, Murph."

"I didn't want to kill him, but I had no choice. I actually liked the big guy."

"So did I until tried to kill me. How long have you been undercover?"

"Three months. I'm renting a house in Clarksburg and posing as a marketing rep for Coors. That's how I got to know Albrecht. He learned of my Marine background and invited me to come into the militia."

"Did you know about that basement bomb?"

"No. Not until you broke in. I knew there was going to be something big planned for Washington DC, but he apparently only let his leadership in on his plans yesterday."

"And me."

Murphy shook his head. "You're here three days and learned more than I have in three months."

"I guess because Albrecht and I have a history in counterterrorism, he decided to move me up the ladder quickly. From what I gathered; I was to work with him on his plans. I guess I screwed things up by getting too nosy. But in case you haven't learned, he plans to detonate that small, new-fangled EMP bomb over Washington, D.C., knocking out all electronics which will paralyze the government, the Pentagon, congress...everything."

"I had heard rumblings to that effect. Who are you working for?"

"The National Security Advisor. I have a history with him as well."

"Did you pick up enough to get the NSA to share what you know with my higher?"

"I'll make it happen. When I get back, I'll be meeting with him in Washington."

"Thanks."

"Aren't you worried Albrecht will find you out?"

"I've been keeping a low key and not breaking into buildings. Just there to pick up what I can."

"How are you going to explain Bear taking a bullet?"

"That he was right about how dangerous you are. You cold-cocked me, took my gun, which is yours, and shot him. You then escaped in your SUV."

"Good story and I think it will sell. But you're going to have to show some kind of bruise where I took you out."

"Then hit me."

"Really?"

"Take your best shot."

I stood a moment thinking about it, then hauled off and punched him in the eye."

"Damn! You hit hard for an old dude."

"Sorry about that. Just don't arrest me for assaulting a federal officer." I then looked down at Bear. "Did he have a family?"

"A wife and adult son. This is going to haunt me for a long time."

"How will it be explained to them that he died?"

"Albrecht will likely tell his family it was a training accident on the firing line. He will apologize and offer to help the wife personally and financially. I heard the militia actually did have a fatal accident last year. Don't know much about it, but someone drowned in a creek during an exercise."

"It wasn't any accident, John. The guy was a mole and Albrecht found him out. I don't know who he was working for."

"Albrecht is a mad man."

"I made that very statement to myself when I heard he was going to detonate a bomb. Just watch your back, Murph. You don't want to find yourself facing a bullet like I did tonight." "Yeah. I might be pulled back in after my boss hears about this. Officially, I don't know the specifics of Albrecht's plan. I could leave any time without facing his wrath. By the way, this is yours." He handed off my pistol. And then my cellphone.

"Thanks. I might just go ahead and toss the gun in the river, then it won't be traced back to me if discovered."

"Good idea." He then placed his hand over the left side of his face.

"Shit!" he exclaimed.

"What?"

"My eye is starting to swell and it's almost shut. You could have smacked me in the jaw."

I grinned. "Yeah, I could have."

"Well, help me load Bear's three-hundred pound corpse in the back of my pickup. I have some lying to do this morning."

On my way home, I passed Kurt's place catching a glimpse of Irma opening the store. Irma. I thought she was my friend, but she sold me out to her boss.

> "Buh bye, Irma," I said as I passed by.

An hour into my trek back to Greenbrier County, the sun was peeking over the high ground, promising to be another beautiful fall day. I was beyond tired but the bright yellow ball at the top of my windshield would keep me awake. Suddenly I found myself grinning. I started thinking about what had happened to me…not that almost dying was funny, but there was a bit of irony about it all. It was the second time in just over a year that I had lain facedown with someone preparing to murder me. It took me back to the French countryside outside of Paris where another would-be assassin had a gun to my head ready to pull the trigger but was himself then killed by one of my friends. Deja Vu all over again. My life has been full of Deja Vu moments. I didn't need any more like this one.

When I arrived home, I emptied my SUV of the ruck, my .308 and night vision device, the unused snacks, and opened the hidden compartment in the luggage area where I had placed my XDM. The Sig 9 mil was sleeping with the fishes in the West Fork River.

I took a shower, grabbed a breakfast bar and made a cup of coffee via our Keurig. Then I picked up the phone and called the National Security Advisor. He was on the freeway on his way to work when I dinged him.

> "I'm home now, Ben."

"Well, you must have gotten out early this morning."

"You could say that. I actually went AWOL."

"You'll have to explain that."

"It's something we need to talk about, but better done in person."

"You want to come this way?"

"Yes. As I don't trust the mail, just have my check ready to pick up."

"Your check just for the weekend?"

"My first and final check."

"You're not returning? I thought you were working your way into the organization and would be our resource over at least the next few months."

"For several reasons, that's not going to happen."

"I want to hear them."

"Again, I need to tell you in person."

"Okay. If you're coming up here, when?"

"Can you work me in tomorrow? It's imperative I make it as soon as possible."

The Constitutionalists

"You sound serious. You either learned something you don't want to talk about over the phone or something critical is happening with that organization very soon."

"Both."

"Then I will clear my calendar for you tomorrow afternoon. Make it one o'clock."

"See you then."

I knew by now that Murphy was doing his best to explain to Albrecht what had happened down by the river where he and Bronson were supposed to plant me. He'd be furious that Bear ended up dead and Murphy allowed me to escape. I hoped he wouldn't take it out on Murph. And I hoped when all had settled down there, Albrecht would not come looking for me. Adriana wasn't home and I didn't know when she would be, but I didn't want him coming to burn my house down with me in it. I believed he was insane enough to do that.

He wasn't the first counterterrorist operative I had known who had gone off the deep end. Some of the things we did would have easily broken the average Joe. Two operatives I had known committed suicide, several had fallen victim to PTSD, and I knew of three guys who fell off the grid in isolated places somewhere in Montana and Arizona never to be heard from again. Ben Marshall had told me Albrecht had left his post under dishonorable conditions. I supposed that had apparently further fueled his hatred of the government and its policies.

Col. Lee Martin

As Kurt Albrecht knew I would be alerting someone high up in the government about the imminent launch of an EMP bomb, he would try to stop me the best way he could as soon as he could. It would not be difficult to find my house. Most everyone in the county knew about our house which was at one time called Wolf Laurel, one of America's premier country inns. If he made his move to come after me, I figured he would bring his roughest, most dependable people with him. It would not be the first time Wolf Laurel had been under attack. Terrorists had stayed at our place and taken it over; when the Secret Service betrayed their president while he was staying at our place the last month of his term, the hundred bullets fired into its walls ripped up the place; and just the previous year a domestic terrorist sent two goons to kill my wife in revenge for me killing his caregiver.

I still had more than 24 hours before I'd be leaving the house for Washington. I figured if Albrecht was coming, it would probably be during the hours of darkness. He had a business to run during the day and then on top of that, he'd have to put together a team of trusted men who were not above committing murder.

However, I was so tired with not having any sleep, except when my bell got rung from Albrecht's rifle, at 8:30 that morning I set security and went to bed. I would leave Lionel with Joey another two days and retrieve him upon return from Washington.

At 2:30 that afternoon, I woke up and made two calls...to Joey to see if he would keep my pooch a while longer and Adriana to tell her I was home. No one had come to burn the house down while I had slept. Maybe that night would be different...but I'd be ready. All that day, I imagined what kind of dialogue had ensued those early morning hours before dawn at Camp Constitutionalist. Did Albrecht blow his gasket and take it out on Murphy? And how would he have conveyed to Bear's family that their husband and father had lost his life?

I had also been thinking about Gail Delancy. Considering everything that had gone down around her, especially learning about the bomb, would she end up staying with both Kurt and his organization? I figured she was afraid to leave him. After all, she was privy to the plan to strike Washington as was the rest of his staff. Nobody sitting in his briefing room was going to leave him. They were all in too deep. I took it the rest of the organization was not going to learn of the November plan until they received the call to mobilize. But I wondered how that was going to work. Would there be a pyramid roster where Albrecht starts it off, then platoon and squad leaders call their people? Monthly training was one thing but could he depend on the bulk of his people taking off work and leaving their families to drive to Washington? Then what would be their purpose in traveling there considering it was all about the bomb? Maybe it would be Albrecht's show of force.

But then when I had dumped all my information on Ben Marshall, it was going to be his responsibility. I was done.

Chapter Thirteen

It was a quiet night. No bad guys. However, I kept waking up anticipating there could be at any time. But I was back up at seven and after my bathroom chores, I went out to have a hearty breakfast of biscuits and gravy at Bob Evans. By ten I was on my way to Washington.

The president's man, the National Security Advisor, was located at the Eisenhower Executive Office Building off the west wing of the White House. I was glad on this day he was not at his White House desk. As I was not a fan of the sitting president, I preferred not to be put in position where I might run into him.

Marshall had told me I had to park in a lot off F Street since the office building had no parking garage. At 12:45, I pulled into the lot then hoofed it down the street to his office. Once inside, I was passed through security, not setting off any alarms, and then sent to the information desk where I learned the floor and location of the NSC. The cutie behind the reception desk told me to go on in as Mr. Marshall was expecting me.

When I tapped on his door, he said "Come on in, Bruce."

I did so and closed the door behind me. He stood and greeted me with a handshake. "Good ol' dependable Bruce McGowan. You're here exactly at 1:00. You always were prompt, arriving

The Constitutionalists

the exact minute you said you would. Please have a seat. Some water?"

"No thanks, Ben." I then apologized, "I'm sorry. I've been calling you Ben all along and as you are the National Security Advisor, I need to refer to you as…"

"Bruce, we go way back. To you I'm Ben. I'm not much on formalities. Hell, I'm even on a first name basis with the president. But I see him every day at the end of which we enjoy a drink."

"Do you really like this guy enough to drink with him?"

He laughed. "I'm his daily advisor on security. Whether I like the old dude and his policies or not is not important. My job is to see to the security of the United States and its citizens. He didn't appoint me anyway, my being a carry-over from the previous administration."

I now remember why I always liked Ben. He was candid, funny, yet as sharp as they come.

"Okay, Bruce, now that you're here, I take it you quit the mission on me. You said something about going AWOL. What does that mean? Did you do something to piss Albrecht off?" He then paused and stared at the bruise on my forehead. "What the hell happened there?"

"Before I get into that, I want to ask you…did you ever cross paths with Albrecht in your former life?"

Col. Lee Martin

"I didn't know him but I knew of him just like I knew you. With my years of law enforcement experience, people like me at the higher levels stayed up on who was who in the justice and state departments' counterterrorism divisions. I had heard good things about him, but I never dreamed he would become a government-hating loose cannon in his retirement."

"You had alluded to the fact that he did not retire from government service on very good terms. What was that about?"

"He was under explicit orders to hunt down and bring in a Taliban kingpin in Afghanistan who had reportedly exploded the IED that killed six American troops in a restaurant. An Afghan informant told of plans that other bombs would also be set in venues frequented by Americans. It was the state department's intent to gain information of when and where they were planned to be detonated. Under no circumstances was Albrecht to terminate the terrorist…just capture and interrogate him using any and all techniques to elicit information. Nevertheless, Albrecht raided the man's home, killed him outright along with every member of his family while they were having dinner. When asked why he took the action he did, disobeying orders, he simply said, "It would have been a waste of time. He would never have divulged anything." Then making light of it, he added, "What the hell's the difference anyway? Just another camel humper that needed to die." So, he was pushed into forced retirement. He could no longer be trusted.

"And then what's ironic, after he got canned, he became a terrorist himself."

"What do you mean a terrorist? He just heads up a militia that hates the government."

"It's what you guys think. But his real mission is to punish this lame government you work for." I paused for effect and leaned into him. "He's planning to set off an EMP bomb right here in America's city."

"You're shitting me."

"I saw the bomb, Ben. I broke into a heavily guarded and secured building where I found it. Unfortunately, they found me sneaking a peek at it. I had taken photos of it on my cell."

"Whoa. You're going to have to start from the beginning."

And I did. I told him about Albrecht offering me a leader position in the organization, after I had gained his trust, then about the secret meeting where a looney scientist from California was giving a lecture on his bomb and its effects, and finally where in that meeting Albrecht laid out his plan to shoot the bomb up over the city of Washington to knock out the electrical grid for who knows how long. However, both he and the mad professor said it was not a nuclear bomb and nobody would die.

"My God, Bruce. You actually sat in on a meeting and heard all this?"

"He envisioned that I would be a tremendous asset with my experience and would partner with him to bring down the government."

"Has he now gone mad?"

"Pretty much. He's a narcissistic maniac who says he's not afraid of being captured as long as he is successful in putting Washington on its knees."

"Does he realize that an EMP will cause death in indirect ways?"

"I made that abundantly clear to him. He said basically that's the spoils of war. People sometimes have to suffer and die at the cost of bringing down evil regimes."

"How did you get away? Did you just walk out?"

"He surmised I was working against him when I was found breaking into his building and that I would be reporting what I saw and heard to whoever sent me. He then had two men to take me out in the woods to whack me."

"Okay, but you're here. I definitely want to hear this story."

"One of the two men is named John Murphy, undercover special agent for the FBI. When the other man was ready to blow my head off, Murphy shot and killed him. As Murphy was not in on the meeting about the bombing, he doesn't know much. He asked that when I give you all the

The Constitutionalists

information, which I just did, that you share it with the FBI director."

"And that I will do. The Bureau's JTTF needs to raid that compound ASAP and bring Albrecht in. Your testimony about what you saw and heard will be important in securing a warrant, leading to his arrest and a search of both the compound and his business. I will of course immediately notify the president, chief of staff and director of Homeland Security in addition to the FBI director. Good work, Bruce. In just three days you have uncovered a plot to bomb the nation's capital that will in essence destroy its entire electrical grid."

"Okay, how about feeding me a little information?" I asked.

"Like what?"

"When you and I talked initially, you told me you suspected Albrecht was planning some kind of activity against the government, perhaps attacking some government buildings and the like. What was your source of this information?"

"Several people. First, ATF had a man embedded in the organization for a couple of months and he was discovered to have had a drowning accident in a creek nearby, supposedly from participating in a training exercise that involved the creek. Albrecht reported the man had separated from the others in an exercise and went missing. "He must have slipped and hit his head on a rock," he said. The ATF said the agent's personal effects that were turned over to the police who investigated his death were missing along with his badge and ID. Albrecht obviously suspected he was a plant.

"Earlier this year, the IRS performed a full-blown audit of one J. Hoyt Nelson, a wealthy owner of several businesses in Clarksburg, also the county commissioner, who was found to be financially supporting the militia group. He had previously been mixed up with the now defunct militia group, the Mountaineer Militia. Nelson was also a friend and partner with the leader of that group who ended up going to jail. In tracking his money, the IRS found receipts for scores of AR-15s and a couple tons of ammonium nitrate, ANFO and titanium, which together makes a damn powerful explosive."

"And so you decided to put me inside…a used up, expendable former operative who you only committed to pay $5,000 a day…"

He smiled. "There's no one else in my book who could have brought back information like this and lived to tell about it. Anyway, that's damn good money. No salaried government cop makes anything close to that."

"So, do you have a check ready for me? You owe me 15 grand, boss."

"This country owes you a hell of a lot more than that, my friend…ten times that."

"Well, good then. I'll take it."

As I knew Ben had to immediately have a pow-wow with the president and the list of directors he mentioned, our meeting needed to break up. And I needed to get the hell out of town before the afternoon after work traffic started. We had talked about the EMP effects on the Washington grid, but if I didn't hurry, I'd be facing a grid that would soon be affecting me…something called gridlock.

Chapter Fourteen

That next morning, I went to Joey's house and picked up Lionel. Although he seemed happy to see me, he acted like he didn't want to leave my brother. When I dumped him in the front seat with me he began scratching at the passenger's side window and howling. Both he and Joey had that sad, puppy-dog look in their eyes. However, after we settled in at home, I fed him some puppy chow and then we set out on a run through the countryside.

Since I do my most active thinking on a run or a long drive, my mind was back on Albrecht and his group. I was trying to imagine what his next move would be. He hadn't come after me, probably knowing that I expected it. However, he also knew unless he brought some beefy bubbas with him, he wouldn't stand a chance uno a uno. He might wait a calculated amount of time, believing I had all but forgotten about him, and then utilize the tactic of surprise to come pay me back for my treason. I was more concerned he would try something after Adriana had returned, putting her in harm's way. I don't get excited about killing anyone, unless the person was trying to kill me, but I could make an exception with Kurt Albrecht. He was just a two hour ride up the road.

But then late that afternoon, any apprehension I had about Albrecht was quickly quelled. Ben Marshall had not wasted any time. It was on the evening news. The FBI's JTTF had broken through the entrance gate at the Constitutionalists' compound and as the camp's security was in the process of fleeing, over 30 SWAT agents began a search and sweep. Only one person was arrested in a building called Barracks One. Kurt Albrecht. It was only him they were looking for anyway. There was film showing Bureau agents sweeping through every building including the mystery building with the basement. A news reporter was interviewing the SWAT commander about the particulars of the search.

"What is the FBI was looking for and what have you found?"

"We received reports that the militia group who occupies this camp once a month had plans to conduct hostile operations against the federal government. We were looking specifically for bombs and bomb-making materials."

"And what did you find?"

"Nothing. Not a weapon, not one round of ammo, and no bomb. In search of the organization's mess hall, we didn't even find a can of beans. Everything has been cleared out."

"Didn't this used to be a 4H camp?"

"Yes, and it looks like one today."

"What happens from here?"

"We have the alleged head of this militia group in custody. He'll be questioned and then it's up to the attorney general what happens from there. That's all I have."

Col. Lee Martin

Neither did Albrecht waste any time. In anticipation of a raid on the compound, he had erased every bit of evidence there was even a militia group located there. Because I had escaped and would be reporting my findings back to Washington, he and his people had trucked the racks of weapons, the ammo, and the EMP device to another location outside the compound. Where that was…was anybody's guess; probably a cave, as there were many in that area.

I knew what would be happening from there. Albrecht might be arraigned but then ultimately released for lack of evidence. I wagered he would be back in his store by the weekend. Now he would have a new reason to be pissed off at me. Not only was he compelled to vacate his camp, but his plan to detonate the EMP would have to be scrapped…at least for the time being.

An hour after the broadcast, my cellphone rang.

"Well, Bruce. It looks like Albrecht pulled one over on us. I guess he knew when you escaped his clutches that you'd turn over to us what you learned there. He had to scramble to get everything out of there. And I got chewed out by the president. He said, "Now the FBI has a hell of a lot of egg on its face. Director Nelson is pointing his finger at me and you for giving him erroneous information. I expected you to do your homework on that place before the Bureau went charging in there."

"Everything I told you about was there. I took photos of the bomb, although they obviously erased them. Albrecht had to be working night and day to get it all out of there."

The Constitutionalists

"I know the shit was there, Bruce. I'm not blaming you. But the government's case against Albrecht won't go anywhere. The only way it could was for you to testify as to what you saw; but then it would come down to your word against his. Without the evidence…the bomb and bomb-making material, plans on paper, photographs and et cetera, there will be no case."

"You forget about Special Agent John Murphy. He had been underground with them for three months. He at least knows there was a bomb, whether or not he was in the know as to what would be done with it."

"Bruce, the Bureau can't locate him. He has disappeared. Agents went to his rental house to look for him. His belongings were there, but not him."

"Sounds like Albrecht might have had him killed."

"I don't know. Maybe he found out Murphy was undercover or got pissed that you escaped under Murphy's watch."

"I ended up liking Murphy. The guy saved my life. If he's found dead, I'm going after Albrecht myself…that is if and when he gets released."

"Let the Bureau take care of their own, Bruce."

"There were six other people in that room besides me who heard Albrecht's **briefing…his chief of staff, five members of that staff and flaky scientist Mendelssohn, creator of the** bomb. If the Bureau can pull them in and put them through some intense interrogation, one or all will sing."

"Do you have their names? I'll give them to the director."

I rattled them off, but I had no idea where they were from.

"You gave me five names; you said there were six."

"Did I say six? I was never very good at math."

I had purposely left Gail Delancy off the list. As I knew where she worked and Albrecht was going to be in the pokey for a few days until his attorney got him released, I would go see her myself. I didn't want the feds descending on the hospital and picking her up in front of the medical staff. Maybe I could convince her to provide the Bureau with a sworn statement and then set up a meeting with an agent. But then I thought…giving that statement would put her in a dangerous position with Albrecht. He would go after her, and then she would come up missing. Therefore, I was banking on the others at that table to corroborate my statement.

"The Bureau will dispatch agents to hunt these people down," Ben said. "They shouldn't be too hard to locate given that the Clarksburg-Harrison County area is not that densely populated. If they end up turning on their leader, I believe a case can be made. This Mendelssohn character will be especially important to find. Any idea where he came from in California?"

The Constitutionalists

"Albrecht only said that he was from Berkeley. I don't know if he meant the city or specifically the university," I remarked.

"Interesting that Albrecht is a far-right conservative in his politics but then this bomb-maker is from a super liberal part of the country."

I nodded. "Of course anarchy can occur from the left or the right, depending on which form of hated government is in power. It can make for strange bedfellows."

"Well, civil disobedience is one thing; terrorism is another. That EMP bomb has to be found. Any ideas?"

"Did SWAT locate his cabin?"

"Yes. They went through it with a fine-tooth comb. No bomb, no plans, no evidence at all of any subversive activity. There were two nasty dogs that tried to eat them up, but they were carted off to the pound."

"Harpo and Chico."

"What?"

"Never mind. How about his store?""

"Same there. He kept nothing about the militia in his store office. Agents were also all over the woods around that compound. Nothing. You'd never know anyone occupied that entire compound last weekend."

"Then there's a secret location somewhere or one of the people I mentioned is storing it all. I'd start with this guy Gages. He was in tight with Albrecht."

"I'll advise the director."

"And go look in all the caves."

"Right.

"Anything else for me?"

"Not at this time. If you can think of anything significant you saw or heard that might help, call me."

"Will do."

That next morning, I called Samaritan Hospital and asked to speak to Gail Delancy. I was advised she was with a trauma patient. I didn't want to talk with her over the phone; I just wanted to find out if she was there. A few minutes later, I loaded Lionel up in the Suburban and set out for Clarksburg. Two and a half hours later, stopping only for Lionel to take a pee break, I pulled into the parking lot. As it was a nice cool day, I dropped the window glasses a few inches to assure Lionel was comfortable and proceeded into the ER. I was praying he wouldn't get angry that I had left him and chew up my seats.

The gray-haired lady at the desk behind the glass partition asked, "May I help you, sir?"

"I'm just waiting for Gail."

"Gail Delancy?"

"Yes."

"She's with a patient in ER."

"When she comes out, just tell her an old friend is here."

"Will she know who's waiting?"

"No, it'll be a surprise. I haven't seen her in a while." That while was four days.

The lady smiled and nodded.

I took a seat in the waiting area and watched as patients came in and out for nearly fifteen minutes. A few had cuts and bumps from apparent accidents and many just sickly looking, coughing and blowing noses. One large fellow in flannel, bib coveralls and a John Deere cap sat with a bloody rag against his head. It reminded me that I hadn't had any treatment for the nasty knot and bruise on my forehead from the butt of Albrecht's AR. I probably should have gotten an X-ray. However, as the swelling had gone down considerably, I guessed that I was going to live.

Then I saw her whisking along a hallway. Quickly, I moved in on her and softly called her name, "Gail."

When she turned, she suddenly turned pale. "Bruce," she replied.

"Got a moment?"

She glanced at her watch. "I...I have a lunch break coming up. I take it you want to talk."

"If you have a few minutes for me."

"Let's go to the cafeteria."

I followed her further down the hallway, where she told another nurse, "I'm going to take my lunch now, Brenda." She then led me to the cafeteria.

Not a word was spoken as I followed her through the line. She chose a salad in a plastic container. I reached under the glass overhang and pulled out a large sub. What I didn't eat, I'd share with Lionel. Of course I would be defying Adriana's orders that he was to get no human food. Oh wait; Adriana was in Florida.

I paid for her salad and then both of us poured ourselves cups of water. She led me to a table by a window away from where others were sitting.

"Are *you* okay?" I asked her.

"I should ask you the same question. That's a concerning hematoma on your head."

"Compliments of your boyfriend."

"I assume you mean Kurt. He's not my boyfriend, Bruce."

"He's now probably somebody else's boyfriend at the correctional facility."

"He would be deserving of that. I know that he sent you out with two men who were to kill you. I heard you escaped and am so glad about that."

"No more glad than me. Apparently, I busted one of their heads and shot the other."

"You did?"

"Wasn't that the story?"

"Kurt never talked about it with me."

"I saw in his EMP briefing how shocked you were when he talked about placing the bomb over Washington."

"I never went for any of that, Bruce. As a matter of fact, immediately after that meeting, I left. The next thing I heard was he and everyone else in the militia loaded the entire compound up in trucks and pulled out."

"Anticipating a raid by the feds."

"He called me the next day to tell me how disappointed he was that I took off. He also said you were a plant working for the government."

"That was true, Gail."

"So, what are you doing here?"

"Two reasons. First, do you know where he took the bomb?"

"I don't have a clue. He just said it's in storage."

"What kind of storage?"

"I don't know. I think maybe a warehouse or storage unit. He never said. I'm sure he knew he could no longer trust me."

"He was having me killed. I would be looking out for myself if I were you."

"All he did was threaten me if I ever let it out he was going to put a bomb on Washington."

"What did he say specifically?"

"That I would disappear from the face of the earth."

"Then you're not going to like my second question. Would you talk with the FBI and give them a sworn statement about what you witnessed in the briefing room?"

"Not a chance, Bruce."

I nodded. "I can't say I blame you. He's likely to be released unless people come forward to give their statements, such as the other members of his staff."

The Constitutionalists

"And they won't. They're all attached to his hip. He's known them for at least five years. They will all stick together."

"Until they get put into an interrogation room and threatened. The FBI is damn good at what they do."

"I think they're a bunch of traitors to the American people, siding with all the liberal politicians."

"Is that you talking or Kurt Albrecht?"

"Do you not think I have a mind of my own? Why do you think I joined the Constitutionalists in the first place?"

"I didn't mean any offense, Gail."

She sighed and said, "Sorry, Bruce."

I changed the subject. "So, you work in the ER I see."

"Yes. I'm a trauma nurse. I assist the ER doctors when they're doing things like attending to serious injuries, sewing people up and the like. Gets a little hairy at times."

"What days and hours do you work?"

"I'm here six days a week from ten in the morning till nine at night. Off on Wednesdays."

"Eleven hours a day?"

"Sometimes longer if I need to respond to an emergency five minutes before it's time for me to get off. I just can't leave in the middle of caregiving."

"Of course." I then paused to take one last bite of my sandwich. "Well, back on the matter. I gave the person who hired me the names of Kurt's staff; however, I didn't give him yours. But, the FBI may find out anyway. If they come see you, what will you do?"

"I won't ever testify, Bruce. Even if Kurt is locked up, he has people who can get to me."

"I hear you. Whatever you do, just be vigilant. I have a feeling he will be at your door if and when he gets out. He'll be making his rounds to all of his so-called staff to assure nobody testifies against him."

"Well, again, it won't be me that does."

I nodded, then wrapped the remainder of my sub up and laid my hand on hers. "The questions aside, I just came up here to see if you were alright."

She smiled. "And I appreciate that, Bruce. You're a kind and considerate man. Like I said, too bad you're married." She stood and added, "I need to get back to work."

When we had walked to the lobby, she gave me a hug and said, "Take care of yourself, Bruce." As she walked down the corridor, I was thinking how the green scrubs didn't do her shapely body any favors; but she still looked sweet. No, it wasn't too bad I was married. But if I wasn't, she would be a good candidate to chase after.

Chapter Fifteen

With the time I had to wait to see Gail and our lunch in the cafeteria, I had taken longer than I anticipated. However, I was pleased to find that Lionel had neither chewed up my seats or dumped on my floor. He had however either rubbed his wet nose all over my windows or licked them, leaving them in a filmy mess. But he was happy to see me, especially with a half of a sub in my hand.

"Good puppy, Lionel. Here's you a treat. Don't tell your mom."

It was two-twenty on my dash clock when I left the hospital. When I passed by Kurt's Store, I was sure I recognized a couple of vehicles I had seen in the compound parking lot, so I decided not to stop for a Coke. Irma might just slap leather and shoot me for getting her boss locked up. I assume she knew I had turned out bad, my being a plant. She and the people who worked there were unconditionally loyal to Albrecht. But it mattered little. I was sure he'd be released soon either for lack of evidence or at the hands of some charitable prosecutor.

No sooner had I put the store in my rearview mirror, one of the vehicles, a gray Dodge Ram, began pulling out behind me. There was no immediate reason to be concerned as it was just a good ol' boy leaving the store for home with his six pack and pouch of Red Man. People would be coming and going every ten minutes. But a guy with my history is always suspicious.

I had the driver's window down, allowing the intoxicating, cool air of autumn into the Suburban as the outside temperature was neither warm enough nor cool enough for either the heater or the A/C. But then Lionel began looking at me and whimpering.

"What is it, boy?" As though I expected him to answer me.

He would look at me, look at his door, then look back at me again.

"Oh, I get it. You want your window down also."

I thought about taking it all the way down, but then wondered if he might try to jump out or even fall out. He was a fairly new pup and not exactly predictable, given that he had taken off into the countryside twice when we opened our front door to go for a walk. That was when my walk turned into an all-out run. But, thankfully, each time I turned on the afterburners to give chase, I was able to catch him.

"How about if I drop the glass just a little?" And I did…about six inches. He seemed okay with that.
When the road joined Route 60 a few miles down the pike, I noticed the gray truck was still behind me. As it had been more than ten miles since passing the store, I was becoming suspicious. However, the truck was still keeping a distance of a dozen car lengths. If the driver was following me, did Albrecht from his jail cell make a call to dispatch the guy? Was he intending to follow me all the way to Wolf Laurel? If he did, was it to just see where I lived or was he planning on whacking me when I got out of the Suburban?

Ahead on the left was a BP station that had once been a Pure. As I was now down to a quarter of a tank, why not fill up, I said to myself. When I pulled over, the gray Dodge with two heads in it sailed on by.

"So much for that, Lionel. My paranoia was off-kilt, I guess."

After hanging up the nozzle and printing my receipt, I pulled back out onto Route 60. But then I had only gone a half mile when I saw the Dodge again in my mirror, entering the highway from behind a building. That's when I lifted my XD from the holster and laid it in the seat with Lionel. Glancing again into my mirror, I said aloud, "Okay, boys, what do you want? Let's find out."

After driving another mile, I turned right onto a farm road numbered 4357, which I knew passed by a farm owned by Joshua Himmler, a Mennonite friend of mine; I decided to pay Ol' Josh a visit…except I wouldn't park right in front of his house. True to my suspicions, the Dodge also turned right onto the county road, following at the usual 10-12 car lengths.

Joshua's barn, a weathered red-turned-gray dwelling, sat off the farm road about a hundred feet, having a narrow road of its own all the way to the back. After turning down the road, I quickly swept my SUV around the side of the barn to the rear where I was no longer in sight. The pickup didn't follow; however, its driver braked to a stop outside of the split rail fence at the edge of the property. I then dismounted and with gun in hand, stood at the corner of the barn where I could clearly see the truck. Their windows down, the men sat inside, motionless, waiting for what, I didn't know. I then slipped

The Constitutionalists

around the opposite side of the barn and using a small grove of conifers for concealment, ran along the outside of the fence to the rear of their pickup. Having made their rear bumper apparently unnoticed, I ran at a crouch upon the driver's open window. He turned toward me about the same time his left jaw caught the butt of my pistol. I then pointed my .45 at the passenger's head.

"Since your pal here has suddenly fallen asleep, you now have to do the talking. What's your name, maggot?"

"Uh, Marve...Marvin Hastings." Marve was a red-haired kid about twenty-two.

"Why are you following me, Marve?"

He was stumped for an answer. "I...I..."

"Aye, aye. I got it, Marve. Now, take your time. Who sent you to follow me?"

"The Major."

"Major. Would that be Major Gages?"

He nodded. "He posted us at the commander's store to watch for your Suburban."

"And what were you intending to do once you caught up with me?"

"He just said to find out where you live."

Col. Lee Martin

"He could have done that by going on the internet. He risked you boys' lives for nothing. You know I nearly shot you two. Are you armed?"

"Yes, sir."

"Toss your gun out the window...handle it with two fingers."

When he did, I reached around his unconscious friend and found a .45 in its holster. "What's his name?"

"Billy Bonney."

I chuckled. "Funny. Tell Billy the Kid I took his gun and how close he was to my shooting him in the head."

"What are you going to do with us?"

"If it was night and there was no one around, I'd shoot you and plant you two in the ground."

"But...but you won't now?"

"Thank the Lord for the daylight, kid. Here's what I want you to do; you go back and tell Major Gages never to send anyone after me again." I then tapped the muzzle of my pistol on the window frame. "If he does, I will drive back up to Clarksburg and put a bullet from this gun into his head."

Marve looked at Billy. "Is he alive?"

The Constitutionalists

"He's alive. When he wakes up, you kids go back home. Do yourself a favor and distance yourselves from both Albrecht and Gages. You don't want to wind up where they're going."

"Yes, sir. Thank you."

Without a word, I turned and walked back to the reverse side of the barn and stepped into the Suburban. Lionel had been pitching a fit that I had left him in the truck.

"Sorry, little buddy. Had some business to take care of. Let's go home."

I knew it would be happening. I had forecasted it. As soon as I arrived home, I received a call from Ben Marshall. "What you said would happen, Bruce, did. Albrecht is out. Charges were dropped for insufficient evidence."

Commanding a militia group that had, to this point, behaved itself would not keep him behind bars. Militia groups themselves were not illegal unless they took their activities into the public realm or there was confirmed evidence they were conspiring against the government. Nothing on paper nor on Albrecht's computer alluded to any subversive activities. He had protected himself well. Papers, plans and an EMP bomb were nowhere to be found. Ben Marshall said he had given the names of the co-conspirators, namely Albrecht's staff, to the FBI director and his agents would be pulling them in to grill. I was betting that at least one of them would turn state's evidence. However, as they knew Albrecht was not above killing someone who betrayed him, they might rather perjure themselves than face his wrath.

A week later, Adriana finally came home. She had flown back into Charleston, where I picked her up on the 8th. As the bump and bruise on my forehead were now gone, there was nothing I had to explain.

"What's the story on your mom?" I asked her.

"She finally got her insurance issue straightened out and will now pay for a health nurse to come in four times a week. Dad and a neighbor lady will look after her the rest of the time. She's on a walker now."

"Well, it's so nice to have you home." I smiled and placed the back of my hand on her lips. She kissed it.

Fall was still aflame, its glorious colors on the mountains now finally peaking. As we navigated the curves of West Virginia's turnpike, she said, "I love the palms, the magnolias and oleander down where Mom and Dad live, but there are no more beautiful trees and flowers than right here in West Virginia. How are the mums doing?"

"Beautiful. The reds, purples and yellows are especially stunning this year. The maples and oaks are also in their finest glory, more so than I can remember."

"I can't wait to see them." She then leaned into me and kissed me on the neck. "And I can't wait to show you later how happy I am that I'm home. A month away from you is too darn long. But how's our boy Lionel?"

I was agape at how quickly she had gotten off the subject of me and onto our dog. I deserved more than five seconds.

"He's been missing you. He goes to our bedroom, lays on your slippers and whines sometimes."

"Oh, the little darling. I'm so anxious to see him."

"Well, I missed you, too."

"Are you jealous?"

I smiled. "Maybe just a little."

"Has anything happened around here while I've been gone."

"No, not really." I didn't lie. It wasn't around home that anything did happen.

"Well, at least you got to do something out in the woods. I hope that went well for you."

"It turned out well. I bagged a few coyotes and nobody shot me."

"That's a good thing."

And that's all I was going to say about that. I supposed I was being dishonest with her by not telling her what had happened to me because I took a part-time job for the National Security Advisor. How long would it be, though, until she found out about it? If I did tell her, I would soft-sell the story to the point she'd think nothing about it. Of course, I'd leave out the part where I nearly took a bullet in the head.

Col. Lee Martin

However, now that she was home and Kurt Albrecht was out, I'd go back to worrying.

She was still smiling at breakfast the next morning. I must have done something right the night before…three times if I remember correctly. Lionel sat at my feet at the breakfast table begging, waiting. Maybe I'd miss my mouth and a piece of bacon would fall on the floor. Keep dreaming, Lionel. Not going to happen. But then, a couple of times, Adriana reminded him, "We don't give you people food, sweetie."

"But" he whimpered, "Dad shared his sub sandwich with me." At least, that's what his eyes said.

After my breakfast had settled, I went for my morning run. When I do, I only take a bottle of water with me…no phone, no wallet, no gun. Adriana generally told me I should take my wallet and cellphone in case I had a heart attack. I could dial 911 and have my ID with me so I could be identified if I'm found unconscious.

"You don't have to get all morbid, you know," I'd say. Today was no different. She mentioned it again. "But those things are too bulky in my gym shorts, my dear." She retorted, "Then run with a fanny pack."

I said, "Do you know how fruity that looks on a guy like me?"

Anyway, I won out and left everything at home.

The November air was fresh and crisp, and my lungs enjoyed every moment of it. That morning, I pushed it harder than I

The Constitutionalists

had in days, going four and a half miles over lush, green farmland. I felt less like a jogger and more like a high school cross-country runner. I still had the heart and legs of a forty-year-old.

When I arrived home, I downed a half-liter of Gatorade, kicked off my Adidas, and settled back in my recliner. Adriana told me my cellphone rang, and when she picked it up and answered it, there was no one there. It rang again fifteen minutes later and then quit. I had a bad feeling about that. Was it just a prankster, or was someone checking to see if I was home?

But a few minutes later, when Adriana took Lionel outside for a bathroom walk, my cell rang again. The text read unknown caller.

"Hello."

For a few seconds, no one responded.

I then said, "Okay, listen to me, maggot. Your game-playing is over. I warn you not to keep doing this." But just as I was preparing to end the call, a voice said, "Hello, McGowan." I knew the voice.

"So they let you out, Albrecht."

"I made an error in judgment about you, Bruce. I should have known better than to trust you, a former federal agent. Your little charade sabotaged my plan."

"And you, a former agent yourself, became an insane domestic terrorist. You sent me out with people who were to kill me, but it didn't work out, did it?"

One of which you supposedly killed. But I didn't believe it from the get-go. I saw right through the story that you and Mr. Murphy hatched. Poor Murph. I kind of liked the guy till I found him out."

"What do you mean found him out?"

"I'm not stupid, Bruce. And I do my homework. Special Agent John Murphy stopped breathing four days ago."

"You son-of-a-bitch."

"That may be, but I don't take kindly to betrayal. You, of all people, should know that. You think you stopped me, but you only offset my timing. What I have planned will still go down. Of course, you won't be around at such time I carry it out."

"Which sounds like a threat. Don't even think about going there, Albrecht."

"You won't have a clue about when, how or where it will happen. You might just be walking out of church and the bullet will find you."

"You were always talking about consequences, so you come within a hundred yards of me and yours will be fatal."

"I don't need to be at a hundred yards. You know what kind of shot I am at five hundred."

"I'm not going to continue trading threats with you, prick. This conversation is over." That's when I ended the call.

When Ben Marshall told me Murph had been reported missing, I suspected he had done away with Murphy. I didn't know if he had a wife and children, but I would try to find out.

It was time for Kurt Albrecht to die. I didn't have anything on my calendar the upcoming Saturday; I may as well go on another hunting trip. This time the target would not be a defenseless coyote.

Chapter Sixteen

Wednesday morning an old friend called and asked me if I'd be interested in being a fourth at the local country club golf course. It was exactly what I needed to take my mind off the Clarksburg matter. It was going to be a sixty-degree day with low humidity, no wind, and a one-ten tee time. Perfecto! The old friend was Dr. Henry (Hank) Smith, a psychiatrist on staff at the Bolt Springs Mental Wellness Center just over the state line in Virginia. I had gone to the local military school with Hank a half century before and we had stayed in touch especially over the past fifteen years. As he was by nature a very competitive guy, I always had to laugh when this counselor of neurotic and psychotic people came unglued when I would beat him on the links. One time he actually threw his club into a pond. Still, he'd give me a call when he was ready for another ass whoopin'.

At eleven-thirty, before we met the other two players at the golf shack, we sat down for a hot dog at the canteen. I hadn't seen Hank since late summer. He was my age, a bit rotund, bespeckled and slightly balding. I always had the impression that when I was in a conversation with him, he was not listening as a friend but as a clinician. He would never take his eyes off mine as though he were looking right into my soul. It didn't exactly unnerve me; I just found myself being careful I didn't say something or behave in such a manner that he may think I was either full of neuroses or bullshit. Every once in a while, I might say something in jest like, "Have you always had that twitch in your left eye?" Or "I noticed you've been slurring your words. Not a stroke coming on, is it?" When I mentioned the eye twitch, it wasn't twenty seconds until he excused himself to the restroom, likely checking it out in the mirror. I love getting inside the heads of head doctors.

After we had gotten our food, we began talking about our wives, adult children, people we knew, things about the world of politics that piss us off, and retirement, which he was considering. But just for my own edification, I brought up what I referred to as a hypothetical scenario.

"I'm just curious, Hank. You know I worked at one time for the government in counterterrorism."

"Yes, interesting line of work."

"It was. I myself often had to get into the mind of the terrorist."

"I'm sure you did, which helped you determine his next move. And then what little I know about counterterrorist agents, you may have had to pull the trigger on someone. There could be psychological aftereffects in doing that. Is this conversation about you?"

"Let's say I know of somebody you just mentioned, hypothetically of course."

"Of course."

"This guy pursued terrorists all over the world…the Middle East, Northern Africa, South America, Asia…assassinating scores of people. He took lives via sniper fire, raids, bombs, poisonings, every creative way imaginable. Often there was what we refer to as collateral damage…innocents killed…women, children, families. Maybe people died where he did not actually pull the trigger; he ordered air strikes on villages or with drones on enemy base camps. Then he retires and is no longer a man of action…no longer a killer. Tell me about what can happen to that mind."

"These are things you did."

"Well, yes…but this is not about me.'

"Sure," he replied, slowly nodding. "I get it. But, you obviously have something very real on your mind, Bruce, or you wouldn't be bringing it up. So, are you saying this person is experiencing some psychological issues and/or behaviors?"

"He definitely is, but before I tell you where I'm going with this, what are some residual effects that could occur after fifteen to twenty years of taking people's lives, regardless of them being terrorists?"

"What I see is that this person had been on a high all those years, experiencing a power unlike anything else. From his own hand he's able to snuff out another human being's life. I once counseled a convicted murderer who told me the only time in his life he felt important was when he had murdered someone. Your guy lived an exciting life that involved mystery, suspense, dominance and unrestraint. But then suddenly, all that power is taken away. It's like taking a drink away from an alcoholic or a drug from an addict. And so, what suffers the most is his ego. He has to find a way back to the world in which he is the most comfortable."

The Constitutionalists

"Okay, that all fits. I understand it's a power thing."

"What is this person doing now?"

"Over the past three years, he has been the leader of a 300-man and woman militia group."

"Have you had an occasion to observe him?"

"I have watched him stand before his people with outstretched arms shouting out venomous threats against the very government for whom he worked. As people cheer and chant his name, their eyes are wild with adoration. When they are in training exercises and performing to his liking, he plays the role, standing like a General Patton on the battlefield, hands on hips, smiling, complimenting them. But then there is another side of him. An angry and cruel side. Anyone who disobeys him or betrays him, he will punish. From what I understand, he has killed two government agents who he found out were planted by the government in his organization."

"When you began this conversation, I was sure this was about you. Patients will often give me hypotheticals or talk about someone else having the issue, but it is actually them. However, this last bit of information informed me it actually is someone else." He then looked at me over his glasses. "That is the case, isn't it?"

"Yes. Not to worry. He's a real person, just not me."

"What you see here is classic narcissism, Bruce. The leadership role has helped him restore that sense of power. Killing the two people you mentioned was like icing on the

Col. Lee Martin

cake. Metaphorically, they represented the government he hates. It also allowed him to experience the taste of blood yet another time. Let me ask you a question. I know you're retired, but has your former employer asked you to…"

"To take this man on? Yes. However, after I had infiltrated his organization, he found me out."

"Bruce, from what you told me, this man is not only dangerous but has psychopathic tendencies."

"That I did figure out. I was just trying to learn what makes him tick."

"Has he come after you?"

"He has. You see, I knew this guy years ago. We were in the same counterterrorism division. He asked me to come in with him, confided in me, telling me the plans he had hatched against the government. But then when he discovered I was working for Washington, he set me up for the kill. Fortunately, I was able to get away."

"Is he now wanted by the government?"

"Yes, but he is staying on the run."

"Well, my friend, I like you too much to see you end up dead. I'd end my contract with the government immediately and go back to just being local golfer Bruce McGowan."

"I am planning to end things as we speak." I didn't tell him how.

After that, we got off the subject of Albrecht, although I didn't mention him by name. I'm not sure why I even opened a conversation about him as I had pretty much figured out everything he told me on my own. Maybe I just needed it reinforced by an expert in his field. In my own way I thanked him for allowing me to bounce my concerns off him. I didn't throw the golf match, but I didn't allow myself to play my best. He beat me by a stroke. I guess I was just trying to prove to myself that unlike someone else, my ego hadn't suffered in my retirement.

Chapter Seventeen

That Friday, I heard again from Ben Marshall. The Bureau had found Mendelssohn. Dr. Hans Mendelssohn had left West Virginia sometime after Albrecht found out I had escaped being murdered. I imagined Albrecht had told the bomb maker to get lost, and he expeditiously returned to California. A former professor at Berkeley, Marshall told me he had been dismissed the year before for making anti-administration statements. Because there are federal and state laws that prohibit the manufacturing, possessing, and distributing of explosive devices, Mendelssohn would have concrete walls around him for at least 10 years. However, he would likely be offered a plea bargain in exchange for his testimony that would reduce his sentence.

Retired Marine Major Tom Gages was located where he worked as an insurance office manager in Clarksburg. When at first he only admitted being in the Constitutionalist militia and knowing nothing about any plans to detonate an EMP bomb, Bureau agents informed him that if convicted of a federal crime, he would lose his retirement pension the 61st day after said conviction. Considering he needed both his insurance salary and pension to sustain his invalid wife, he quickly changed his story, admitting he had sat in on Albrecht's conspiratorial briefing. However, he expressly denied any previous knowledge about either the plan or the bomb. A search of both his home and office turned up nothing that would incriminate him.

The Constitutionalists

Simultaneously, two other of Albrecht's subordinates were also pulled in and questioned…militia staff members Schwartz and Donovan, who were likewise privy to their commander's briefing. After agents had put the fear of God in them, they provided the written statements that incriminated Albrecht for planning to detonate an electromagnetic pulse device over the city of Washington, D.C.

Acting on all statements secured from all the above over a three-day period, the Bureau once again materialized at Albrecht's door to arrest him. However, Albrecht could not be found; he had obviously gone on the lam to avoid re-arrest. Considering he had friends in a hell of a lot of places, he could be difficult to locate. Which meant my plan that weekend to go find him and kill him was off. In our conversation, Ben told me the attorney general's case would be even better consolidated with my testimony.

"Uh, Mr. NSA, do you not have enough witnesses who were in his briefing to make a case?"

"Why wouldn't you want to testify? The fact he tried to have you killed would add more theater to the case."

"Theater? What the hell, Ben. What I experienced was a bit more than theater."

"I didn't mean it that way, Bruce. It's that your testimony would better solidify the case against Albrecht."

"It's time I shared something else with you, Ben. My wife would have been vehemently against taking on your request. She still thinks I was merely going on a coyote hunt with an old acquaintance. Since my retirement, all those times the government pulled me into some counterterrorist matter, she was on pins and needles until I came home. And what was worse, sometimes I'd come home shot up like a WWII, B-17. I have promised her faithfully that I would not take on another mission. So, if she finds out I went undercover in a militia organization bent on bringing down our government and almost getting myself killed, it will be my marriage that's shot up. I'd prefer you and the attorney general to keep my name out of it. I feel bad enough having kept all this from my wife. Our marriage has been built all these years on honesty and truthfulness. No secrets."

"Well, just remember, Bruce…when it comes to wives asking questions, you have the right to remain silent. Anything you say can and will be used against you."

"Funny, Ben. I'm serious about this."

"Okay, Bruce. I hear you. For the time being, I'll keep you out of the equation. But I can't promise that at some point, your name might come up, and you'll be subpoenaed by the state to testify."

"I'll cross that bridge when I come to it. But of course, the feds still have to find Kurt Albrecht."

From the abyss of my mind, Albrecht's words continued to ring in. "You won't have a clue about when, how, or where it will happen. You might just be walking out of church, and the bullet will find you."

The Constitutionalists

Threats have never bothered me. Terrorists, both foreign and domestic, and adversaries bearing grudges, have told me in person, over the phone, and in every way imagined they were going to kill me. It never bothered me. For the most part, I went after them, not giving them the chance to get to me. But Kurt Albrecht was in defilade somewhere, and although he wasn't about to come out in the open, he could whack me from any vantage point. He had been the same super G man that I was, going through the same training, hunted down, and terminated the worst of humankind. And he was pissed at me. I wasn't worried about me; I was worried that the bullet meant for me might find Adriana. Even if his bullet did find me, a high-velocity round can travel through one body and into another. Somehow, somewhere, I had to find him. And there was only one other person who could help me do that.

I hadn't told Ben about Gail. Even though I can be callous and ruthless at times, I guess I have a soft heart for some people. I knew the FBI would locate her, maybe go to the hospital and pull her into a room to interrogate her, embarrass her in front of her co-workers, and maybe get her fired. But that wasn't my only reason. Maybe I felt sorry for her. I knew she didn't belong in that organization and had been hoodwinked by the charismatic Kurt Albrecht to come in with him. And they had had a personal relationship. But I also saw the look on her face in Albrecht's briefing; she was stunned, even thunderstruck, that he would be planning to detonate a bomb over Washington.

I also had the feeling, even though he had put the fear of God in her, he would not give up on her. It was evident he liked her…a lot.

Two days later, Adriana received a call from her dad.

"Hey, sweetie, can you come back? Your mom's in the hospital again."

"Why? What happened?"

"She couldn't get her breath this morning. Thank God the health nurse was here. We called 911, and they admitted her. I was told it's something called a pulmonary embolism from where she had the surgery."

"Oh, no. That's serious."

"That's what they say. But she's breathing okay now, and they're gonna keep her there a few more days. She's been a little delirious and wants to know why you're not here. She doesn't even remember you were here to help her."

I was standing near Adriana when she received the call and saw that she had exploded in tears. "What is it, sweetheart?" I asked.

"It's Mom," she sobbed. "She's worse. I have to go back down." She then told me what had happened.

Turning her attention back to her dad, she said, "Don't worry, Pops. I'll make some flight arrangements and come either this evening or tomorrow."

She ended her conversation and dabbed at her eyes. "I expected when they reached this age, stuff would happen with them. First, my dad has a heart attack, and Mom becomes his caregiver, then she goes down. It's never going to get any better."

"We talked about this. You have to convince them to move back here. We have plenty of room."

"They won't do it. That's why they moved to a warm climate in the first place. Dad freezes when the temperature drops below 60."

"Well, book the two of us. I'll go down with you."

She shook her head. "No. You'd be bored to tears down there sitting around with Dad. All he wants to do is sit watching the TV and smoke cigars. You stay here with Lionel."

"You just can't keep going back there. You're the town's mayor. You were gone three weeks this last time."

"But I was easily handling things by phone and Zoom. However, you're right. I need to do my job in person. Maybe I should just go ahead and resign."

"No, sweetheart. You've been the most admired mayor this town's ever had. The people would put up a fuss if you did."

"We'll see. But I'd better go ahead and call the airlines."

I worried that Adriana was wearing herself thin, flying back and forth as she was. After returning this last time, I noticed there were tiny worry lines around her eyes. We hugged tightly before she boarded her plane, then gave each other a

Col. Lee Martin

doleful final look when she passed through security. I immediately regretted not going with her. I could have sat there with her dad those long days watching ESPN, even if it was bowling or curling. I'd do anything for her.

It was a long hour and a half from the airport back home. What made it seem even longer was the rain, which was blowing sideways. Then there's no more dangerous stretch of road than the West Virginia Turnpike, especially when there are pockets of standing water. I read all the time about people being killed on that winding, poorly graded road from either hydroplaning or hitting sheets of black ice. I brought Lionel with me this time, and he didn't disappoint me. He had held his bladder the entire way so that I wouldn't have to get out of the vehicle in the hard rain and walk him into the bushes.

It took about twenty minutes longer than usual to get back into town. But by the time we did so, the rain had stopped. I took Lionel home and fed him, then went out for a nice but lonely late dinner at a popular restaurant called Food and Friends. Back home at ten, I was beyond tired. I walked inside, almost expecting Adriana to be there, even though just a few hours before, I had kissed her goodbye. The house was quiet and lonely. It always felt like a morgue when she was gone. I took Lionel out one last time, then went to bed. But when I did, my mind wouldn't turn off. I kept seeing Albrecht's face when I closed my eyes and heard in my head his threatening words. It was then I knew what I had to do. I reminded myself at first light, I needed to call my brother to see if he could keep Lionel for a few days. I had to go back to Clarksburg.

Chapter Eighteen

After dropping Lionel off at Joey's that Thursday afternoon, I set out for Harrison County. In the past two weeks, I had gotten pretty damn familiar with the winding road. A couple of hours later, as I passed slowly by Kurt's Store, I looked for his white Ford pickup. Of course, it wasn't going to be there, especially since I saw sitting back off the road under a large poplar, a black official-looking SUV with a push bar. It was either a Bureau or an unmarked state police vehicle. I cruised on by and then drove on into Clarksburg.

It was just after four-thirty when I arrived at the Microtel. I was driving Adriana's Toyota as I wasn't taking any chance on one of the good ol' boys or even Kurt Albrecht himself recognizing my Suburban. I checked in but when asked how long I'd be staying, I told the desk clerk with the Pekinese face I didn't know. Put me down for three days.

I hadn't eaten lunch so I had a burger at a bar a block down the street with a Heineken. Basically, I had nothing planned until about 8:45 at which time I would camp out in the hospital's ER parking lot waiting for Gail Delancy to come out. I wasn't looking to intercept her; I was waiting instead to see if Kurt Albrecht would materialize. If he didn't, I would at least learn what kind of car she was driving and follow her home. Maybe that's where he was hiding out. If he wasn't, I was sure he knew where she lived and could be waiting for her. As she had told me what her hours were, I expected her to exit the ER any time after nine.

And so, sitting about a hundred feet away, at two minutes past nine I saw her exit from the emergency entrance door. To be sure it was her, I spied her through my night vision device as she walked to a blue Honda Civic four door. Waiting until she pulled away, I then followed her at five to six car lengths back. I had hoped no one was watching me watching her, and then would be calling the police.

After she turned off the main drag onto Jefferson Avenue and then Buchanan, I realized that in total she lived only a mile or so from the hospital in a small one story house on narrow Jackson Street. As she was pulling into her driveway, I found a spot at the curb two houses down. Again, I was hoping a neighbor was not noticing a strange car on the side of the street with someone sitting behind the wheel. Looking around, I didn't see anyone watching from a window or taking an evening walk. I didn't intend to be there that long, anyway.

The windows in the house were dark which didn't mean there wasn't someone already inside with the lights off. Through my powerful night vision sight I zoomed her in as she left her car, stepped onto the porch and unlocked her door with the aid of her cellphone flashlight. Once inside, she flipped her switch and lit up the room. Moments later, other lights went on throughout the house visible through the Venetian blinds which covered every window.

When I was in the counterterrorism business, I often employed my sound radar device, a handheld, high-tech monitor called Nosy. I hadn't had any reason to use it over the past nine or ten years, so before I left my house, I replaced its 9-volt battery and tested it. I had stood about 75 feet away from the house, placed the earphones on my head, and aimed it. I had put Lionel inside

The Constitutionalists

and then called out to him, which caused him to bark, telling me in doggie language to let him out. It still worked fine. I could understand every word he said.

Looking around once more on the dimly lit street for anyone who may be watching my car, I put on my headset and aimed Nosy at Gail's house. At first I could hear only the clatter of dishes and running sink water, but then within a half-minute the sound of voices, a man's and a woman's. It took me a moment, however, to realize the voices were coming from a TV. After I had sat for another ten minutes, I was satisfied Albrecht hadn't been waiting inside for her. I then put Nosy away.

But it wasn't just about Albrecht being a threat that generated my concern for her. An attractive woman living alone in a poorly lit neighborhood and coming home in the dark almost every night bothered me. However, it was her life, and even though she was none of my business, I still feared for her. I'd fear for any woman, young or old, who lived as she did. She should have had at the very minimum a bright motion-detection light installed on the outside of her house.

I wasn't going to sit there at the curb the entire night, but I did give it another hour and a half. If Albrecht intended to materialize, I figured he would already have been there. I doubted he would come in on her in the wee hours of the morning. However, as he probably thought I'd have told law enforcement about his relationship with Gail, surveillance would include her house. He wouldn't risk being spotted there. Still, I had to give this a shot.

It was a few minutes past eleven when I cranked the Toyota and moved on.

Col. Lee Martin

I slept in until eight the next morning, which felt good. Normally, I'm up by six-thirty, but when you have a dog who wants out to pee at five in the morning and whimpers till you let him, well there ya go. Lionel was Joey's problem this morning. I then partook of the motel's continental breakfast, having some scrambled eggs and sausage from the serving bins, and sat with my coffee and a complimentary copy of the local newspaper from the lobby. I don't often read the newspaper. I'm with Mark Twain, who said, "If you don't read the newspaper, you're uninformed; if you do, you're misinformed." Or something like that. I do, however, get my news first from one of the Charleston stations, then switch over to the major conservative network.

But as I sat reading and drinking that morning, I took account of one of the headlines, "*Local Fugitive Remains at Large.*" Was it about who I thought it was? I read on. Local businessman, Kurt Albrecht, who is better known as the leader of a large militia group known as The Constitutionalists, is being sought by both federal and state law enforcement for conspiring to commit crimes against the United States government. Although he had been released from jail on the 5th of November because of insufficient evidence, the FBI has since questioned several close members of the group, learning more about Albrecht's alleged subversive plans, the specifics of which have not been disclosed to the public. A new warrant for his arrest has now been issued. Albrecht himself is reportedly a former government agent…

The article went on to describe Kurt Albrecht as well as his vehicle. And if anyone had any information as to his whereabouts to contact either the FBI or local law enforcement.

I had not been to the militia compound since I was forcibly removed from there during the early morning hours the day after Albrecht's briefing about the EMP. Since I had nothing to do or any place to go during the hours of daylight until Gail Delancy left for her home in the evening, I decided to give the place a look. The FBI had combed the compound in minute detail and provided its report up the chain, ultimately reaching the NSC, but I wanted to take a look myself…mostly out of curiosity.

About five miles to the south, I came upon the gate, which had been padlocked, probably by the FBI. Now, there were no gate guards checking me as I came in, and the compound was not bristling with activity going on inside, which was occurring the last time I was there. After parking my vehicle off the side of the road, I found I could easily scale the gate and walk on in. Briefly eyeing the barracks off to the right, I then turned my attention to the mess hall. I found the door unlocked and once inside, a large roach scurried past my foot and disappeared under the large refrigeration unit. Ben was correct. Not a can of anything was left in the cabinets or the large refrigerator and the storage room was bare as well. The table where I had sat a couple of meals with Albrecht's staff brought back recollections of conversations, we had there…back when he thought I was his friend and trusted ally.

Upon leaving the chow hall, I went to the range. Just as I was told, there was not one casing to be found. It summoned memories of my days in officer basic at Benning when after a firing exercise, we presented our unloaded weapons to the range officer and shouted, "No brass, no ammo, sir." I caught myself smiling in remembering that. The only evidence a rifle range was even there were the silhouettes of shot-up human figures at various distances down range. I then went on down the trail to the makeshift urban village. The storefronts still stood as wooden props where at one time would be soldiers pretended to be augmenting the police and rousting rioters. Now, everything was quiet, even ghostly. I wasn't particularly looking for anything. I knew the Bureau agents had performed a thorough search for evidence, so I didn't expect to find any clues as to Albrecht's whereabouts.

As I was moving toward where Albrecht had kept his quarters in barracks Building One, I was suddenly descended upon by two men carrying ARs over their shoulders. "Stop where you are, sir!" one of them barked. I did.

"What are you doing here?" the other asked. "And keep that pistol holstered."

"Just looking around," I replied.

Both men, maybe 35 to 40, were dressed in khaki cargo pants and black jackets. One was red-headed, and the other a skinhead. The bald guy had a photo in his hand and was looking me up and down.
"Who are you?"

"My name's Bruce McGowan. And you?"

"If it's any difference to you, we are investigators with the West Virginia State Police working with the JTTF. You are trespassing on property that has been seized by the federal government. Did you not see the no trespassing sign?"

"No, I did not." And I didn't.

The Constitutionalists

"Show me some identification."

From my cargo pants I pulled out my wallet, making sure they saw my ID card denoting I was retired from the Department of State. Along with it was my retired badge.

"Well, Mr. McGowan, do you have a reason to be here?"

"I showed you mine, now show me yours."

They looked at one another and then pulled out their badges.

"Please answer my question, Mr. McGowan."

"I was working undercover in the Constitutionalists group for the National Security Council, specifically NSA director Ben Marshall."

"Was?"

"I suppose I still am, although I have turned over all the information on the militia that occupied this compound that I had at the time. I just came back for another look."

"You're looking for what?"

"I'm not sure…maybe Kurt Albrecht himself."

"Well, I assure you he's not here. We thought you might be him. Are you officially looking for him?"

"Not officially, but we have some unfinished business I need to address."

"Unfinished business? I don't understand," the red-haired officer said.

"Well, to put it bluntly, he wants to kill me. He tried to do that a few days ago because he found out I was working for the NSC. I fear he was successful in killing an FBI agent who was also undercover."

"Sounds like an intriguing story, McGowan. So you want to get even."

"I want to find him before he begins planning another attack against the government."

They looked at each other again. "We heard about that. What kind of an attack, if you don't mind us asking?"

"The president who heads the NSC hasn't released that as yet."

"But you know."

"Yes."

"Well, we know the JTTF has gone through this place looking for records and plans for some kind of attack against the government; I doubt if you'll find anything of significance, Mr. McGowan."

"Like I said, I'm just looking. Maybe I'll remember something I didn't think of when I provide my own statement. I got hit in the head pretty damn hard by Albrecht and the blow caused a little memory loss."

The red-head nodded. "Sorry that happened. Alright, then. Look around all you want. Let us know when you leave, sir."

"Will do."

When the officers walked away, I continued toward the barracks building and then opened the door of Albrecht's small office he had set up. I had been there before sharing a drink with him...me a beer, and he a bottle of Scotch from which he ended up shit-faced. It was where I first learned of the EMP bomb. His desk in the middle of the room was nothing more than a simple table without drawers, and his bed was a single military-looking bunk. For an egomaniac, drunk with power and vain glory, I expected his desk would be something lavish and masculine and bed, at least a queen, to accommodate one of his female militia members. Especially Gail Delancy. But as I had been there twice before, I knew what it would be.

I sat in his straight-back chair at the table for a few minutes, thinking. The butt-stroke on my forehead had scrambled my brains. I hardly remembered being carted off to where I was to be shot in the head and dumped into the river. Everything that Albrecht had told me there and in the briefing room with the bomb-maker and his staff seemed to still be hiding in defilade. "Damn!" I exclaimed, stomping my foot.

Thanks to my boot, It was one of those eureka moments. A floorboard beneath me moved ever so slightly. It was loose. Taking out my Ranger knife, I dug the blade into the crack between two boards. A six-inch by two-foot section of the plank board popped up. When I pulled the wood up from the floor, I saw something the Bureau agents had missed…a stack of papers. I then picked them up and laid them on the table. Bingo!

What lay before me was a veritable treasure trove of incriminating evidence.

Chapter Nineteen

I just briefly skimmed the papers and their headings at the table, reading Albrecht's printed captions such as Target Washington, EMP Technology and Structure, EMP Coverage/Range, Expected Casualties, Damage to Electrical Grids, and Political Ramifications. I decided rather than to read the documents there, to take them back to my room at the Microtel and read them in depth. Then they needed to be handed off to the attorney general via Ben Marshall. But how would I get them to him? The documents were too sensitive to fax. The public would be in panic if anyone got wind of a plan to detonate a bomb over Washington, D.C.

I didn't inform the two-state investigators of my findings. On the way to the gate, having shoved the documents inside my shirt, I merely said, "Well, it does look like the JTTF combed the place sufficiently. How many curiosity seekers or militia types have gotten into this place over the past couple of weeks?"

"Counting you? One. Our people have turned away at the gate a couple of reporters and three militia members who told us they hadn't been informed that the feds closed the compound down."

"Well, sorry to have breached your security."

"No problem, Mr. McGowan. Have a good rest of the day."

I had another fast-food dinner at a chicken restaurant, then grabbed a brew at a local grocery to take back to the room. I wondered how Albrecht had allowed these documents to remain in his floorboard. Because he was in a hurry to evacuate the bomb and get the troops out before he knew a JTTF element would be swooping in, did he forget about them? Actually, I think it was a matter of timing. Murphy had returned with his shiner to tell Albrecht I had escaped their clutches, assaulted him and shot Bear Bronson. Not buying his story, in a fit of rage, he had Murphy killed, maybe doing it himself. Realizing I would be going straight to the man who engaged me with my information, he knew he had to move the bomb and get Mendelssohn out of camp. He then had his warriors grab and move weapons, ammo and equipment out of the compound as they were leaving. Someone, maybe Gages, carted the bomb and launcher. Marshall said when the JTTF arrived, nearly 300 people and their vehicles were scurrying like ants. As the feds moved in and cornered Albrecht, he not wanting to risk getting caught with his plans, hid them in the floorboards. At some point when he was released, he would return to retrieve them. That seemed to be the only explanation I could come up with. Otherwise, his leaving the documents on site made little sense.

Once settled in my room with my beer and the documents, I began reading. One report showed a diagram of the bomb, which included the armature cylinder containing the high explosive, stator winding, surrounding jacket, and a W-54 warhead. It was clearly Mendelssohn's own invention, which did not appear conventional. There was an explanation of how it was either to be detonated or fired by a missile high into the atmosphere. It would be fired, in this case, from a strategic location in the Washington area to detonate over the city, with its focal point being the White House. There would be an intense electromagnetic burst, which would neutralize all communications systems, vehicle control systems, and controls on defensive missiles and bombs. Electronics would be affected not only in the nation's capital but also in the cities of Baltimore and Philadelphia. Pentagon systems would be killed as well. Electric mass destruction could also be realized at the National Crime Information Center outside of Clarksville, which, in essence, would also affect the Clarksburg populace.

Transported on 14 November from the militia compound to a warehouse in Alexandria, Virginia, via a covered single-drop flatbed truck were the vintage M29 Davy Crockett missile firing system and the E-bomb, both purchased by anonymous Washington and Clarksburg, West Virginia businessmen. On 15 November, the truck would move into the State of Maryland to high ground 1.2 miles from Gaithersburg, where at 1000 hours, the EMP bomb would be launched two nautical miles into the troposphere. It would detonate at about 20,000 feet center mass over Washington, D.C. via a synchronized timed fuse.

In thinking back to my Army days, the Davy Crockett system was never used in combat, only firing two test missiles into the western desert. It only saw about ten years of service. Where did the financiers get it, and would the planned launch have been successful? How tragic would it have been for the system to only launch the bomb a few hundred yards and wipe out a community? It was not supposed to be a nuclear weapon, but the blast and shock wave alone would kill a great many people and destroy both homes and businesses in the D.C. grid.

If the statements provided by Albrecht's loyalists were not enough to convict him, I had in my hand something that would. I would be visiting the CJIS the next morning to hand-deliver the documents to the FBI.

At 8:30 that evening, I parked Adriana's Toyota on Jackson Street in a different location at the curb near Gail's house behind an older BMW. As of that evening, there were several cars parked on the street, likely belonging to guys who were doing a little Friday night partying. I shouldn't be noticed. Nine o'clock came and went. So did 9:15 and 9:30. Maybe Gail had stopped off at the store or a friend's house. But then at 9:40, she pulled her car into the driveway. Again I watched as she exited and walked up the steps to her porch. She put her key in the lock and then opened the door. That's when I placed the listening device on the dash and turned it on. I heard her footsteps on the wooden floor, then saw the living room illuminate. A second light came on, and I heard the sound of a cork popping from a bottle again. There was then the sound a glass makes when set down on a countertop. No voices this time from the TV or otherwise. However, about ten minutes later, she began talking with someone on her cellphone. There was laughter and a lot of gabbing about someone at work.

I again sat in the car until 11:00, watching several young men, as I had guessed, leaving a couple of the houses. One who had stumbled a bit on the sidewalk, obviously having too much to drink, slid in behind the wheel of the BMW. Before I pulled out behind him, I called 911 and gave the operator the license number. "He's heading west on Jackson and doing a bit of weaving." The response was, "Thanks for the heads-up, sir, officers should be intercepting him on 14th Street."

It had been a good day. I had found some real evidence that Albrecht was planning to detonate the E-bomb over Washington. Gail was safe in her house, hopefully for the night. And a young drunk would not be killing someone on the street that night.

Saturday morning was cold. The temperature had dropped to 30 overnight, and I was glad I had packed my coat. After a bowl of cereal at the breakfast bar and a cup of coffee, I returned to my room and called Ben Marshall. He was a six-days-a-week guy at the office, and I figured I would catch him there. I was wrong. However, he did answer the phone.

"Are you having a good Saturday morning, Bruce?"

"All is good here in the doubya vee. Wait a minute…do I hear seagulls in the background?"

"I'm in tropical Ft. Lauderdale with my family for the weekend. What's up with you?"

"I'm in tropical Clarksburg."

"And you're there why?"

"Add a few more days to my contract."

"Again, why?"

"I took a little tour of the now closed militia compound."

"Did you not have enough of it when we put you there undercover?"

"I know the Bureau agents did a clean sweep when they raided the place, but they forgot to look under the rugs…actually floorboards."

"You found something?"

"A stack of Albrecht's records and notes about his plan to shut down Washington, D.C. with the E-bomb."

"Fantastic. More ammunition to put this guy away…if and when we find him. You're not up there looking for him, are you?"

"If I happen to see him, I'll send your regards."

"Bruce, I told you to let the feds and locals handle this."

"Oh, you did say that, didn't you."

"Go home, Bruce. I'll have a couple more days pay sent to you. You never fail to come through."

"I need you to do something for me."

"Name it."

"Call your Bureau contacts for them to get me admitted into the CJIS building. I need to get Albrecht's documents to them and just can't walk in. That way, they'll get them to you and the attorney general. I knew I couldn't fax them to you or send them in the mail. And I didn't want to make another trip up to D.C."

The Constitutionalists

"I'll make a call, Bruce. When that's done, go home."

"I intend to tomorrow."

"Why will you wait till then?"

"Goodbye, Ben. Thanks in advance for making the call." I then ended ours.

Just before eleven, Ben texted me to say I was to be expected at the CJIS. Once inside, I would be directed to the bureau's Criminal Justice Information System department.

I had never been there, but man, was it impressive. I found the main office building alone to be something like 500,000 square feet. Constructed in a modular design, the building was nearly the length of three football fields. In doing my homework about the place on the internet, I saw it had a 600-seat cafeteria, a 500-seat auditorium, and a 100,000-square-foot computer center. After entering the complex, I went through security and picked up my visitor's pass. At the information desk, I found I was expected and was issued a separate pin-on ID with my name on it, then directed to the eighth floor where I was to meet Special Agent Marco Rivera. When I exited the elevator, a lovely young thing greeted me at he door and gave me the warmest of receptions. "You must be Mr. McGowan."

"That I am."

"Please walk this way."

I followed her down the hallway. If I did walk that way, I would be taking quick little sandpiper steps and wiggling my derriere. I'd also be getting some strange looks from the other guys on the floor.

When I was directed to Agent Rivera's office, he stood and shook my hand. He was short, with coal-black hair and an olive complexion. He was a nice-looking chap. "Good morning, Mr. McGowan. Welcome, and please have a seat." He spoke with a slight Hispanic accent.

I sat in one of the chairs that faced his desk. Looking past him through the window, I saw that he had a nice view of the West Virginia countryside.

"Your reputation precedes you, sir," he said. "I actually received a call from the director in Washington, D.C.. He said he knows you."

"You, of course, mean Don Habersham. Don and I were special agents in the same office in Gulfport, Mississippi for a short time. Our paths then took a different turn. He grew up to be the Director of the FBI, and I grew up to be a house husband."

"You forgot about your service in the State Department as a counterterrorist operative."

"Well, I didn't forget about it. I just never talk about it. What is your job here?"

"I supervise a unit of investigative analysts performing research on suspected foreign and domestic terrorists."

"The reason I was sent to see you."

The Constitutionalists

"And I understand you have something for me regarding one Kurt Albrecht."

"Did anyone bring you up to speed on this guy?"

"Our analysts have been conducting investigations on him for over two years in conjunction with our office in Charleston and the Pittsburgh office that has oversight on the entire state of West Virginia."

"Then you're the right person to give this to." I handed off the manila folder containing Albrecht's documents. He took them and I could almost see the same glee in his eyes that a child has on Christmas morning.

"I understand some incidents occurred at the Constitutionalists' compound that involved you."

"I was doing some undercover work there for the National Security Advisor."

"But you are retired. How did you…?"

"The people with whom I used to collaborate and who still work in various government law enforcement capacities seem to remember that I'm still alive. I get calls every once in a while."

"I heard that you were the best in the counterterrorist game. Apparently, there are not many in today's world who could measure up to your reputation."

"You're embarrassing me now."

"You did your job, then followed up when the compound was shut down to continue your investigation. You then discovered these documents. That's not only being thorough; it's being tenacious. It is both an honor and a privilege to come face-to-face with someone of your stature.

"Thank you for your kind words, Special Agent. But I do have a question. Do you know if an agent named John Murphy was ever found? Albrecht had boasted he had him killed for being a mole."

He dropped his eyes. "I didn't know him as he was brought in from Virginia. But yes, his body was found in some woods by a couple of hunters, stabbed through the heart."

I shook my head. "Horrible. I was thinking the other day that Albrecht, in hunting down and killing terrorists, had obviously developed the kind of personality disorder that made it easy for him to kill anyone for any reason, especially when someone crossed him. He ordered me killed, you know."

"Yes. That got around. It also got around that you killed one of them yourself."

"No. Murphy did when my would-be killer put a gun to my head. Murphy saved my life. Now that his death is official, it grieves me deeply."

"Sorry, Mr. McGowan. It grieves all of us when we lose one of our own."

"Do you know anything about his family?"

"No, I actually heard he didn't have one. He was pretty much a loner."

I shook my head and then said, "Sad."

We had about twenty minutes of small talk after that, mainly about our own families, and then I stood. "I guess I need to get out of your hair, Agent Rivera. Thanks for taking these papers off my hands."

He nodded.. "I don't know how long you'll be in the area, but if you need anything from me or the Bureau, here is my card."

We shook hands again and said our goodbyes.

I started to blow a kiss to the pretty receptionist on the way out but then thought just throwing my hand up was much more appropriate.

Chapter Twenty

After I left the CJIS facility, I stopped at a local restaurant serving blue plate specials for $6, complete with rolls, sweet tea, and a choice of dessert. It looked to be a popular haunt for the good people of Clarksburg, as I had to park in the back of the building and then stand in line at the door for a table. However, fifteen minutes later, I was seated.

While waiting on my food, I began looking around at the faces. I could swear the young man in the jean jacket and close-cropped beard with his wife and young daughter was wearing a face I had seen in the compound. As a matter of fact a couple of other faces looked familiar as well. Most of the members of the Constitutionalist group would in fact be from Clarksburg and around the county. People I had observed in that compound were every age from twenty to seventy, all considering themselves patriots, hating the current government enough to follow someone who planned to do something about it. However, none of them knew it involved detonating a bomb over Washington. They only despised the government enough to curse it, have meetings about it, and demonstrate in mass, carrying their black militia banner, the one with the sword and griffon. It gave them a sense of purpose as a red, white and blue American. I couldn't imagine that with the exception of Albrecht and two or three others, anyone in that militia group wanted to destroy Washington, its grid and its ability to defend the United States against countries such as Russia, China and North Korea.

The Constitutionalists

I had consumed most of my meal, which by the way was hearty, when an unmistakably recognizable face came through the door. Major Tom Gages. And he saw me immediately. As the restaurant had a seat yourself policy, he decided on a table that was open next to mine. It was intentional.

Talking just loud enough for me to hear, he said, "You actually decided to show your face again?"

"I show it every day, Gages."

"But it's here in this county you can get it shot off with double buck."

"I heard you sang like a choir boy to the feds to save your ass."

"I despise rats. I especially despise rats who wrangle their way into an organization like ours and then backstab its leader."

"Speaking of that, was it you who stabbed Murphy to death?"

"Murphy. Another weasel. You'd like me to confess to it so that you could run back to whoever hired you and tell them. Well, I won't give you the satisfaction."

"So, where's Albrecht hiding?"

"I'm sure you'd like to know."

"I guess you don't even know, yourself. You see, you're the worse kind of rat...the Judas Iscariot kind. You ratted him out and he's gotta be pissed at you. Maybe he's out there somewhere looking for you."

"You helped to bring down a good man and destroy a patriotic organization. Yeah, he's out there somewhere and if he knew you were sitting in that chair, he'd come in here and blow you away with a 12 gauge. I might just do it myself."

"Then you are as insane as he is, Major."

"You need to get your ass out of this place before I take you outside and demonstrate how Marines handle snakes."

"I was a rat a couple of minutes ago. But, if you're aiming to prove how tough you are. I'll be outside as soon as I finish my banana cream pie."

Gages then turned his head away without a word and picked up his menu.

After not paying Gages another second of attention, I finished up my pie, paid my bill at the cashier's counter, and headed out the door. The day had warmed, and the bright, early afternoon sunshine felt delicious against my skin. When I had reached my car, I suddenly felt something else...a hand grasping the collar of my coat. Gages swung me around and was preparing to land a punch. However, I ducked his fist and gave him a straight punch of my own, squarely into his nose. Blood gushed immediately, but that didn't stop him. Like a bull, he came charging head-first toward my chest. I think that's the way Marines fought. But as he stumbled forward, I sidestepped and

The Constitutionalists

rammed his jarhead into the brick wall of the restaurant. As he writhed on the ground, trying to get to his feet, I put my foot on his neck. "Better stay down, Major. You're going to hurt yourself even worse than you have." But then he wanted to get ugly. I saw that he had reached inside his jacket and pulled out a 9 mil. When he tried aiming it at me, I pressed harder on his neck and he dropped it on the ground.

"I'm going to let you up, Gages, so you won't drown in your blood. Now don't try anything else."

"Alright...you're choking me." He gasped for air. But he lied when I moved my boot off his neck and grabbed for the gun. I then stomped his right arm with my boot and he cried out in pain. I heard and felt his bone crack beneath my boot. He laid in position for a few seconds then tried to stand up. But with a busted arm, he couldn't push himself to his feet, I helped him up by grabbing him by his jacket. As I leaned him against my car, he looked pitiful...bloodied forehead from the brick wall and broken, bleeding nose from my brick fist.

"Go see a doctor, Major," I said, and tossed him aside. I then opened the door to the Toyota, slid in behind the wheel and turned the key. As I was pulling away, I saw him pointing at me, yelling something about killing me next time.

Back in my motel room, I sat in the side chair and thought about the altercation I had just had. Tom Gages never thought when he got up that morning he'd be getting his ass kicked. He'd go back to his insurance office and tell a different story to save face, the tough guy Marine he was. He was either knocked down by a hit and run driver or he fell down the flight of stairs somewhere. He wouldn't admit somebody my age beat the crap out of him. But hell, he's the one who started it.

Col. Lee Martin

I watched a little of the news at five, then just after 5:30, called Adriana. Her mom was doing better but the P.E. had taken a lot out of her. I could hear the exhaustion in Adriana's voice and really felt for her. I was anxious for both of us to get back to our normal, sedentary life…not that romancing Mrs. McGowan was anything sedentary. But we missed each other and were beyond anxious for her to get home.

I was going to give my surveillance of Gail Delancy one more night. I couldn't explain it but I just had a feeling that something was going to pop. But then I was almost at the point I didn't care anymore. My whole purpose in going after him was the phone call he had made and that he might decide to carry out his vendetta at Wolf Laurel, my country home. Was he that maniacal or was his focus still on making Washington, D.C. come to a screeching halt? There could be a thousand places he was hiding. Wherever it was, he wasn't going to be far from his bomb. He would devise a new plan even if he had to carry it out by himself.

Once again at 8:45, I sat in the Toyota on the side of Jackson Street between the driveways of two houses. As if on cue, around 9:10 Gail steered her car onto the driveway and parked. After exiting, she ascended the three steps to her porch and unlocked her door. I was still wishing she had installed a motion sensor light, but this night, it appeared she was safely inside. However, I didn't even need to set up my listening device when I heard the scream. It was hers. Like a bat out of hell, I sprang from the car and ran to the house. She screamed another time and as I bounded through her front door, gun in hand, the next scream was reduced to a muffle. Someone had his hand over her mouth. When I flipped on the wall switch and flooded the room with light, there he stood. Albrecht had one hand over her mouth and the other was holding a pistol to her head.

"Drop the gun, McGowan. Drop it or a bullet goes in Gail's head."

Her eyes were as big as shooter marbles.

I dropped the gun onto her couch and then said, "Why are you doing this, Albrecht? Leave her out of it and just make it about you and me."

"I knew you'd be back tonight. You see, I also sat in my car the past two nights watching you watching her. She was bait for the both of us. You were thinking I might either be here shacking up with her or would come here to threaten her. You might be a hard-nosed bastard, McGowan, but you're also a bleeding heart…to a fault. I knew you liked Gail and didn't want to see her mixed up with the likes of me, the leader of an organization prepared to take down this commie, socialistic government with a 2 kiloton E-bomb." He grinned, devilishly. "This is not going to be your night, Bruce." He then looked beyond me and said, "Major?"

The sharp pain on the back of my head was the last thing I felt.

Chapter Twenty-One

For a second time in two and a half weeks, I was awakened by a slap in the face while tied to a chair. This time the surroundings were different. As I looked around, still groggy and my head hurting all over like a toothache, I discovered I was in one large room, maybe a warehouse with a thirty foot ceiling and a smattering of small windows high up on the walls. The windows were allowing light to filter into the place which was the only way I could tell it was daylight outside. Someone had strapped me to the chair with what seemed like an entire roll of duct tape that covered my upper torso and legs. My wrists were bound together with plastic straps. The only parts of me I could move were my head and lower arms.

Looking around, I saw no one. What looked like Albrecht's Ford truck was parked inside the building about twenty yards from the chair. I took it that it had been parked there the past couple of weeks and he was driving something else so that it wouldn't be spotted on the road. And off to my left was the la preuve…the bomb, the tangible evidence of Albrecht's intent to destroy the Washington, DC electric grid. I learned that word, preuve, while in Paris the year before.

It was then I heard the large entry door slam shut, followed by two sets of footsteps. The two men belonging to the footsteps walked to where they stood in front of me. Gages looked like someone had beat the shit out of him. Actually, someone had. A large bandage was glued to the top of his head, both eyes were black and swollen, and his right arm was in a sling. In his left hand was what looked to be a walking stick.

"I see you took my advice and sought medical treatment, Major."

He then stepped up to me, swung the stick and cracked me on the side of the head. The blow dazed me to a point where I thought I may be losing consciousness again.

"You're weak, Marine. You couldn't beat me in a fair fight, so you tie me to a chair and whack me with a stick."

"Keep talking, McGowan. Maybe I'll cut your damn tongue out before we kill you."

"Now, now, Tom," Albrecht said. "I was planning to keep McGowan in suspense about what we'd do with him. The cat's now out of the bag."

"How does it feel to lose everything, Kurt? Your freedom, your command, your reputation, your girlfriend, and I'm sure in time, your business."

It was he who hit me this time. His fist found my left jaw. I don't know why I kept pushing the envelope. His blow hurt like a bitch.

"Damn but that felt good," he said. "And so, here you are again…sitting there all tied up in a chair with a killer headache. This time will be different, McGowan. Won't be anyone coming to your rescue. I will personally guarantee that."

Col. Lee Martin

"What did you do with Gail Delancy? The last time I saw her, you were holding a gun to her head."

"Oh, she's fine. Probably back to work today, a little traumatized I suspect. But I'm not worried about her. She won't go to the police or FBI. She saw what happened to you and that put the fear of God into her. Or the fear of me…same difference. And just what were you doing sitting outside her place, anyway? Stalking? Peeping in her windows?"

"Just what were you doing inside her place?"

"Watching out for her in case perverts like you were watching her."

"So, your concept of looking out for her is breaking into her house, waiting to attack her, then putting a gun to her head?"

"Just shut your freaking mouth, McGowan."

"So, what are you going to do…put a bullet in me where I sit?"

"You're not going to die that easily. We're going to play a little cat and mouse game. I'm actually going to let you go."

"I think I see what's coming."

"The major and I are going on a little hunting trip. We'll take you from here and drop you up on the Shawnee, which is a series of hills bearing the same name as the tribe that once lived there. A lot of Indians and whiteys were killed in skirmishes up there, so you should feel honored dying where they did. But, you'll not only have to survive the two of us and all the bullets we'll be throwing at you but the rugged hills of Shawnee as well. We know that triple-canopy terrain like the back of our hand. It's where we have taken our troops on maneuvers a few times. We'll of course have the advantage with our high-powered rifles and scopes. However, although you may think of me as cruel, even deranged, I'm actually a very just and compassionate person. I wouldn't leave you out there in no man's land without protection. You're going to have with you that trusty XD we took from your holster. Does that not sound fair?"

"It sounds to me like there's a caveat to your plan."

"How insightful, Bruce. Yes. The magazine you'll have will contain only one round. One bullet. But I caution you to use that one bullet resourcefully. You might have to use it on the bear that may be tracking your scent. Of course, if you shoot it, you might only piss it off. And then you might just get lucky enough to hit either me or Major Tom, that is if you see us. But your one bullet has to be true. We won't kill easily. Even if you get into a position where you do kill one of us, that leaves the other. However, after a couple of days without food and you find yourself winged by our rounds in the arms and legs, which we will do, you might just use that one bullet on yourself. But I hope you won't resort to that. I want your head in my crosshairs when I finally fire the fatal shot."

"Now I know you're mad, Kurt. I think that hunting down terrorists and killing them made you a nut job, a psychopath. For somebody to waste his time and effort on a person who was merely serving his country as a plant getting intel on a militia group, you're taking this all too seriously. You need to get a life, man."

He then stepped into me and placed his face within inches of mine. "I had a life. I was the leader of a patriotic organization, respected and admired for what I was doing. I thought you were going to help me carry out my plan. You were a friend, a confidant. I shared that plan with you. But you betrayed me. You were working all along for the iniquitous, loathsome government I despised. And then you got away from me, running back to the people who hired you with information about my mission. I had to shut everything down and hide my EMP before the feds swooped down into my compound like vultures. You did that, McGowan. You caused me immense consternation. That's why you are now my mission...to play a cat and mouse game with you. It'll be fun. And just as a cat takes small bites of a mouse to where it can no longer resist, I will be taking pieces of you before blowing your brains out." Little bits of spittle sprayed me every time he formed the letter b.

He was indeed mad. I was watching and listening to someone whose brain had blown a gasket. The gerbil had fallen off the wheel.

"Uh, Kurt, I'm not trying to get Major Tom here in trouble, but didn't he betray you as well by turning state's evidence with the feds? He knew he'd be going to jail with you if he didn't, so according to my sources, he provided to them specific information about your E-bomb. Can you really trust a guy like that?"

"Major Gages and I have talked about that. I know you gave your people the names of those in the room during my briefing, Tom being one of them. The FBI did interrogate him, but he did not tell them anything. If someone said he did, they are lying. Tom is loyal, as all my people are loyal. That's why the charges against me were dismissed. Nobody is going to stand up and testify against me."

"They don't need to, prick. The FBI now has tangible evidence of your plot that includes the EMP bomb."

"And how would they have that. I have either hid or destroyed everything on paper. Sorry, McGowan, but your people have nothing."

"Hmmm, maybe I shouldn't tell you this because you might just take my one bullet away. But I will anyway. The Bureau boys didn't find something on their sweep of your compound that I did."

"And what could that be."

"Your comprehensive plans to include bomb description and data you hid under the floorboards in your room at the barracks. It contained not only your handwriting but fingerprints as well."

Albrecht glared at me, face reddened and mouth pursed into a scowl. He looked ready to just go ahead and put a bullet in my head. However, he turned toward Gages and said, "Blindfold him, Major. Then rip off the tape and push him out the door. Time to go hunting."

I knew it was a Jeep that he had tossed me into because Albrecht told Gages to "Toss him into the Jeep." Gages then tied my wrists to the front passenger seat assist bar and then climbed into the small back seat. I had earlier overheard Gages tell Albrecht he had taken a few days off "to do this," but "It's worth it." Did that mean they would have me out there dodging bullets for more than a day? The nights would be chilly and they hadn't given me any food. I shouldn't have any trouble finding water, considering it had recently rained. But then I thought the whole thing was absolutely ridiculous. If they wanted me dead, just shoot me. However, they wanted to make a game out of it like children who try to make a cookie or candy bar last longer by nibbling on it a piece at a time. My guess was, they intended to get their jollies by shooting pieces off me a little at a time before the final kill. I'd bleed out, run and then drop.

We must have gone five or six miles over rough roads making at least three turns. As I couldn't see when a pothole loomed ahead, I wasn't able to brace myself. For the most part, I just bounced around, bumping my head a couple of times on the Jeep's roll cage and sound bar. Those little impacts did nothing but exacerbate my headache.

The Jeep then came to a stop and as Gages cut my bindings and removed the blindfold, Albrecht pointed a handgun at me. "Get out," he said. So I did.

Then with both a .308 and a .30-06 trained on me, I stood looking around. It was definitely triple-canopy forest in which I'd be lost without a map and a compass or better yet, a GPS. Unable to gain any sense of direction, I had no idea where to run. But, I was a Ranger in the Army and very good at land navigation exercises. Whether the jungles of Panama or Vietnam, I could still feel my way along taking note of terrain features such as hills, streams and rivers, trails, and when in open areas, follow the sun and stars. So, with that experience, under normal conditions I knew I could find my way into civilization. However, my two pursuers closing in on me and taking shots at my body when they caught sight of me through their scopes, might make me not only lose progress but my focus. But there were only two of them. Unless they were master trackers, I could be anywhere in those woods. And it was a huge mess of woods.

But no sooner than I had thought that, to my surprise two trucks pulled up, each containing four men bearing everything from ARs to sniper rifles. And I could tell immediately they were experienced hunters. I took it they were also members of his now defunct militia. Albrecht addressed them. "Alright, boys. This man here is an enemy of the people…a man who has committed treason and deserves to go before a firing squad. You will be that firing squad. You just have to get him in your sights. I want to kill him but not all at once. I want you to make him bleed a little at a time. Shoot pieces off him. Then I will place the final bullet. This could end today but it could take two or three. Have fun out there."

"Don't listen to him, people," I said. "If you do this, you will be committing murder. I am not your enemy. I'm a retired civilian who has worked for federal law enforcement. This man is a psychopathic sadist of the worst degree who thinks maiming and killing human beings is a game. Don't play this game with him…"

They didn't let me finish before breaking out in laughter. Did these nutso mountain boys actually realize what they were planning to do or were they just caught up in Albrecht's madness, thinking they were hunting down some enemy agent? That's what Albrecht had made me out to be.

Albrecht tossed me my gun, then threw the clip containing the single round over my head. I watched where it landed in a clump of weeds. "Okay, McGowan, you have one minute to go find that magazine and disappear into the woods. Ten guns will then be bearing down on you." He turned to his men. "Spread out and make a wide sweep. Good hunting, my boys."

I stood for another few seconds wondering if they would cut me down if I didn't move. Realizing any one of them would take his shot and put a bullet in my arm or leg, I hustled to where I saw the magazine land, felt around for it in the weeds maybe ten more seconds, then found its cold steel. I had no sooner picked it up and sprang into the woods when the first round from one of the ARs whizzed past my head and hit a massive oak to my front. I knew I'd be running but didn't think they would. They would be spread out in a line, walking determinedly, scanning the forest for any movement. I had seen a movie a few years back where during the 1940s a young Black man who was guilty of nothing but being a Negro, was trying to escape a band of Mississippi fun-seekers pursuing him through a swampy forest. And now in real life, a mad man with his merry men were doing the same with me as their target.

Chapter Twenty-Two

As a former infantryman, one of the training exercises to which I always looked forward to was something called E&E, Escape and Evasion. Having experienced maybe a dozen of these at Ft. Benning's Ranger School, Panama's Jungle Survival Course and the Everglades to mention a few, there are tactical skills one never forgets. I had to E&E for real in Vietnam when my Special Ops team was overrun by an 80-man sapper element. One tactic we learned was a retrograde maneuver where we stopped, hid using available foliage for concealment and then doubled back after the aggressors passed by. But you also have to know your enemy. Given the fact that this group of woodsman had formed a line and was sweeping the forest straight-on, after I had covered a hundred yards or so, I took off at a 90 degree angle. To stay on that angle, one has to spot a visual target such as a large tree or rock formation. When it is reached, sight in on another terrain feature and move to it. It's easy when sighting with a compass and shooting azimuths, but I didn't have one. The only compass I had on this trip was on my watch and Albrecht had taken it. What I didn't want to happen was to veer off that angle and end up running into my pursuers.

I stopped for a few moments by a large sycamore to listen. In the woods when one can't see but a few feet in front of him, listening is the most important natural skill a person has. Someone likely knew that I had trailed off to the right and was thrashing through the brush on his own. I didn't think it was a deer. I waited, and as I did, whoever or whatever it was stopped. Now we were both waiting for one or the other to move. Two minutes later, it was I who did. I began making my way as silently as I could, being careful not to snap a twig. That is when I heard the report of a rifle followed simultaneously by a bullet that tore through my open Greg Norman jacket at the pocket. I dropped quickly. The first shot still reverberating through the forest, the gunman fired a second round which zipped by my right ear then ricocheted off the large rock to where I had perched myself.

Running to the reverse side of the large rock at a crouch, a third bullet zipped wildly over my head. I kept running, this time aimlessly. However, they must have enveloped me. Someone else was now firing from another vantage point. This time the round took a piece of my left bicep. Seconds later, blood oozed through my sleeve. Apparently, however, I ultimately must have outrun their line of sight as I found lower ground that dropped dramatically into a small stream. I then jumped the creek and trekked up a small hill, falling into a three-foot-deep depression where a large root ball had come out of the ground. That's where I began ripping brush from out of the ground and pulling it over me.

They had apparently seen the direction I fled as I could hear them coming…two, maybe three of them. I heard one of their boots splashing into the water and then after they had crossed the stream, they stopped to talk.

"Where the hell did he go?" one of them said.

"I just had him in my crosshairs and then it was like he disappeared into thin air," said another. "The guy's good; I'll give 'im that."

The Constitutionalists

"Who do you suppose he is…some commie spy?"

"Don't know. He looks like he could be."

I stifled a laugh. These guys were pieces of work.

A minute later they moved on. I waited until I could no longer hear them and still sitting in the hole, looked at my wound. From my pocket, I took my handkerchief and shoved it into my sleeve to put pressure on it. I then pulled out my .45 and for the first time checked the magazine. Just one bullet, like Albrecht said. I hoped at some point it would find him.

I thought a couple of fallen trees looked familiar close by where the chase had started. If I was correct about that, the vehicles had to be close by. As I began making my way back past the rock where I had sought shelter and the sycamore that had taken the first round, I saw a clearing. And then the firebreak where three vehicles sat…two pickups and an olive drab green Jeep Wrangler. Making a dash for the Jeep, the figure of a man with a rifle aimed at me stepped out. He was just a kid, maybe twenty, fresh-faced with a couple of days growth. His eyes, wide and bold, told me he was scared.

"Don't move, Mister. I will shoot you."

"I thought you were supposed to."

"I…I ain't lookin' nobody in the eye and pullin' the trigger. I ain't never shot nobody anyway."

"And you don't have to do it now."

Col. Lee Martin

"You…you just need to get back in the woods, Mister. Now go on."

I shook my head and said "No. I'm going to drive that Jeep out of here, son."

But suddenly, a shot rang out from the woods that creased my right thigh. After ducking behind the Jeep, a second round took off the side mirror.

"You'd better run, Mister."

And I did…across the other side of the firebreak and into the forest. I felt yet another round pass by my head. They weren't supposed to be shooting at my head this early in their game. After ducking behind a massive oak, I heard Albrecht's voice. I listened. "What the hell you doing, Wendell? You had him, boy."

"I…I didn't want to kill him."

"You weren't supposed to kill him…just wing him. I take care of the killing. That's why I left you here with the vehicles in case he circled back. You blew it."

"Sorry, Kurt. I…I just couldn't pull the trigger, is all."

Albrecht clinched his fist and shook his head. "Just go sit in the truck, Wendell. The rest of us will handle it."

He then gave a look into the woods and fired consecutive rounds to where he thought I had disappeared. Touching the

The Constitutionalists

talk button on his radio attached to his coat, he said, "Come back to the vehicles. He's now south of the firebreak."

South, I said to myself. At least I had a direction. But that's all I had. The sun was now setting, and the land was darkening. In an hour, the woods would be totally dark. I had to find a place to dig in for the night.

I figured Albrecht and the team would sleep in the vehicles but was sure he'd send out a roving patrol with night vision goggles to look for me. He would do it in shifts. But at night, the defense has the advantage. I could find a fallen tree and camp out in its branches for both warmth and concealment. The temperature in early November can dip below freezing, and even though I might not freeze to death, hypothermia could settle in. My light jacket wouldn't provide much warmth.

As I ventured further back into the woods, I found a tarp that someone had dumped along with other garbage, such as broken dishes and even a small refrigerator. It was also a good place to set up for the night. The tarp would keep me warm, and three cardboard boxes I found could be broken down and provide the concealment I was looking for. Before I settled in, I took some cord I discovered and wrapped it around a dozen empty beer cans I had filled with pebbles, then tied it all off to some trees. The makeshift boobytrap would provide me with early warning.

Now, I was nursing the wound on my thigh. It was more of a burn or scrape but still bleeding a little, although my cargo pants had helped clot the blood. Albrecht was doing what he said he would…nip at me with well-placed rounds to make me hurt and bleed before the final round came. It was the sadist in him.

After wrapping myself with the dirty tarp and pulling the flattened-out boxes over me, in hindsight, I thought that might be the first place someone would look. I knew it was fruitless to be walking through the woods to try to find my way out. It was the darkest of nights and what was left of the waning moon was clouded over. All I would be doing is wandering aimlessly, bumping into trees. So, I had to remain stationary. Lying as still as I could, gun in hand, it was going to be a long night. I wasn't sure I'd be sleeping or even dozing, but if I did, hopefully, my rattling boobytrap would not fail me. What would tomorrow bring…more wounds, this time serious ones? Would I be able to evade the hunters and find my way to a main highway or anywhere near civilization? I had no idea what time it was but knew it was early in the night. Lots of hours left to do nothing but think.

I guess I had lain in position for about two hours when I heard someone approaching farther to the south. Apparently, one of the rovers had enveloped me and was working his way back in my direction. I could hear the crunch of weeds and branches beneath his feet but then he would stop. Seconds later, he moved again but then stopped once more. It was apparent he had seen the boxes which may have looked to him as a makeshift tent. He was curious. And then he was suddenly upon me. He hadn't tripped my alarm. If he removed the boxes and tarp, he had me. As he was bent on putting a round in me, would I then waste my one bullet on him?

I waited. He waited. But then he grunted…and snorted. I then knew he wasn't a man at all. He was a bear. With one huge paw, he swept the boxes away and began sniffing me. I was remembering what I had always heard about being approached by a bear…don't run. Stay still. But in doing so, I had the muzzle of my XD within inches of the bear's nose. If it opened its wide mouth to take a bite of me, I'd have to shoot. The round might not kill the big guy, but it would certainly piss him off. For what seemed like an eternity, neither of us moved. Finally, I just said, "Boo!" And that was all it took to scare the varmint off. As he ran crashing and thrashing through the woods, a loud boom sounded, cutting through the night air and reverberating endlessly throughout the forest. Whoever fired the shot obviously heard the bear running, thinking it was me. I wasn't sure the shooter hit the bear as I could still hear its footfalls on the forest floor. Nonetheless, when the excitement was over, I pulled the flattened boxes back over me.

Then, adding insult to injury, it began to rain…not a drizzle…a deluge. In no time at all, the boxes were soaked to a point where they had lost their shape. Forty-degree rainwater trickled down onto me in several places, including my neck, which caused me to shiver. With the exception of the roving guards, the hunters were comfy inside their vehicles. As I was only about a hundred yards from the vehicles, I thought about getting desperate and slipping up on the Jeep, flinging open the door and shoving the muzzle up against Albrecht's head, shouting "Okay, game over. I win," then putting my one bullet in his head. But then I thought maybe I was getting a little slap-happy and not being rational. It was the only bullet I had, and there was sure to be a hail of bullets coming my way. But I'd probably get shot down by one of the men on patrol, anyway, before I'd get within twenty feet of the vehicle. I'd just have to take my chances in getting away at first light.

As I lay there, I also wondered if one of the men looking for me would have slept on what he was doing…hunting a human being he knew little about…and arise rethinking his role in the game. Most of these mountain boys were Christians and had to have ingrained within them a sense of morality and human decency to realize what they were doing. However, charismatic Kurt Albrecht was as influential as any Jim Jones or David Koresh, although he was not leading his people as a religious zealot. And then I couldn't imagine these working men taking a vacation to go hunting for an undetermined number of days. What kind of mesmerizing power did Albrecht have over them? Or was he paying them each a tremendous amount of money? I knew the man had turned into a devil, but had these people become devil worshippers? He must have sold them on how evil I was and needed killed. The entire scenario made no sense.

Chapter Twenty-Three

Before dawn, while the forest was still dark, I got a jump on the day and began feeling my way through the woods, keeping my hands in front of me to be sure I wasn't bumping into trees. I could see just enough, however, to know I was walking in the opposite direction from the vehicles on the firebreak. The terrain had begun to change a little as the morning light started streaming in through the trees. And it seemed there were now less trees. I found myself stumbling a bit, partly because the ground was more rocky than before and because I had had no sleep. Maybe I was also a little weak because I was starved for having nothing to eat for over twenty-four hours.

But then another shot rang out as a fiery shard of pain hit my left shoulder a split second later. The bullet had traveled into the shoulder under the collar bone and out through the front. The impact had knocked me down, and almost immediately, I felt myself losing consciousness. But I had to stay awake and alert. Someone would be on me, knowing that I was down, but then, if I didn't quickly find some way to stop the bleeding, every drop of my blood would soak into the ground. After tearing off my poplin jacket, I bunched it up into a ball and pressed it against the wound. Most of the blood was coming out of the front part of my shoulder. Thank God it was not spurting out, which would have meant the bullet hit an artery.

As I lay in a mess of weeds, some of which were sure to be poison ivy, given my luck, I kept drifting in and out of consciousness. However, I was able to get to my knees and then to my feet to stumble on ahead. After a few seconds, I began running again at a crouch, keeping as low as I could to make myself as small a target as possible. Two more rounds spit past me, ricocheting harmlessly into trees. Finding myself back in a triple-canopy forest, there seemed to be more trees than openings. That was good in a way because the trees provided both cover and concealment.

After what seemed like a mile, which was more than likely about three hundred yards, I started getting faint, almost feeling what people with diabetes described as low blood sugar. But then I saw a fallen tree, half of which was not touching the ground. With all the strength I could muster, I began digging into the soft soil beneath it until I had enough of a space to crawl into. Once I had positioned my body to where I was sandwiched in between the trunk and the ground, I allowed myself to drift into a state of unconsciousness.

I don't know how long I had laid there, but it now looked like noonday. Too weak to move, I just decided to remain there. That is until I found myself covered with ants. Biting ants. Or were they termites pouring out of the rotted bark of the tree. Finding enough strength to roll out from under the trunk, I pushed myself to my knees again and began crawling away, at the same time, beating the ants off me. I knew one thing...I needed some water.

Moments later, I heard voices. Two men traveling close to one another were within about twenty yards from where I dropped back into the prone. If it was just one manhunter, I might have been able to surprise him, take him down and pound him with his own weapon. Even then, I may not have had enough strength to make that happen. However, they continued on

The Constitutionalists

their path in another direction. In a couple of minutes, they were out of earshot.

Half walking, half crawling, I trudged on through the forest until I saw that the terrain was dropping off. And when the ground begins to descend, there is hope for a thirsty being. Not a hundred yards later, I found what my body needed…a stream. It wasn't much of one, but it was wet. I practically fell face-first into it. After I had drunk what I needed, I placed my shoulder into it. That might not have been the most sanitary thing to do, but the cool water felt good. God was providing.

And then, speaking of God, he was obviously looking out for me. Not fifty yards up a moderate grade to the opposite side of the stream, I spotted a cabin. From my vantage point, I couldn't tell if anyone was inside. I listened. No voices or other sounds coming from the cabin. But I was thinking…if Albrecht knew those woods as he said he did, he had to know the cabin was located there. It didn't appear to be broken down or abandoned, but was it occupied?

Slowly and with as much stealth as I could manage, I slogged up the hill toward the cabin. After stopping behind a large tree perhaps thirty feet away and then checking to ensure no one had set up close by to ambush me, with all the strength I had left in me, I dashed to the front porch. I then banged on the door and waited, hoping no one had heard my hammering. No answer. I tried the latch. It was locked. However, there was a window to the left of the door which I tried to raise, finding it locked as well. My bloodied jacket already rolled into a ball, I smashed the glass, then reached in and unlatched it. The window was a bit swollen in its track, likely having been stuck for years, but I finally got it raised. After climbing through the open frame, I looked back outside to see if anyone had followed. Nothing moving.

I then checked out the inside. It was a hunter's cabin, maybe occupied only on certain weekends. There were two more rooms with two bunk beds each and a bathroom, a thousand square feet altogether. Keeping an eye on the window I came through, I looked for alcohol or something similar to pour onto my wounds, now three wounds, one serious. In checking all the cabinets, including the bathroom, I didn't find anything. But I did find another kind of alcohol…Wild Turkey. Since I don't drink the stuff, pouring a third of the nearly full bottle onto my shoulder was no loss to me. But then I screamed, sounding like a 10-year-old girl when it hit the wound. I may have lost a smidgen of my manhood. Looking into a drawer in one of the bedrooms, I found a tee shirt that I ripped up and slung it tightly around my armpit and over my shoulder, covering both my entrance and exit wounds. The flesh on my bicep that had suffered a bullet wound warranted another tee and a splash of the Wild Turkey.

My medical issues were now addressed, and I began rummaging around for something to eat. The fridge contained a couple of bottles of Blue Moon, some moldy cream cheese, and a container of ketchup. What I wouldn't have given for some fries to go with that ketchup. But I did find an unopened can of Spam as well as a can of pork 'n beans. After I had opened them both, I ate every morsel, chasing them down with one of the Blue Moon beers. Wonderful breakfast food.

Back in the bedroom I hadn't visited, I found a wall unit that looked similar to a gun cabinet. In fact, it was. When I opened the door, I caught myself smiling. A beautiful pump shotgun. Taking it out, I checked for shells. My smile faded. It was

The Constitutionalists

empty. I checked the cabinet drawer, and it was empty as well. I pulled out every drawer in the cabin, finding none anywhere on the premises. My luck hadn't gotten any better, except I now had two guns and one bullet.

That's when I heard voices outside the cabin. I stood at the front wall and took a quick peek out the window. They were Albrecht's men. I heard one say, "Do you think he's inside? The window's busted."

"Either him or whoever owns this cabin. Let's try the door."

After I heard their boots on the wooden porch, one of them knocked. A few seconds later, they tried opening the door, of course, finding it locked.

"Since the window's busted out, let's go through there."

"But that's breaking and entering"

I almost laughed. I couldn't believe they were hunting me down to ultimately murder me, and one of them was worried about a B&E on somebody's cabin in the woods. Morons.

As I knew they were coming through the window, I hustled back to the bedroom, where I found the shotgun. Once I was positioned, I could hear the window being raised and more glass fragments falling to the floor. Then, for a half minute, I could hear them walking around in the main room.

"Check the back rooms, Jerry."

When Jerry opened the door I was behind, he first said, "Nobody here." But then he got smart and looked on the door's reverse side and found the barrel of the .12 gauge pointed at his chest. "Damn!" he exclaimed.

"Hand me your weapon, Jerry. Now!"

Without hesitation, he handed off the AR. I closed the door behind him.

"Now put your hands on the back of your head and yell to your friend to come in here."

He did as ordered. "Uh, Chuck. Come here a minute."

"What's goin' on?" I heard his approaching footsteps.

When Chuck opened the door, I swung the AR and gave his chin a horizontal butt stroke. He and his weapon hit the floor hard.

"You see what happens when you cooperate, Jerry? That could have been you lying there." I pointed the rifle at his head and added, "Pick up Chuck's weapon and hand it off to me."

He complied quickly so that he would not find himself in Chuck's position.

"Now stand with your hands against the wall. Remember that the muzzle of this rifle is against the back of your head."

The Constitutionalists

"Just don't kill me, Mister. We wasn't gonna shoot ya. We was just doin' what Kurt asked us to."

"You already did shoot me, Jerry. Or somebody did."

"It weren't me. I swear to God."

With the muzzle still pointed at him, I took my left hand and began painfully searching him. My shoulder hurt like a son-of-a-bitch. Jerry also had a 9 millimeter on him but nothing else. I shoved the gun in one of my cargo pockets. "Lay down on the floor, hands on your head, while I search Chuck."

When Jerry had taken the prone, I went over to Chuck and patted him down. He didn't have another gun, but I took from a sheath on his belt a menacing-looking knife.

Both men were in their upper twenties, nice-looking chaps, who had obviously become willing disciples of their influential leader. What was it that Albrecht had over these young men to compel them to go on a human hunting spree?

When Chuck finally came around and saw that he was tied up alongside Jerry with some twine I had found under the sink, he sat wide-eyed and stoic.

"Hello, Chuck. Have a nice sleep?"

"Who are you, Mister?"

"You've been chasing me through these woods, and you don't have a clue who I am."

"All Kurt said was…"

"That I was some kind of commie spy, or maybe I was a convicted child rapist who escaped prison. You tell me who I am, Chuck."

"He never really said; just that you were a traitor who deserved killin' But he told us not to kill you."

"But you were only to play this sadistic game called Wing the Bad Dude, huh? Why the hell would you two sign on with him to do something like that? You look like nice, respectable young men."

They looked at one another and Jerry said, "We're sorry, Mister."

"I have a name, fellows. It's Bruce. I'm a retired FBI agent and former counterterrorist operative who used to do pretty much the same thing Albrecht did for the government. He was just pissed off that I ruined his plans to detonate a bomb on Washington, D.C. He was bent on destroying our government, boys. I may not like who's in charge, including the president and Congress, but I'm not going to fire off an electromagnetic bomb that will affect millions of good citizens. Kurt Albrecht is a madman. Now, does that tell you anything about him?"

Chuck's eyes filled with tears. "Yes, sir. And I'm sorry we went after you like we did,"

"Yeah, sorry, Mr. Bruce," Jerry repeated.

The Constitutionalists

I then told them everything that Albrecht was planning and my role in getting him taken down. A lot of people were going to be hurt and could die from the destructive effects of the blast. He was a madman. They listened intently. I hoped I was reaching them.

"Okay, I need to get out of here and back to civilization. Will you help make that happen?"

"Yes, sir," Jerry replied.

"How can we do that?"

"I'll tell you."

Chapter Twenty-Four

Jerry Stuart lifted the walkie-talkie off his orange vest, one of the radios that Albrecht had handed out to each of his hunters. He pressed the talk key. "Boss, Jerry here."

Seconds later, I heard the response. "Yeah, Jerry."

"Chuck and I have the target in custody."

"Custody? You weren't supposed to take him prisoner."

"Had to, Boss. He's shot up pretty bad."

"What's your 20?"

"A cabin several hundred yards south of where the trucks are parked."

"I know the cabin. It belongs to Homer Dawson. You say he's shot up?"

"Yeah…shoulder, arm, leg. Chuck and me came across him."

"Alright. Looks like the hunt will end earlier than I figured. The firebreak we're parked on leads to another one near the cabin. We'll get back to the vehicles and be there in one zero. Out."

So, Kurt and the rest of his crew would be pulling up to the cabin within ten minutes. I'd be waiting.

"Okay, fellas, I'm going to untie you if you promise not to cause me any trouble."

"Don't worry, sir. We want this to be over as much as you do."

I chuckled. "I doubt that, Chuck."

"What do you want us to do?"

"I want you to be standing on the porch so that when he arrives, he won't suspect anything. Jerry, I'll have your AR with me inside the cabin. Chuck, you'll have yours with you, but your magazine will be empty. You tell Albrecht that I might be dying and want to talk with him and Major Gages only. Give Albrecht my pistol, telling him you took it from me. Then he won't be expecting that one bullet he allowed me to have to come flying his way. You stay outside with the rest of the men and tell them what we discussed. If they hear gunfire inside, just tell them Albrecht is finally ending the game."

"Are you going to kill them?"

"That will be up to them."

I cut the twine off them with Chuck's knife and stood them up. "You boys go on outside and get ready. You know what to say when they arrive."

They then unlocked the door and stepped out onto the porch. I stood by the window and listened to them talk. Jerry was wondering how the hell they got themselves "involved in this shit."

Chuck said, "I thought Kurt was right about what he was doin'…that he was goin' after a bad dude. Turns out he was just pissed off because this Bruce guy ruined his plans. I had no idea Kurt was going to bomb Washington, D.C.."

"Do you think Bruce just told us that and he really is some kind of foreign spy or child molester?" Jerry asked.

"Nah. He could've killed both of us. You listened to him. He's believable."

"The boss will be pissed. He'll know we gave him up."

"I don't care anymore. I just wanna get the hell out of here."

That was all I heard out of them. They had stopped talking because they heard what I heard…the sound of truck motors. Albrecht was not far.

Seconds later, three vehicles came to a stop on the trail twenty yards from the cabin. Through the window, I saw Albrecht and Gages exit the jeep while the others stepped from the trucks. "You boys stay here," was the command. As he approached the cabin, Albrecht had his rifle at the ready. He stopped on the steps and eyed his two men on the porch. Gages was behind him with an automatic sticking out of his arm sling.

"Where the hell is your weapon, Jerry?"

"Uh, inside…laying' on a table."

"You left your rifle in there with McGowan? What the hell were you thinking?"

"He's in there unconscious. Lost a lot of blood."

"That man in there is a tricky bastard. We could be walking in there facing a hail of bullets from your gun. Damn, boy."

Chuck then handed him my pistol. "Here's the gun we took off him. Are you goin' in to finish him off?"

Albrecht looked at Gages and held out his hand. Gages then pulled from his belt a grenade and placed it in his hand. Albrecht pulled the pin, opened the door and tossed it in. That's when I lunged through the window, frame and all, then hit and rolled onto the porch like the old airborne trooper that I was. Gages fired at me, and I felt the bullet whiz by my temple. I fired back. A headshot. Between the eyes. His body rolled off the porch. A second later, the grenade exploded inside, blowing the door into Albrecht and, at the same time, peppering my back with small bits of collateral shrapnel and debris.

Albrecht then swung the barrel of his rifle in my direction. Although I had pointed my AR center mass, my bullet struck his gun at the trigger guard, taking with it a piece of his hand.

Col. Lee Martin

He yelped and then shouted to his men, *"Shoot him! Shoot him!"*

As two or three of the men brought up their weapons, Chuck held up his hand. "No! Don't shoot! We were wrong! He's not our enemy!" They looked at each other, then lowered their weapons.

Albrecht, now furious, holding his wounded hand, yelled, "Are you all going to betray me, your leader, your commander?"

One of the men, someone I remembered seeing in the compound a few weekends before, reacted by firing a round that harmlessly struck the outer wall of the cabin. As I was ready to return fire, it was young Wendell, the kid who had allowed me to run off the evening before, who swung the butt of his rifle, catching the man on the side of his head. The excitement behind me, I turned back to Albrecht. He wasn't there. He had scampered to his Jeep and was preparing to pull away. I fired at the Jeep, my round going through the canvas top. I assumed I had not hit him as the Jeep continued.

I then ran to one of the trucks, a jacked up Dodge Ram, and asked "Whose truck?"

"Mine," one of them said.

"He's getting away. I need to borrow it."

"I'll come with you," he replied. "I'll drive."

"Then come on." I jumped up in the passenger's seat as he slid in behind the wheel.

When he pulled out, spinning his wheels and spitting rocks, I saw that Albrecht's Jeep was now nowhere in sight. But my driver was wasting no time going after him. He was thirty-ish with a short, dark beard and missing a couple of teeth. He looked like a nice young man, but I wondered if one of the rounds that had torn into my flesh came from his gun.

"What's your name, son?"

"Wyatt."

"Do you know these woods and trails?"

"Somewhat. I know there's a county road up ahead that goes into Clarksburg a few miles down."

"It's probably where he's heading."

"Well, we'll be able to see in a mile or so. Coming off this hill, it opens up, and you can see the road a long distance."

We didn't talk for a minute or so, but then he asked, "What's Mr. Albrecht got agin' you, Mister?"

"My name's Bruce, Wyatt. It's a long story. All you need to know is that Albrecht has gone off the deep end. If you think about it, why would somebody enlist a bunch of men to go hunting another human being like you would a wild animal?"

He nodded, thoughtfully. "Yeah. And why would guys like me fall in with him and carry out his orders?"

"I hope like hell you all learned something today about blindly following somebody like this madman. I take it you were a member of his Constitutionalist militia."

"Yeah. I was. We shouldn't a done what we did. We just got all caught up in it."

"You may not know this, but his plan was to shoot off a bomb over Washington, D.C., that would knock the power out over a three-state area that would cripple the government."

"I dunno, man. Maybe the gov'ment needs to be crippled. Theys a bunch of commies runnin' things."

"Wyatt, a lot of innocent people would lose everything…even their lives. Just think about how devastating a bomb like that would be. Think of the children and the elderly."

He nodded. "Yeah, maybe you're right. Makes me think about my two kids."

I could tell he was affected by our conversation. He was like many of the rest of his group…a poor, dumb hick who had fallen under the spell of a charismatic tyrant…someone who had convinced them what they were doing was not only patriotic, but necessary to protect their liberty.

When we reached the top of the hill where we could see the road in front of us winding down the mountain, Albrecht's Jeep was not in sight. He couldn't have been that far ahead of us, which meant he had taken another road. I was angry at myself for taking my eyes off him back at the cabin; however, somebody was shooting at me at the time.

"Wyatt, as we're close to Clarksburg, my car is parked in a subdivision on the west end of town. If you would take me there…"

"Yeah, I kin do that. It's the least I kin do for what we done to you."

Chapter Twenty-Five

My car was still parked where I had left it on Jackson Street, but what I found amazing was the key was still in the ignition. In my haste to go help Gail when she was accosted by Albrecht, I had not removed it. Not only that, but my noise detection device, which was not cheap, was still in the seat and my .308 still in the trunk. And this was in a neighborhood I had thought was the ghetto of Clarksburg.

Rather than go back to my room at the Microtel, if I still had one, I drove myself to the hospital. Bloodied, muddy and my shirt half ripped off me, I went on to the ER without cleaning up. My shoulder especially needed immediate care. I was sure infection had set in.

I did get some looks when I entered the ER, but I didn't care. One thing I didn't have was my wallet that contained not only my identification but my insurance card. Where it had gone, I didn't know. I could have lost it in the woods or it could have been taken from me. I couldn't prove who I was much less if I had any insurance. However, my saving grace was Gail, who seeing me sitting and looking like a homeless person in the lobby, ran quickly to me.

"My God, Bruce. What happened to you? I know Kurt took you somewhere, but did he do this to you?"

"Every bit of it." I then told her my story in twenty-five words or less.

"I can't believe it. He actually put you out into the woods and had his people hunt you?"

"As far-fetched as it seems, yes."

"Come with me. We have to get you treated."

After gently taking off my shirt, which was stuck in places to my skin with dried blood, she began cleaning me up with soap and water and antiseptic. "This is bad, Bruce. Your shoulder is infected. The good thing is, you picked up a handful of maggots which have eaten much of the infection."

"Maggots?"

"Don't worry. That's not as bad as it sounds. Another good thing is that the bullet went on through your shoulder without hitting a bone or artery. You may have some muscle impairment, however, after you've healed up. We've got to do an MRI to be sure. And I see a chunk of skin was taken off by another bullet on your bicep."

"You're noticing the blood on my leg. A bullet also grazed my right thigh."

"You need to get completely undressed to have you checked all over."

I grinned. "You'd like that, wouldn't you?"

"Stop that. This is serious." I did get a smile out of her.

Col. Lee Martin

Following the MRI and an X-ray, a physician entered the room. He was balding, around fifty, and wore glasses. "Mr. McGowan, I'm Doctor Amos Cartwell, a staff physician here in the ER. Nurse Delancy filled me in on your wounds. I need to tell you that all gunshot wounds must be reported to the police. There's an officer on the way. How did this happen?"

"A hunting accident."

"Hunting accident. You were shot three separate times, Mr. McGowan. We also dressed wounds on your back where we pulled out small bits of metal. It appears from some type of explosion. So, let's have it. I need the real version."

And so, in as few words as possible, I told him.

"That's a bizarre story. Is that the truth?"

"It is, doctor."

"Well, this is a new one on me."

"Me as well."

When I had been bathed, disinfected, and patched up, I was placed on one of the emergency room cots. No sooner had that been accomplished than Lieutenant Oliver from the Sheriff's Department stood at my bedside. Gail stood at the door.

"Okay, Mr. McGowan, the nurse there vouches for you, telling me an incredible story of you being the victim of a manhunt up on the Shawnee. Now, why was that happening?"

Again, imparting the story I had told Gail, I started from the beginning, which was when the National Security Adviser to the president asked me to infiltrate the militia called the Constitutionals. I told the lieutenant how I managed to do that, but the leader, Kurt Albrecht, a former counterterrorist operative like me, who had invited me in with him, found out I was a government plant.

"I know that name Albrecht and about the militia group. They have been on our radar for a couple of years now. His name also went on the FBI's most-wanted list last week. And doesn't he own that store out on the Clarksburg Highway?"

"That's correct." I then continued my story as to how he and Gages took me out into the wilderness with their band of merry men and made me a game, sadistically hunting me down and putting bullets into me.

"Damn. Who the hell in this day and time would do something like that. Down-right barbaric."

"I escaped and captured a couple of his people. They helped me set a trap for him. When I shot and killed his friend Gages, who, by the way, tried to kill me, Albrecht escaped.

"This kind of shit only happens in the movies."

"And here in Harrison County."

"Did you get the names of these men?"

"Only a few first names. But believe me, when they finally saw Albrecht for who he was, they very quickly found Jesus."

"Just give me those first names and we'll hunt 'em down."

"You might think me a pinhead, Lieutenant, but I'm going to let it go."

He narrowed his eyes and shook his head. "Why the hell would you do that?"

"There were only two people who had planned to kill me. The others just wanted to pick at me with their rounds. They are just a bunch of dumbasses who got caught up in a manhunt game their very domineering leader was playing. He had convinced them I was a traitor to our country."

"You said you were at one time a counterterrorist operative?"

"Yes; retired FBI before that."

"I understand you had no identification on you. Can you even prove who you are? I can't go on what the nurse said about you. Hell, I don't even know how she knows you."

"Call the CJIS down the road and ask for Special Agent Rivera."

"I'll do that. The doc says they're going to offer you a bed for the night to especially watch that shoulder wound.

Something about a possible P.E. That's fine because I want you to stay around for a while. I still need to check you out."

"Be my guest, but I don't think I'll take the doctor up on his offer. I need to get back home down in Greenbrier County."

"Ah, Greenbrier." He then began a lengthy story about how he and his wife spent three days at America's Resort, The Greenbrier Hotel Resort. They played golf, rode horses, ate at Prime 44 West, and a dozen other things. "Love that part of the state." He then paused. "But, I don't want you to go anywhere just yet. Listen to the doctor."

"We'll see," I said.

There was no way I would stay the night. Anyway, I had some phone calls to make and things I had to get taken care of. Gail lent me her phone. I called my bank, which had a local branch in Clarksburg, and canceled both my debit and credit card. The branch manager said she would process temporary ones and have the new ones sent to my address. I then called my health insurance company and told them I didn't have my group number, but a hospital would be calling for coverage information. I wouldn't worry about a driver's license until I arrived home. I called the motel where I was staying, telling them I had had an accident and lost my credit card. However, as the bank had given me my debit card information after providing them with my sign-in and passcode, I was okay there. What I missed the most, however, was my cellphone. I would waste no time in getting a new one at the AT&T store I had seen down the street from the hospital.

Col. Lee Martin

Before I could break away, however, one of Lieutenant Oliver's deputies called him to say someone saw a couple of rugged-looking guys in a pickup unloading what appeared to be a body wrapped up in a blanket at the door of Freeman's Funeral Home, then took off like a bat out of hell. No one could provide a description of the men, nor did anyone get the tag number. Found on the dead man was his wallet, which included his retired Marine ID card identifying him as Thomas Gages. He had been shot in the head.

Oliver said, "Now that we have a corpse, you're not going home any time soon, Mr. McGowan. You admitted shooting him, and your story needs to be verified somehow, or you're going to be under arrest."

Chapter Twenty-Six

After I had politely informed Dr. Cartwell that as gracious as the invitation was to stay the night, I must decline, I did tell Lieutenant Oliver I would be returning to my motel room for the night. If he needed me for anything else, I would be catching up on the Z's I had lost the night before.

Gail had a forty-five-minute dinner break at five thirty, which she always took off of the hospital's campus, mainly to get away from the sick, the injured, and the smell of phenol. That evening, she was going a couple of blocks down to a Chick-fil-A. I asked her if I could join her. I, not having had anything to eat since my Spam and Bean breakfast, was famished.

Before I met her, I bought the new phone, had it activated, and drove to my motel for a hot shower and change of clothes. The guy at the phone place looked a little uneasy about me, my having on a ripped and bloodied shirt with a huge bandage on my shoulder. The motel still had my room under my name and hadn't thrown my bag out in the street. I found some time before meeting Gail to call the woman I had failed to call the last twenty-four hours. She was almost in a state of panic.

"Where have you been?" she asked. "You always call me every night we're apart from each other. I tried calling you, but the message was that you were unavailable."

"Sorry, Babe, I lost my phone."

"How did you manage to do that?"

"Well, when you're camping out in the woods, all kinds of things can happen."

"You were back out there with your friends on a hunting trip?"

"Yes. More guys came along this time. I couldn't resist the invitation."

"Did you bag anything? That's the term you use when you kill something, right?"

"Right. As a matter of fact, I did. Just one." I was talking metaphorically, which is kind of like telling white lies. The absolute truth would have infuriated her.

"Bagging only one was hardly worth the hunt."

"I almost got a second one, but he escaped."

"Well, tell me next time you decide to go traipsing through the woods."

"I don't plan on going back out. I like my easy chair too much. So, how are things in Florida this time?"

"Fine."

Whenever a woman says 'fine,' it ain't.

"About the same, huh?"

"Both of them have been difficult this time. But, I'll spare you the details. I know you're having a better time than me."

If only she knew. "Well, just hang in there. Any idea when you'll be back home?"

"Maybe next week," is all she said.

I knew she was beyond ready to come back, but I was hoping she could put up with her parents just a little longer. I didn't want her to come home to see the bandages on my body, which would be a clue that I had either been shot up or was in a bad car accident. I know it was selfish of me, but I didn't want her to freak out. One thing I would not do, however, is keep my charade going indefinitely. When the time was right, I'd tell her everything.

At a quarter past five, I was back at the hospital waiting to walk with Gail to the Chick-fil-A. But as soon as I entered the door, I found that it was she who was waiting for me. "Ready?" she asked.

"Hungry," I responded.

As we were walking the short distance to the restaurant, I was mildly concerned we might see a Jeep Wrangler following us. Obviously, he was now driving the Jeep, which likely belonged to one of his friends. The FBI and police would be looking for his registered pickup. Albrecht also knew where Gail worked and likely knew as well when she took her dinner break. I didn't think he would approach her at the hospital or even in the parking lot since security had good nighttime visibility of the hospital's surroundings. But would he return to her house as he did two nights before?

When we arrived at the restaurant, we ordered our food and sat down at a booth. I then eased into a conversation about my wild couple of days in the woods, filling her in on some details I hadn't shared with her at the hospital. I let her know that Albrecht was now driving an O.D. green Jeep Wrangler and that I had wounded him in the hand. She needed to be on guard because he may be looking for a little patch-up work from a nurse…offsite.

"Do you have a gun?"

"Of course. I used to be a member of a militia group, remember? The operative term is *used to be.*"

"Then I'd carry it with me. I know you can't have it with you in the hospital, but as soon as you step into your car, take it with you into the house."

"I'm already doing that."

While she was digging into her Cobb salad, I was wolfing down my sandwich, a large order of waffle fries and large lemonade. I ate so fast, I didn't give my mouth time to even taste anything.

"You're ravenous. Forgot to eat today?"

"I was busy doing other things, like running for my life."

It wasn't funny, but she formed a smile.

"Will you be staying here longer?"

"*Here* meaning in the Clarksburg area?"

"Yes. I know you declined a night or two in the hospital. Are you still staying at the motel?"

"Yes. That's part of why I wanted to talk with you. Since I didn't name you as a witness to the EMP conversation, nobody in law enforcement even knows you were part of the militia. I'll keep it that way, but I need some help from you. Because it didn't come out that Albrecht and Gages kidnapped me at your house, Lieutenant Oliver doesn't know you're involved in any way. You're merely a nurse at the hospital who took me into the ER. As you heard, I admitted to shooting Tom Gages. I could be arrested for murder unless you divulge that they broke into your house, attacked you, and then me. He'll ask why I was outside your house and what connection I had with you. He needs to know it's all tied into you being in the militia and witnessing firsthand the EMP discussion. I suspected Albrecht might come to threaten you; he thought you planned to testify. So, will you be my witness?"

"I will have to think about that, Bruce. I have a good job which could be in jeopardy. Let me ask you something…was that the first and only night you were parked outside my house?"

"No. There were two other nights. I knew you worked at the hospital and learned your shift. Sorry if this sounds like

I was stalking, but I knew you two were an item, and I had hoped to find him there."

I could tell my admission caused her to be angry. "You were spying on me to get to him?"

"Partly. I was also concerned for your safety."

"I wondered how it was you were there, Johnny-on-the-spot when he attacked me. And, by the way, we were never an item. We were friends and associates. He brought me into the Constitutionalists. But he started getting possessive and even menacing. He thought he could make a move on me. I had just gotten out of a bad marriage and had no desire for any other men in my life. He wouldn't take no for an answer. Anyway, back on the subject, what specifically do you want from me?"

"I'd like you to at least tell the sheriff's department that Gages whacked me on the head and dragged me out to woods. You have to tell them what happened at your house. That will bring credibility to the story I told him. It will provide reasoning as to why I ended up killing Gages."

"Do you know what you're asking me to do?"

"I know very well what I'm asking…that you expose yourself as a witness to save me from going to jail for murder. It was pure self-defense, and they need to see it as such."

"Then I'll be linked to him, the militia, the Washington, D.C. plot, and to you."

"Appears that's so, Gail."

She laid her fork down and took in a deep breath. Saying nothing in response for a few seconds, she finally nodded. "I will tell the sheriff's office that I used to be in the militia, which is true, and I met you there, who I found out later was an informant, also true. Because you and I became friends, Kurt was jealous and thought we were having an affair. That's partially true. He did mention you after he saw us sitting at the breakfast table together. However, as you and I talked, I told you Kurt and I had been close. Since you were looking for Kurt anyway, being a fugitive from justice, you staked out my house in case he went there. You heard me scream and ran inside, finding him there with a gun to my head. That's when Gages came up and hit you on the head; then they threw you in their vehicle and left. I'll tell the sheriff's department that much. I will not tell them I witnessed Kurt's briefing about the Washington, D.C. plot. That information will get back to the FBI, and I'll then be called in as a witness. After providing a sworn statement, Kurt will then kill me."

"Gail, your statement won't be needed. Others in that room have already provided statements. I also found the written plans in Albrecht's room there in the compound. He knows that, and it is one of the reasons he's out to take me down. He'll keep trying. But if he brings it to my doorstep, I'll be ready. What I'm worried about is that my wife could get caught up in all of it. That's the main reason I came up here…to bring the war to him."

"Thinking, of course, you'd find him at my place."

I nodded.

Col. Lee Martin

"And so you did."

We walked back to the hospital, and I saw her inside.

"Okay, I will talk with Lieutenant Oliver and tell him what we discussed."

"Thanks, Gail. Again, as far as the FBI is concerned, you were never in that briefing room to learn about the bomb. Thanks for being a friend."

"Thank you for trying to come to my rescue," she replied.

"Remember to keep your gun handy, especially when getting in and out of the car at night at your house. Have it in your hand when you walk inside; you never know who might be there."

"Does this mean I won't see you again?"

"Quite possibly, unless I take another bullet before I leave for home."

"Don't say that, Bruce."

I gave her a smile and clasped my hand around hers. "Take care, Gail."

She then gave me a hug, one that lasted much too long.

Chapter Twenty-Seven

I was to leave the bandage on my shoulder for at least four to five days, then go to a clinic or hospital to have a fresh one applied. I was still hurting, now even worse since the anesthesia had worn off. I thought maybe it was something like a couple of beers, some Tylenol, and a good night's sleep would address. However, after drinking one Heineken and laying my head on the pillow, I was down for the count.

I think I must have slept twelve hours, as it was a few minutes past seven when I awoke the next morning. My shoulder ached horribly, and even my bicep, which had a small piece of flesh missing, was sore. Down in the breakfast area, I took a dose and a half of the acetaminophen sample Dr. Oliver prescribed with a plate of eggs, bacon, and biscuits. Within twenty minutes, I began feeling better.

Back in the room, I sat in the sofa chair and watched cable news to see what the rest of the world was doing. Overnight riots in Detroit, eight deaths by gunshot in Chicago, Democrats and Republicans trading insults, and the president stepping on his tongue again. Nothing new.

After turning off the TV, I used my spiffy new phone to make a couple of calls. The first was to Special Agent Marco Rivera. Thankfully, I had placed his card in my jeans I was wearing when he handed it to me. I took perhaps fifteen minutes filling him in on my vacation in the woods, how I managed to get there, and that I ended up killing one of them.

"Good. We can now take Gages off our person of interest list. I'm glad you made it out of there, Bruce. Sorry about the wounds. I cannot believe someone would put together a hunting party to go kill another human being. That's insane."

"There is a Lieutenant Oliver with the local sheriff department who may be on the verge of arresting me for Gages' murder. A call from you to tell him I'm one of the good guys would help. I promised I wouldn't leave the area for a couple of days."

"Not to worry, Bruce. You won't be arrested, but you may have to testify at a coroner's inquest if held."

"I can come back for that. By the way, Albrecht was last seen in a green Jeep Wrangler rather than the truck that's listed on the wire. No tag info, though."

"Got it. I'll put the word out. My advice, Bruce, is to go back to safe and peaceful Greenbrier County, play some golf, and…oh wait…I guess golf is out for a few weeks."

"Funny, Marco. Anyway, good talking with you. Now go nail Albrecht."

My second call was to Ben Marshall. But, whoever took my phone took all my contacts. I had to start from scratch. In calling the main number for the NSC, I went through a typical menu of single-digit numbers, and then when I did get a voice,

The Constitutionalists

it was yet another recording. Finally, I made it to an operator. Unfortunately, I was passed on to the wrong department and had to start the sequence again. Fifteen minutes later, when I landed a live person, I asked to speak to The National Security Adviser. I was then advised that I would have to leave my number, and 'someone' would call me back. "No, I want Ben Marshall to call me back," I said, just a wee bit frustrated. She said, "I'm sorry, but it has to be one of his assistants."

"Look," I said. "Tell him Bruce McGowan is calling." Expecting an immediate apology at the mention of my name, all I got was, "I will leave his assistant a message."

"No!" I barked. "Leave it for him. Here's my number!"

Well, that didn't end well. All I could do was wait, being the insignificant little snit that I was. And I did for almost an hour.

When my phone finally rang, I saw it was a 202 number. I answered "Hello" rather tartly.

"Bruce, is that you?"

"It is, Mr. National Security Adviser. You gotta get a better contact system. I can't tell you what trouble I had getting through all your menus, recordings, and operators."

"All intentional, I'm sure." He then chuckled. "But you have my direct line. Did you delete it or something?"

"Or something."

"What's the something?"

I then began my story with a play by play. "And that's how I lost my phone. Amen."

"My God, Bruce. Unbelievable. Can you send me a typed version of this. I know a guy who can write the screenplay."

"I'm glad you're taking this so seriously."

"Sorry, Bruce. This is nuts. I've never heard of such a thing happening except in fiction. It reminds me of The Hunger Games or Battle Royale. And you say you killed one of them?"

"He was Albrecht's right-hand man."

"Then that must have pissed him off even more."

"He'll still be coming after me. Of course, in doing so, he'll risk exposing himself."

"The Bureau is putting him on their 10 Most Wanted list. He'll have to find an even bigger rock to crawl under."

"I can handle him coming after me. I'm just concerned his doing so will put my wife in danger."

"I understand, Bruce. Hopefully, he won't be out there long. As to the large building you were taken to where you saw the EMP weapon and launcher, do you have any idea where it is?"

The Constitutionalists

"I was unconscious when they took me there and, as I said, woke up tied to a chair. They then blindfolded me and took me to a point maybe three miles from there. I might be able to find the location where they let me out and put me on the run. I would suggest the Bureau put a drone in the air from there and send it out to cover a five-mile radius, looking for a building the size of a 10,000 square-foot warehouse."

"If the local resident Bureau will set it up, can you accompany agents to the location?"

"I can. If it's possible to be done in the next day or so, all the better. I'd like to get back home. And while I'm here, how about being a sport and committing to another three or four days of salary plus pay my motel bill."

"The least I can do, considering what you went through. I'll contact the director today. And don't lose my number."

Ben had worked fast, and so had the FBI director. A few minutes past 4:00 that afternoon, I received a call from the FBI office in Clarksburg. That office, like other agency offices in West Virginia, was under the control of the Pittsburgh field office.

"Is this Bruce McGowan?"

"Who's this?"

"I'm Rodney Chapin, FBI Special Agent-in-Charge, Clarksburg resident agent office. May I have a moment?"

"Of course, I was expecting a call."

"This is on the Albrecht matter. I have had a discussion personally with the director in Washington, D.C. whose office sent me via electronic file Albrecht's subversive plans. I was already aware that he was on the 10 Most Wanted list and considered an enemy of the state. The director also apprised me of what happened to you over the past 48 hours, and I must say I was astounded that something like that could happen in our very backyard. However, I understand when you were assaulted by Albrecht, he took you to some type of warehouse where you saw the EMP bomb that he planned to detonate over the nation's capital. The building is supposedly in proximity to where you went through the harrowing experience up on the Shawnee."

"That's correct, Agent Chapin. I have also discussed the matter with Special Agent Marco Rivera at the CJIS."

"Yes, I know Agent Rivera. But let me get to the reason for my call. I'd like to meet with you this evening, if possible, to talk about what we have planned. I can either come to where you are, or you can meet me at my office."

"How about here at the Microtel? I'm in room 240."

"Is nine too late for you?"

"Not at all."

"Perfect. See you then."

Chapin, a black agent-in-charge in his early 40s with a military-style haircut and thin mustache, was dressed casually in a gray sport coat, open-collared shirt, and dark slacks. I offered him something to drink from the mini bar, but he respectfully declined. The room had two chairs: a nice, cushy one and a straight one behind the desk. I offered him the soft one, but he went ahead and pulled out the desk chair.

"I understand you're retired FBI, Mr. McGowan."

"That's correct. State Department counterterrorism operative after that. All behind me now."

"But you still take on federally requested missions on contract?"

"Not usually. I just agreed to infiltrate this militia mostly as a favor to the NSA, who is an old acquaintance from past federal law enforcement days. Interestingly enough, I had also collaborated on occasion with Albrecht who worked in counterterrorism for another team."

"We've been watching this militia group for some time now and for the past year, Albrecht, as the leader of that organization, has been on the Bureau's radar. We were also brought up to speed by the Pittsburgh field office about his plans to conduct subversive activities against the government. We didn't know, however, that the plans involved an EMP bomb."

"I guess then you know pretty much everything."

"Yes. Now, we need to locate that bomb. I believe it was your idea to put a drone in the air up on the Shawnee."

"Even though I was blindfolded before being dumped in the woods, I believe I can find where it was. From that point, I think a drone covering an aerial view of five miles in all directions will pick up the building. Of course, there could be a number of buildings in the area. Where does your drone come from?"

"The CJIS has a couple. They're just a little larger than ones you can buy on the market."

"When do you want to do this?"

"How about in the morning at 0930? We'll pick you up here. I'll have with me a drone operator and two special agents. I'll be in a Tahoe 4X4. The second vehicle will be a Bureau pickup. You're sure you can find where you were?"

"I think so. I do know my way to the cabin where two of Albrecht's men helped me get away. That's where I ended up after Albrecht turned me loose in the woods to run for my life. But, even from the cabin, the building shouldn't be all that far. I don't believe they tracked me more than three or four miles."

"Then if you can get us to the cabin, we can begin from there."

"I'm 90 percent sure I can backtrack and get us there. If not, we may have to drive over every county road and firebreak, which might take all day."

"Whatever it takes."

When Rodney Chapin left, I made sure to call Adriana. As she had no idea I was still away from home, I didn't tell her. There were a few questions about what I was doing around the house and how Lionel was doing without her. I had to get creative in answering her, mainly staying generic with my responses, like saying, "Life is good as always at Wolf Laurel." I was sure it was. I just wasn't there to be enjoying it. Neither was Lionel. But after tap-dancing around her questions, changing the subject, and a bit of lovey-dovey silliness, our short conversation came to a close.

I hadn't been off the phone for two minutes when there was another knock at the door. Initially, I thought Agent Chapin had returned to ask me something else. No one else knew I was even staying at the motel. Maybe housekeeping. However, before I opened the door, I looked through the peephole. Letting out a long sigh, I flipped the lock and opened it.

"Gail. What are you doing here?"

"Can I come in?"

"Is there something the matter?"

"No. I just wanted to talk."

"I thought we said everything we needed to at the restaurant."

"Please?"

I stepped aside and gestured for her to come in. I didn't have a good feeling about her being there.

She immediately went to the sofa chair and sat down.

"What's on your mind, Gail?"

"Do you have anything to drink?"

"Like a Coke or ginger ale?"

"Something stronger I can mix it with a soft drink. You have mini bottles of the hard stuff, I presume."

I looked in the bar and saw several bottles of whisky, vodka and Scotch. I pulled out one of each and held them in my hand. She looked them over.

"That Seagrams Seven will do. Maybe a 7 and 7?"

Reluctantly, I pulled out a can of 7 Up and gave her a glass. "I'll let you mix it. There's some ice in that bucket."

"You're a gentleman." She put two ice cubes in the glass, and after popping the can and twisting the cap from the mini bottle, she poured them in.

I sat down at the desk chair. "Alright, Gail, I'm all ears."

She took a sip of the cocktail and set it down. "I'm scared, Bruce, and just needed a place to go."

The Constitutionalists

"Elaborate."

"Kurt was waiting for me when I got off work a while ago. He had parked that Jeep you mentioned next to my car. When I saw him, I turned around and went back into the hospital. A security guard walked me back out and then I saw he had gone. He could now be at my house."

"Then you need to call the police to escort you home and ask them to stay a while."

"I...thought maybe you'd allow me to stay. I see you have a second bed. I'm off tomorrow and can go home in the morning."

I knew where this was going. "Gail, as much as I'm concerned for your safety, what you're asking is not a good idea. By the way, how did you know I was in this room?"

"If you weren't staying in the hospital as the doctor requested, you were to provide your motel and room number on the discharge papers."

"And you took a look at them...before you left the hospital to find Kurt in the parking lot."

"Well, yes."

"Which tells me you're actually here for another reason. Gail, I told you I'm married. I just can't allow you to stay."

Col. Lee Martin

She narrowed her eyes and set her glass down. "If you think I came here to sleep with you…"

"Am I the first person you thought about? You don't have friends you could stay with tonight?"

"We're both adults here, Bruce. I respect that you're married and would not do anything to make you feel uncomfortable."

"I've always tried to be honest with my wife, Gail. You're a very attractive young woman. If she knew you were even here in this room with me, she wouldn't understand. If you want to talk about something having to do with Kurt Albrecht, go ahead, and then I'll ask you to leave."

She took the last gulp of her drink and then stood. A few seconds later, she walked to where I was sitting and then kissed me on the lips. "Yes, you are a gentleman, and your wife is so very lucky to be married to you. I won't make you struggle with temptation. I'll go. And don't worry…I'll be alright tonight. I do have a friend I can stay with."

I nodded and walked her to the door. "If at any time he tries to get into your house, get on the phone immediately and call 911."

She smiled and walked through the door I had opened. "Goodnight, Bruce. Sleep well."

Okay, I'm a red-blooded American male and would be lying if I said I hadn't been tempted. But being tempted is one thing; allowing myself to submit to that temptation is another. I wasn't sure if I'd be sleeping at all. My little brain might be keeping me up.

Whereas that previous night after the hospital had patched me up, I was so tired I just ignored the pain and collapsed on my bed until well into the following day. However, I had almost forgotten about the debris and small bits of shrapnel that were taken out of my back. Because I normally sleep on my back, I found doing so that second night quite irritating. Even though I had taken my six-hour pain pill at seven, an hour after my dinner at Longhorn, I pushed the envelope by taking it again four hours later when I turned in at eleven. It wasn't just about quelling the pain in my shoulder; the pill would also make me drowsy. And I needed to be put out so that Gail and her lingering perfume would no longer prey on either of my brains.

Chapter Twenty-Eight

After a light breakfast and donning the same clothes as the day before, considering it was all I had, I spent five minutes with the news and readied myself for the Bureau boys' arrival. In my head, I went back over the state, county, and dirt roads young Wyatt had taken out of the Shawnee forest. I remembered the long hill we went down which had given us the looming, panoramic view of the small city of Clarksburg. I knew I could retrogress the route to a certain point, but I wasn't sure about the turns we had taken on the rural route. I should have paid better attention. It was hard to do that when I was concentrating on catching up to Albrecht's Jeep and, at the same time, leaking blood onto Wyatt's seat.

Promptly at 0930, Agent Chapin arrived and temporarily parked under the motel's overhang. The pickup containing two of his agents, Tony Ferraro and Blake Jernigan, dressed in jackets bearing the letters FBI, the drone pilot, Jeff Benton, and the drone itself in the rear bed, pulled in behind Chapin's Tahoe. I took the front seat passenger position in the Tahoe.

"Good morning, Mr. McGowan," Chapin greeted.

"It's Bruce, Special Agent."

"In that case, I'm Rod."

The niceties out of the way, I began directing him out of town and onto the state road that led up the long hill. Four miles later, it was so far, so good. The landscape was familiar. However, that's when things became a bit iffy. I told Chapin to cut off on the dirt road to our left, but then found that it ended a half mile later. We turned around.

"Sorry, Rod."

"No worries. We'll go back to the county road and continue on."

Once we were back on asphalt, I watched for the next dirt road. I knew Wyatt and I had turned right onto the hard road. After we had gone about a mile, which in the country seemed like two, I saw a road intersecting on the left.

"Yes, that's it," I said, pointing. "I remember that river birch, the one with the peeling bark."

We made the left turn but then I had to remember where yet another dirt road intersected. What I thought was our next turn, wasn't. Nothing looked familiar. Agent Chapin said, "I can see why one might get turned around out here." He was being patient with me.

After another half mile, I said, "There." At the entrance to a narrow road to our right, which was probably a firebreak, lay two large rocks, one on each side. I had thought the owner of the cabin might have placed them there to give other hunters notice where to turn. I knew then that the cabin was no more than five hundred feet ahead.

When we had reached a small clearing, there it was on our right. We then pulled up close to the cabin. It all looked much like it was when I left it…front door lying on the porch, the window to the left completely missing where I barreled through it, and what resembled red paint on the porch where Gages had bled out. I was the first to go inside. The grenade Albrecht had tossed through the doorway had wreaked significant havoc. The eating table was upside down, one of its legs blown off and chairs were in pieces; the fridge door was destroyed and hanging loose; sheet rock was missing in several places, exposing the framing. It made me wonder what I would look like had I not blasted through the window.

"Geez Louise!" Chapin exclaimed. "You're lucky to be alive. Obviously, the owner hasn't been back since all this happened. He'll be pissed."

We then returned to the clearing where Chapin's agent-operator Jeff was removing the drone from the bed of the pickup. I pointed to the direction in the woods from which I had half crawled. "You might start your flight there, Jeff. But that doesn't mean the building we're looking for is anywhere nearby."

In less than five minutes, the drone was in the air. We watched the small wireless video screen as the drone's camera took us above the trees and to the north of our position. As the operator sent the drone two hundred yards out, then kept it circling at that distance, he went a hundred yards farther. As he continued changing the distance every hundred yards, still circling to ensure there was both accurate and comprehensive coverage, nothing materialized. That is until he was two miles out and to the east. The camera picked up a house with a detached garage that was three times the size of the house. A driveway situated off a firebreak led to the garage.

The Constitutionalists

"Possibility here," Jeff said, "Of course, the garage could be a person's business, from furniture restoration to auto repairs. But this is pretty far out for either of those as it's pretty damn isolated and would be hard to find."

"Maybe you can send the grid coordinates up your chain and see who owns the place," I said.

"Good idea, Bruce. Hover your drone, Jeff, and pull in the coordinates."

After doing so and handing it off to Rod Chapin, he called the coordinates into his counterpart at the CJIS. We waited just two minutes until the call came back in. Chapin wrote the information on a pocket notepad: "The place belongs to a local businessman, J. Hoyt Nelson."

"Ah, so," I said. "He was Albrecht's money man financing the militia and probably the bomb as well. I wouldn't be surprised if that's the house where Albrecht has been staying, and that garage has to be where I was taken. Are we going?"

"We are."

"Might be some gunplay when we do." I then asked Jeff, "Can you get us from here to there?"

"Yep. I've just captured an image of the trails and roads that lead there. By taking the video screen with us, we can follow it directly to the house."

"Then let's roll," Chapin said.

It took the better part of fifteen minutes to get to a point where we saw the house and garage come into view. Chapin radioed his three agents in the truck. Jeff, you and I will take the front. Blake, you and Tony the rear. You two take your positions first." They answered, "Roger."

"Got an extra gun?" I asked. "Mine's missing in action."

"As this is a Bureau mission, Bruce, we will do this. I know you're retired FBI, but…"

"But an old dude like me will just be in the way."

"Well, I'm not saying that."

"I guess I'll just sit here and watch."

Chapin then gave me one of those "Whatever" shrugs.

When the two men from the truck had made their way through a patch of the woods and enveloped the house, Jeff, the drone guy, joined Chapin, at which time they moved onto the front of the house with guns drawn. On the porch at the door, I saw Chapin knocking and heard him yell out, "FBI…open up, please!"

At least he said please.

Moments later, what looked like an older woman came to the door. After a short discussion, she let them in. I sat in the Tahoe another three or four minutes, then decided to make myself useful. After getting out of the SUV, I began walking like I owned the place to the large garage. It was locked. As I was no longer law enforcement, I didn't need a warrant. But as a civilian, getting inside would be breaking and entering.

I remembered there were two high windows on one side of the building, so I went around to the right side of the garage and found them. It was the place Albrecht had taken me alright. Finding two forty-inch crates lying against the outer wall, I stacked them and then climbed onto the top of them. I was now high enough that I could see in. The window glass, however, was dirty, and I had to wipe it down with my shirt sleeve. That did the trick, and I peered inside. Albrecht's pickup was still there. Straining my neck to see farther down along the wall, I saw it. The EMP bomb. It was no longer crated and looked smaller than I remembered. It was now sitting on a wooden platform.

After dropping to the ground, I trotted to the front door of the house just in time to see Rod Chapin and Jeff Benton coming down the steps. The woman was standing at the open front door with hands on her hips.

"What's happening, Rod?"

"That was the owner's wife, Mrs. Nelson. She would not give us permission to search the garage."

"The bomb is in there, Rod, along with Albrecht's truck."

"How do you know that?"

"I saw them."

"How?"

"Through one of the windows on the side wall. That should be enough for probable cause. Suggest you send Blake or Tony to the office of a federal judge to give you the warrant. You'll need to remain here in case she calls her husband or Albrecht, who will come to move the bomb out of here."

"You're right. Tony, go get the search warrant from Judge Morrissey. I'll make the call to set it up. And go get a flatbed hauler from Benji's Wrecker."

Chapter Twenty-Nine

When Special Agent Tony Ferraro had sped off, Rodney Chapin was already on the phone with the Harrison D.A.'s office pressing for the warrant. Local Judge Hiram Morrissey, always on the side of law enforcement, would come through.

Ferraro would have to accomplish everything and return in at least an hour and a half, so we would just be sitting and watching.

I then said to Chapin, "I wouldn't be surprised if you found Albrecht hiding there. Will the warrant cover both the house and outbuilding?"

"It will. The Nelson woman doesn't know I'm securing one or whether we're even still here. Albrecht should know by now we found the place and will want to get his bomb out of here before we go in. I have a feeling she's on her phone right now notifying him or her husband we were here."

"Knowing the FBI will have the place under surveillance, I doubt he'll risk it. You'll not see him here again. And then he'll be even more pissed that he'll never see his bomb again. So there goes any future plans he might have for it. He and his plans are completely shut down. All he'll have left is revenge. He still might target the government somehow, but no doubt he'll continue to target me for screwing up his mission."

"I'd be very wary, Bruce."

"Don't think I haven't been."

After a long wait of nearly two hours, Ferraro was in earshot. We could hear the whine of the truck's transmission a half mile away, breaking the solace of the forest. Moments later, Ferraro parked the truck out of view of the house. Chapin went to the truck at which time his agent handed off the warrant. "Any trouble?"

"No, sir. It was ready when I arrived at the courthouse. But I had to wait at the wrecker yard; Benji didn't quite have the truck ready for me."

"Okay, after I serve the warrant, drive the truck up to the garage double doors."

"Will do."

I then asked Chapin, "Do you mind if I go with you to the house. I'd like to get a look inside."

"I think that will be okay. Come on."
Agent Chapin knocked once again on the door, and a moment later, Mrs. Nelson opened it. She was still in her bedclothes. "You again? I told you that you weren't welcome here and that you can't search our outbuilding."

"Now I can, Mrs. Nelson. I have a warrant giving us a right to search not only the garage but your house."

"There's not nothin' in this house you'd be interested in. So, you might as well go away."

"We're not going to do that, ma'am. You have to let us in."

She stood for a few seconds without a word, then said, "Alright, make it quick. Anything you mess up, you'd better put back like you found it."

Chapin proceeded on in, and I followed. The only real reason we were searching the house was for evidence that Albrecht had been staying there. Would we find his clothes, more written documents of his planned bombing, or evidence that may incriminate Nelson himself as a co-conspirator, he being one of Albrecht's moneymen?

The house was not stately or characteristic of a place owned by a wealthy businessman; it was apparently just a comfortable little two-story cottage good for an occasional getaway in the woods. I told Agent Chapin I would take the upstairs, and he was good at inspecting the rooms on the main floor.

There were three bedrooms and a bath on the second floor, and I took the bathroom first. The medicine cabinet was nearly empty save for a few toiletries, including a bottle of rubbing alcohol. A towel that had recently been used was draped over the tub, and the toilet seat was up. But then things got interesting. I found that the waste can was half-filled with bloody gauze and rags, along with partial strips of surgical tape. Opening the medicine cabinet again, I took out the alcohol bottle and re-examined it, finding bloody fingerprints on it. I then lifted it out, and after wrapping it in toilet paper, I placed it in one of my cargo pockets.

Col. Lee Martin

The second bedroom on the right was small. The bed was unmade, and I found smudges of blood on a sheet. Albrecht had sprung a leak during the night. Upon opening the closet door, lying on the floor were pieces of dirty clothing and a pair of ankle-length boots. But then I discovered something on the upper shelf I didn't expect to find…my XDM that had been handed off to Albrecht by young Chuck Riley. My favorite of all my weapons. Interestingly, it still had the magazine inserted with the one bullet I was allowed to have. As it was all I needed to see, I went back downstairs and found Chapin wrapping up his search as well. I gave him a nod and he turned to the woman.

"Okay, Mrs. Nelson, I need the key to the padlock on the garage."

"I'm not sure where it is. My husband keeps it somewhere."

"I think I know, ma'am," I said. "Kurt Albrecht has it with him."

She gave us a faux, astonished look. "Who is Kurt Albrecht?"

"You know full well who he is," I replied. "There's a mess of bloodied gauze in the upstairs bathroom from his hand wound."

"I don't know what you're a-talkin' about. That's where my husband cut himself on a saw out in the shop."

Chapin said, "Mrs. Nelson, do you know what aiding and abetting is? It's a serious charge where you and your husband can go to jail for sheltering a fugitive from justice."

Her face turned from an angry beet red to a wanly pale. "I...I didn't know he was any kind of fugitive. We've known him for goin' on five years. He just said he needed a place to stay 'cause there was some kind of problem with his place."

"And neither you nor your husband checked to see what he was storing in your outbuilding."

"I haven't been out there in weeks. If he's a-storing' somethin,' I don't know what it would be."

"We'll tell you what's out there. We're going to be cutting that lock off."

"Now don't you damage nothin' out there."

Chapin ignored her demand, and we left the house. He motioned for the other three agents to join us at the garage. We stood looking at the heavy-duty lock for a few seconds, but with nothing to cut it off, we were a bit stymied.

Chapin then said, "Tony, go see if there's something in the flatbed we can use to break it. I don't want to try shooting it off. Bullets ricochet, you know."

"Roger, boss." He trotted over to the truck and, after rummaging through the back floor and bed, returned with a small sledgehammer.

It took a couple of swings, but on the third smash, the lock gave away. After we opened the double doors, we went inside. When we were in the center of the garage, Rod Chapin let out a low whistle.

"Holy shit, that is one mean-looking little SOB," referring to the EMP bomb. "So that's the devil that was to be shot up over D.C."

"By that Davey Crockett there."

"I'm not familiar with that system."

"Because you're too young," I said. "This thing was decommissioned back in the 90s."

Chapin took a look at the truck. "Will both the bomb and the Davey Crockett fit on that flatbed?"

"I think it will," Ferraro said. "We'll need to find something to secure them and to cover them up so that we don't frighten the good people of Clarksburg."

"Where will you take the bomb?" I asked.

"I have arranged with the CJIS to have them placed in one of their storage facilities for the time being.'

"And then there's Albrecht's pickup," Chapin said.

I nodded. "I'd just leave it here. I don't think he'll be back for it. He knows you guys will have the place under surveillance, and anyway, it's tag and description are listed on the APB."

Chapin shook his head. "The man can't go home, can't come here, lost his truck, his leadership in the militia, probably the use of his hand…I'd be pissed at you too, Bruce."

Chapter Thirty

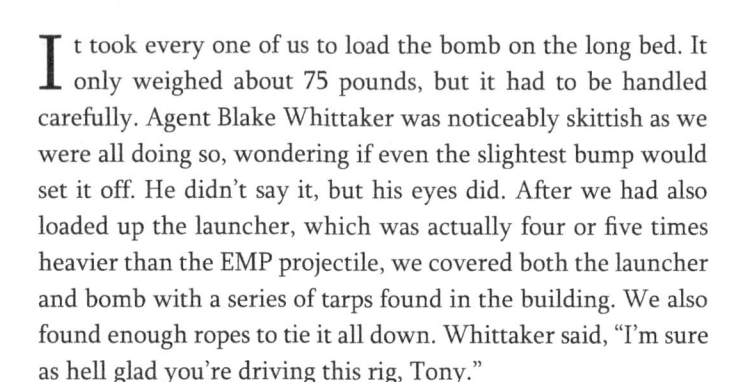

It took every one of us to load the bomb on the long bed. It only weighed about 75 pounds, but it had to be handled carefully. Agent Blake Whittaker was noticeably skittish as we were all doing so, wondering if even the slightest bump would set it off. He didn't say it, but his eyes did. After we had also loaded up the launcher, which was actually four or five times heavier than the EMP projectile, we covered both the launcher and bomb with a series of tarps found in the building. We also found enough ropes to tie it all down. Whittaker said, "I'm sure as hell glad you're driving this rig, Tony."

"Don't worry," I said. "If he hits a pothole and it goes off, any vehicle within five hundred yards of the flatbed will be vaporized along with it."

"Oh that's encouraging." He looked at Rodney Chapin. "Boss, I think we'll be trailing the flatbed about five miles."

Actually, I didn't know what kind of blast there would be. Even though it was a non-nuclear bomb, it would still blow like a multi-TNT round with a shock wave that would be felt fifty miles away. At least that's what I read about EMP bombs. What actual yield this thing had, I had no idea. However, the bomb had been transported several times before it was carted up the bumpy dirt roads of the Shawnee to the Nelson outbuilding. Moreover, as it had been built by Professor Mendelssohn in California, it had also managed the trip all the way across the country.

We were stopped at the gate by rent-a-cop guards at the CJIS complex who were curious as to what we were hauling in. "Just your typical high atmosphere EMP bomb," Chapin said, producing his ID and badge.

"Well, I don't know about this," one of the guards, a sergeant, replied.

"Not to worry. It's non-nuclear."

After a couple of phone calls to someone inside the complex, the sergeant shrugged and opened the gate. "I hope all you people know what you're doing and where you're going. I'm a little nervous about this."

"We just want to transfer it out of our hands and get the hell out of here," Chapin replied. Having said that, he then chuckled. The comment, of course, did nothing to lessen the guard's trepidation.

Rod Chapin followed Agent Ferraro back to the wrecker compound to return the flatbed truck and retrieve his SUV, then dumped me at the Microtel.

"Interesting day, huh, Bruce?"

"Yes, it was. But wait, I have something for you." I dug into my cargo pocket and pulled out the alcohol bottle wrapped in tissue paper. "You probably don't need this to prove Albrecht was staying at the Nelson house, but his bloodied fingerprints will be on it."

"I'll have it run through the lab."

"If I don't see you guys again, it was good working with you."

Chapin smiled and nodded. "I think you can go home now, Bruce."

When I checked out that afternoon, I learned Ben Marshall had come through via the FBI to arrange payment of my motel bill. That included raiding the mini-bar in my room a few times. I was back on the road by three.

As I left town and traveled the fifteen or so miles on Clarksburg Road past Kurt's Store, I noticed there was a closed sign on the building. The parking lot was empty. The iconic store and unofficial militia headquarters were history. It was something else Kurt Albrecht would attribute to me, intensifying his vendetta against me. I knew a storm was coming as he wasn't the kind of person to let bygones be bygones. I reached my hometown just after 4:30 pm and drove straight to Joey's place of business, McGowan and Sons Funeral Home. Even though I had nothing to do with the funeral business…ever…our dad had named it when he retired, hoping both his sons would carry on the tradition. Joey did, and I wanted no part of it. I couldn't fathom drilling holes in dead people and draining their blood, although I've drilled holes in a good many live ones who needed to be made dead. As Joey was generally there twelve to fourteen hours taking them in, embalming them, and then planting them in the ground, I can't remember a day he had to himself. But funeral homes were creepy to me and all I wanted to do was pick up my dog and go home. I was tired, shot up and hungry, having missed lunch again.

The Constitutionalists

"Ah, the prodigal brother returns," Joey quipped. "Where have you been? I was expecting you a couple of days ago."

"Has Lionel been a bad boy?"

"Lionel and I are pals. Okay, he had one accident in the family gathering room and I didn't see it before a mourner stepped in it; but all is forgiven.

"He doesn't do that," I said.

"It was my fault. I didn't take him out for most of the day."

"Well, sorry that happened. I hope it didn't ruin your carpet. "

"It wasn't messy; easy to pick up."

"Okay, enough turd talk; where is the little guy?"

"The last I saw of him, he was sleeping in the casket room."

"You didn't put him in one of those…"

"Heavens no, Brucie. He's curled up by the radiator."

"I'll go get him."

Col. Lee Martin

When I went in, Lionel woke up. I was expecting him to go crazy with excitement, jump into my arms and lick my face all over. But he just looked at me and put his head back down on the carpet.

Lionel didn't say much on the way home. I saw the sad look in his eyes when I pulled away. He watched Joey all the way out of the driveway. I just had to face the bitter truth...my dog liked my brother better than me.

Although I had a security system at the house, I was still wary about Albrecht somehow compromising it and breaking in. After all, he had gotten into Gail Delancy's house and according to her, she had one of the best. Mine was top of the line and a person could cut wires and otherwise disable the electricity in the house; the alarm would then revert to a back-up battery system. However, all looked good and I was confident Albrecht was not laying for me inside.

After feeding myself and Lionel a bit of supper, around seven I made my daily call to the wife. She told me she would be home on Saturday. I had three days to heal up, remove my bandages and put on a face that said I had had a pretty much boring time over the past week or so. Unless she wanted to take a romantic shower with me, I'd be keeping a shirt on to hide my wounds. I may be able to hide my wounds for a while, but the front and rear shoulder scarring would always be there. I knew I would have to find the perfect opportunity to tell her...and soon...tell her what happened to me after the government had once again come calling. I had promised myself long ago that I would never keep secrets from her. Secrets are nothing but lies, even if they don't come out of one's mouth. I remember a quote by somebody that stuck with me… *for* time sees and hears all things and discloses all.

Two days before I was to pick Adriana up at the Charleston airport, I thought I saw an Army green Jeep Wrangler pass me from the opposite direction. I wasn't paying all that much attention and it was by me before it registered in my brain. After finding a place to turn around, I gunned the Suburban to try catching the Jeep. However, it either turned off somewhere or had traveled too far ahead. But then I all but forgot about it. There could be scores of Jeeps in the county, maybe a few that were green.

But that same Friday evening while sitting on our front porch, I saw a green Jeep go by on Seven Bridges Road. I thought it was going rather slow, even though most vehicles traveling on the gravel road did. Was the driver looking over at our house as he passed? All I could see was a male with blondish hair, but the vehicle wasn't close enough to get a view of his face. However, I did practically jump off the porch and charge at a dead run to the edge of the road to see what happened to the Jeep. Did it stop down the road somewhere or go on? By the time I made the road, it was gone. Twice that day a green Jeep had passed by me and disappeared like an apparition. Now I was beginning to be concerned.

I sat on the porch well into the nine o'clock hour with Lionel beside me and a glass of Shiraz. My right arm hung down from the rocker close to the wooden deck where my XDM lay. Lionel had apparently begun liking me again, although for the past couple of days, he had practically ignored me. But that night, he licked my hand and then looked up at me as if to say, 'Okay, now that you're back, don't be leaving me again, Daddy.'

Col. Lee Martin

At nine-thirty, after I had taken Lionel for a walk in the yard, which proved profitable for both of us, we went inside. I then grabbed a couple of doggie treats from the cookie jar. We were pals again.

I retired at about eleven while Lionel curled up in his furry bed on the floor beside me. It was great to get back into my own bed even though the sheets hadn't been changed since Adriana left. I would put on a fresh set the next day.

It was two-forty on the digital clock on my nightstand when Lionel began growling and barking. He never did that. First, grabbing my .45 from the nightstand drawer, I bounded out of bed and ran through the dark living room to one of the front windows. Backing out of the yard fifty to sixty feet away was a vehicle with narrow-width headlights…like a Jeep. However, it hadn't come far enough toward the house to set off the motion sensor floodlight. After turning off security, I then ran to the door and, taking a low profile, stepped out on the porch in a shooter's stance. The vehicle was already on the road and away in a matter of seconds. It was a Jeep, for sure. Albrecht.

The Constitutionalists

Chapter Thirty-One

There was going to be no sleep the rest of the night…for me, anyway. However, I reset security and returned to bed. Turning on our bedroom TV, I began watching reruns of Mannix, MacGyver, and Murder She Wrote. I then looked down at Lionel, who was watching me. I smiled, pulled him up in the bed with me, and began stroking him. "You're a good dog, Lionel." And he was. I think he actually smiled. While we were both kind of getting into MacGyver, I said, "Maybe I should go pop some popcorn, buddy." However, because it wasn't good for him, I decided against it.

It was a long night. Not as long as a few nights ago in the Shawnee forest, though. At least I was comfortable and not running, crawling, and trying to evade bullets. But I'd be red-eyed when I started my morning.

As vendettas are generally motivated by those obsessed with power and position, not wanting to lose face, I supposed vindictiveness was all that Albrecht had left in him. He had lost everything else. But if I hadn't been a key player in that loss, he was still on a path of self-destruction. He had even said after launching the EMP, he expected to be arrested…which proves he was seeking notoriety any way he could get it. The man who would bring Washington to its knees. Once, a man who had found his power by hunting down and eliminating terrorists was now a man turned mad. I had not only caught a glimpse of that madness in his eyes when he gave his speech before his militia but also when he had me bound to the chair in the

Col. Lee Martin

Nelson garage. In the height of his power, this true narcissist stood above his people with outstretched arms, challenging, even commanding them to follow him into his battle against the government. In his defeat, he was now wanting to retaliate against the only person who had stood in his way to ultimate triumph…that triumph being the crippling of the American government.

I had not all that long ago disposed of an old nemesis who had once again surfaced with an intent to lure me into his web so that he could kill me. He nearly succeeded. Now there was someone else who wanted me to pay for my trespasses against him. I guess I bring out the worst in people. Or maybe I should rephrase that…I bring out the worst in the worst of people.

I knew one thing…Adriana was coming home the next afternoon. If I saw that Jeep again on or even near our property, no matter what time of the day or night, I would pepper it with a shitload of angry ammo.

Mid-morning, around ten, the phone rang. Just as had happened before, there was silence on the other end. However, about the time I was ready to let whoever it was have it, he spoke. It was Albrecht once again. "You know now that I am close by," is all he said.

"And you were about to stop a volley of rounds this morning. Don't be playing these bullshit games with me, prick. You're not intimidating me with phone calls like this or sitting outside my house at two in the morning. If you want to have at me, meet me like a man, face to face, like two gunslingers in the street."

"You'd like that, wouldn't you, McGowan? I'm sure you know when you shot me at that cabin, your bullet went through my right hand. I wouldn't be able to pull the trigger."

"Then suck it up and go away for your own good. Better yet, turn yourself in."

"One way or another, you're going to die, Bruce. Like I told you before, you don't know how or when, but there will be a time and a place. I just wanted you to know I'm around." He then ended his call.

Again, the concern I had was for Adriana. He might try something when she and I were together. She had already taken one bullet meant for me. If he had no control over his right hand, in using his left, his aim may not be accurate. But there were plenty of other ways to kill a person.

I didn't know how much longer he would stay around. He had had his say on the phone and made his point a few days ago by putting me out in the woods as game. His plan of action to kill me would depend on two factors…his creativity and his opportunity. But I wasn't going to just sit around waiting for him to make his move. If I would have the opportunity to do so, I would go after him. But then, would he be sticking around Greenbrier County in that green Jeep? I actually didn't think he would stay around at all. He knew I would get smart and ask one of my law enforcement friends to put an APB out on the vehicle, or I would go looking for the Jeep myself. Being a former government operative himself, he was both anticipatory and street-smart. The Jeep was too easy to spot. He would sooner than later be dumping it for a more conservative ride such as a Charger or a Malibu. It would be American-

Col. Lee Martin

made, of course. Now, having no place to stay, he would check around with one of his employees or trusted members of the Constitutionalists for a bed. It wouldn't be Gail as she wanted to shoot him on sight.

And thinking of Gail that morning, I gave her a call. I know I shouldn't have.

"Hello, Gail. Did I catch you busy?"

"Hi, Bruce. Good to hear from you again."

"I'm just calling to see if everything is okay."

"Nice of you to check on me. Yes, it is."

"I wanted you to know that the FBI now has that bomb in storage. Unfortunately, Kurt Albrecht has been lurking around my house looking for an opportunity to kill me."

"Good Lord, Bruce, have you actually seen him?"

"Just the vehicle he's been driving. If you see that green Jeep Wrangler anywhere in your neighborhood, call the police. He hasn't tried anything more with you, has he?"

"He knows better. I still get palpitations just thinking about what happened here and that I may find him inside my house again. But I have my pistol in my hand when I walk in my house after work, ready to fill his gut with lead if I find him there."

"Good for you. Stay on guard wherever you are. He's desperate…has no place to stay now that his cabin, his store, a house in the Shawnee where he had been staying, and the militia compound are under surveillance by the FBI and locals."

"I think somebody's been sitting outside on the street near my house. I can tell it's an unmarked police car."

"Good as well."

"But you're welcome any time to come back up here if you get tired of your humdrum life in Greenbrier County."

I laughed but didn't otherwise respond.

"Well, I was just seeing how you were doing. Stay vigilant."

"I will. I need to get back to work. So, bye, Bruce. Thanks for the call."

As Albrecht had registered his threat, I figured that was all he was going to do for the time being and would be back on the road that very day. But I wasn't going to think about it anymore. I had a wife to pick up. Her plane would be arriving at 3:40.

Adriana practically jumped into my arms as she met me at the turnstile. "Oh, how I've missed you, more this time than the last." She then put a lip lock on me that felt like a suction cup.

"And I missed you, sweetheart," I said after my lips popped back in place. "It's good to have you home."

"I'm making you a promise right now; I will not be going back unless one of my parents is on the deathbed." Then she wrapped her arms tightly around me, drawing me close into her. I winced. My wounded shoulder got caught up in that hug.

When her bags came around, I grabbed them up, one in each hand. After I tossed them into the back of the SUV and Lionel caught sight of Adriana, walking to the passenger's side, he began barking and wailing. Mama had come home.

"And I missed this little boy, too," she said, opening the door. For a solid minute, he gave her a wet facial. "I guess I don't have to wash my makeup off when I get home."

An hour and a half later, we were home. As I had promised I'd take Adriana out to dinner, she went immediately to the bathroom to take a shower. That's when she did what I was afraid she'd do; before she stepped in, she asked me to join her. Showering together had always been one of our favorite foreplay tactics. As soon as I heard the shower, I'd slip in on her. It generally happened once a week, and what happened afterward, with all the rockets going off, almost always put both of us in a state of hedonistic paralysis. Considering I still had bandages on the front and back sides of my shoulder covering my in-and-out wounds, I had to find an excuse not to shower with her. It would be especially difficult for me, being the horny husband that I was, so I had to get creative in my response to the invitation.

"Well, I just took a shower before I went to pick you up," which was true.

The Constitutionalists

Her face now having taken on a pouty look, she said, "You've never told me no before. Is anything wrong? It's always been one of our special pleasantries that leads to, you know what." She could never say the words "steamy sex" or anything she would consider raunchy, although I did hear her say "night of frenzied ecstasy" once when she was especially charged up. She looked hurt.

And then I said something that made me wish I had a speed bump between my brain and my mouth.

"It's…just that I'm not feeling all that romantic right now." And why the hell I came out with that one was beyond me. "Let me rephrase that."

She slammed the shower door. "You don't have to."

"Now don't take it that way, sweetheart." I was digging myself a hole.

I left the bathroom and waited in our den with Lionel. "Well, little buddy, I've stepped in it this time…and it's not in anything you made." I knew I had to tell her the truth, but I didn't want it to be as soon as she came home. I figured the best way was a little at a time. I thought she'd be angrier with me that I had succumbed to another government request, which I vowed I never would…my being shot up was another consequence.

But she was already miffed at me. Should I ruin our evening further by confessing to her? She deserved a better reason I wasn't showering with her, especially considering we had been apart almost ten days. Leaving the situation like it was would only exacerbate her mood. I was ready to take my lumps.

Chapter Thirty-Two

When I heard the shower stop running, I went to the bathroom and picked up the huge, thirsty towel she had laid aside. She stepped out, and I dried her off with it. As she still had an aggrieved look on her face and saying nothing, I said, "Can we talk?"

"About?"

"Come sit with me."

She followed me to the bedroom, and as I sat on the edge of the bed, she took her vanity chair.

"I have to tell you something."

That probably wasn't the best way to start my confession, especially since it caused her eyes to well up.

"Go on."

I then pulled my shirt over my head and exposed my bandaged shoulder and arm. "I didn't want you to see this, but it was inevitable." I then removed the shoulder bandage. Her eyes now widened. "It all started three weeks ago."

As delicately and succinctly as I could, leaving nothing out, beginning with the call from Ben Marshall. I covered the meeting with Albrecht, the coyote hunting trip, his pitch inviting me into the militia, the compound activities, all the conversations I had with Ben, the money he was to pay me, the bomb to take out the Washington grid, the first kidnapping and murder of Special Agent Murphy, and then the hunting expedition up on the Shawnee…the deadly game that got me wounded. It took me more than twenty minutes to convey to her slowly and calmly what had occurred in her absence. I then waited for the explosion.

However, she threw me a curveball. At first, she smiled, and then she laughed. It was a one-eighty from what I expected.

"Why are you laughing? Why aren't you angry as hell with me?"

She then came to the bed and sat on my lap. "When you didn't come to me in the shower and gave me the impression you didn't want me, I thought you were going to tell me you had an affair."

And then I laughed. "An affair? Oh, please."

The laughter was nothing but relief on both of our parts. She was relieved she hadn't lost me to another woman; I was relieved she wasn't going to take my head off for going on another government-requested mission, again coming home with holes in my body.

"I'm supposed to be mad at you," she said. "After I digest all that you told me, I might just be that. You've been a bad boy, Bruce McGowan."

The Constitutionalists

"But, I saved Washington, D.C..."

She smiled and shook her head. "Now that you've gotten your little secret out in the open and are showing me you're full of remorse throw me on the bed and make love to me."

"I think I'll do just that."

And I did…slowly, methodically, and masterfully.

Adriana ended up taking another shower, this time with me.

Around eight o'clock we went out for a late dinner as both of us were suffering post-coital hunger pangs. We sat at a small, intimate table across from each other, smiling and holding hands while we waited for the dinner we had ordered. Meanwhile, I filled her in with a few minute details I had forgotten to mention. But then she asked about someone who I had kind of glossed over.

"This woman, Gail…you actually sat outside her house for three nights. Why were you so concerned for her?" Spoken like a jealous wife.

"Knowing that she had become close to Kurt Albrecht, I went after him, figuring I'd find him at her house or lurking nearby. I went after him because he had threatened to kill me, anywhere, anytime, and I was concerned he'd bring his war here. I didn't want you exposed."

"So, was Gail pretty?" More jealousy.

"I'd say average, not all that attractive." My nose was starting to grow.

"Well, I'm sure she appreciated you looking out for her."

"Right."

Having gotten everything out in the open and enjoying both a very nice dinner and an exuberant evening of sex, I was anxious to settle back in my Big Easy, with my dog and a glass of vino. Back into my sedentary, uncomplicated life as a doting husband and house louse.

It was the warm, morning sun radiating through the window in the den that woke me just before eight the next morning. The last thing I remembered was leaving our bed and plopping into my easy chair to watch the eleven o'clock news. She must have turned the TV off and allowed me to sleep.

She was already in the kitchen making a breakfast of bacon, poached eggs, toast and coffee, Lionel sitting dutifully at her feet, hoping just one small strip of the bacon would pop out of the pan and onto the floor.

"Morning, babe," I greeted, putting my arms around her small waist and then placing my lips on her neck. "Mmm, you smell good."

"That's the bacon, dearie." She smiled. I couldn't help but notice the serene afterglow on her face. I did that.

"It's just so nice having you home."

The Constitutionalists

"It's so nice being here," she replied.

We ate our breakfast while Lionel sat watching us. He had a cute habit of opening his mouth and then clamping it shut each time we took a bite. I felt for the little guy, but his mama's rules prevailed. I often wondered if she relented when I wasn't around. But that was between her and him.

After breakfast we took him for a walk along a less-traveled farm road outside of town where one might see two vehicles pass over a period of twenty minutes. The temperature was fifty-ish, the sky a perfect blue, and the crisp air, intoxicating. In my left hand was Lionel's leash; in my right, Adriana's gentle hand. Nothing could spoil this most perfect morning. One would think.

A couple and their dog out for a walk down a country road in a low-crime state should not have to worry when they hear someone jogging up on them from behind. However, when the runner is not dressed in jogging clothing and is wearing a ball cap with the brim pulled down over his eyes, slowing down to a walk when he's within twenty feet, my alarm is going off. Another quick look behind me, I see he's now brandishing a .22 caliber. The thought immediately comes to mind was that he was another one of Albrecht's boys who had followed us from the house, intending to do a little bloodletting. Adriana, also seeing the gun, let out a slight scream. Lionel, sensing the danger, began growling.

Calmly I said, "Adriana, go over there in the grass and take the dog with you." Quickly doing as I told her, she hunkered down well off the road. The man was between 22 and 25 and had shoulder-length, dark hair.

"You really want to do this, pal?"

"I ain't your pal, mister. Hand me your wallet."

"Are you one of Albrecht's boys?"

"Who the hell's Albrecht?"

I didn't answer. He then followed up with, "I ain't nobody's boy. Now hand me your wallet…and that watch."

I chuckled. "You're robbing me? You're actually out here on this road robbing me? And with a .22?"

"You must be a moron to ask me that. What the hell does it look like?"

"It looks like you're an amateur, boy."

"I don't wanna shoot you, man. Just give me the wallet."

"You would really shoot me for twenty dollars? That's what is in my wallet. You must be in dire straights to try robbing a couple out here in the country. My wife doesn't even have her purse with her."

The man slapped his forehead and began waving the gun around. "Shit, man, why can't you just cooperate here?"

I then took my wallet from my jacket, opened it and lifted the twenty. "Here. Take it. You obviously need it more than I do."

He snatched it from my hand and then said, "Now the watch."

"No. You're not getting my watch. It was an anniversary present from my wife last year."

"I don't give a shit. Just let me have it."

Adriana then said. "Enough. You want it? I'll let you have it, alright." That's when she pulled from her jacket her .357. It was my last year's anniversary present to her. She fired one round into the ground, which to his misfortune, hit a rock and ricocheted into his foot. He screamed and dropped the .22, going down on both knees.

I kicked his gun away and bent over him to look at his left foot. The bullet had entered his sneaker and apparently caught a toe.

"God, woman, you actually shot me." he cried.

"Hmmm. You'd have to be a moron not to know that," she said. I laughed again.

"What's your name, fella?" I asked.

His face, racked with pain, he managed to spit out "Boozer."

"That's not your real name. I just need to have a name to give to the police and paramedics when they come to pick you up."

Col. Lee Martin

"You don't need to call nobody. I…I can walk."

"No you can't, Boozer. Your tennis shoe is saturated with blood."

He then stood up and winced from his pain. I grabbed hold of him by his worn Army jacket.

"Are you gonna hit me?" he asked, almost pitifully.

"No, I'm not gonna hit you, Boozer. I just wanted to look you in the eyes and tell you…next time you accost someone, especially with a cap pistol, you might get shot dead by someone like me. Or my wife there."

He nodded but didn't reply.

"Why did you try to rob us?"

"I…I guess I just needed some money. I ain't eaten in two days."

"What's your real name?"

"Mike…Mike Winters."

"Do you live around here?"

"I'm jus' stayin' at a place beyond them trees."

"Tell you what, Mike; this afternoon, after you get your foot treated, you go to see a friend of mine at a place out on 219 near the country club called Jack's. Jack owns a roadside grill. I'll call him and ask him to give you a meal. I also know he's looking for a dishwasher. It will be up to you to sell yourself for a job." I then released my grip on his coat.

"You'd do that for me even though I tried to rob you?"

"You just need a break. It was my day to give somebody a break."

Tears began rolling down his cheeks. "Th...thanks, mister."

"My name's Bruce. Now, promise me you won't do this again."

He nodded. "I promise, Bruce. Can I go now?"

"Can you walk?"

After testing his weight on the foot, he nodded again. One step at a time, he began hobbling off the road's edge into the trees. Seconds later, he was out of sight.

I felt sorry for Boozer. I had never seen him before, but I figured he was homeless and seeking shelter in the abandoned, broken-down Jarvis house on the other side of those trees. I'd be sending the rescue squad there but not the police.

I then turned to Adriana. She said, "You are such a sweet man, Bruce McGowan. You surprise me every day."

"You, my dear, are the one who's full of surprises. I had no idea you were carrying."

Col. Lee Martin

"Well, I knew you were packing and would soon be putting bullets in the guy. I didn't want that. I actually just meant to scare him, not shoot his foot off."

"Well, I'm proud of you, Madam Mayor." And I was. However, what I didn't tell her was she should never just shoot to warn, especially when the other guy has a gun in his hand. Even if it was a .22 versus a .357. But I didn't want to burst her bubble.

The Constitutionalists

Chapter Thirty-Three

As planned months ago, the two of us spent Thanksgiving in New York City. We arrived on Wednesday afternoon, took a taxi into Manhattan, and checked in at The Blakely.

The carriage ride through Central Park, shopping at the ritzy stores on 5th Avenue, and the Thanksgiving dinner at the Waldorf Astoria made Adriana feel like Queen Elizabeth, so she said. I had all but forgotten about the likes of Kurt Albrecht, almost believing he was now just licking his emotional wounds, maybe somewhere in another country putting together a militia and starting a revolution. At least, I was hoping that was the case.

However, when we arrived home on Saturday afternoon, there was evidence to the contrary. Thumbtacked to our front door, we found a three-by-five-foot black flag…the flag of the Constitutionalist militia. I took it as another warning. Albrecht still didn't have me gone from his mind.

"What does this mean?" Adriana asked me.

"It means I was paid a visit by Albrecht while we were gone." I ripped the banner off the door. "This rag here is his militia flag."

"He really has it in for you. What are you going to do?"

"Just watch the place closely and see that he doesn't do anything that will endanger you."

"What does this Albrecht look like?"

"He's around sixty, maybe six feet tall with greying-blonde hair, driving around in a green Jeep that he's probably no longer in. He's smart enough to go to something else."

"I don't mind telling you, I'm a bit unnerved about this."

"If I knew where this prick was hiding out, I'd go after him."

"No, you will notify the police or FBI. Please don't take any drastic measures yourself."

"We'll see. But I guarantee you he's not going away. He's playing games with me right now, but that will come to an end. There will be a time he'll come after me for real."

"Why is it you always have people coming after you? It's like one of those westerns where you're a notorious gunslinger, and every bad guy with a pistol and ten-gallon hat is gunning for you."

"I'm not letting you watch any more Saturday westerns, my dear."

"You know what? Maybe that isolated cabin somewhere in Wyoming or Montana you talk about might not be a bad idea."

"Well, Madam Mayor, you'd be giving up a lot to move out of here…all that political power, your friends, your church…"

"I didn't say I'd be going out there."

We both then laughed. A little levity was what we needed to take our minds off Albrecht. But regardless of her insistence that I let the authorities handle him, I was going after him.

Adriana was back at city hall the Monday after Thanksgiving. Even though she didn't go there to work in her small office every day, she was always in touch with members of the council by phone or computer on town matters. The people loved her. She couldn't go to any place in the town where someone didn't have a question about something or just wanted to chat. But with her being out and about like she was most days, I had to worry about her. Albrecht had made it apparent that even though he was on the lam, he could slip in and out of town at any point. He could get his revenge on me by making her his target.

However, for the next few weeks leading up to Christmas, I neither saw nor heard anything further out of Albrecht. But that was what he did. He would occasionally surface with some kind of warnings like threatening phone calls, a flag on our door, or a ghostly appearance at the end of our driveway; then, there would be nothing. He was thinking these little psychological ploys would rattle me. But, actually, it was having the opposite effect on me. I thought his little games were childish…a man playing boyish pranks. His madness aside, it was unbecoming of a former federal operative.

Col. Lee Martin

A week before Christmas, Adriana answered my cell phone when I was out on a morning run with Lionel. Here's how she told me the conversation went:

"Hello. You must be Adriana."

"Yes. Who's calling?"

"This is Ben Marshall. I'm the National Security Adviser and a friend of Bruce's as well."

"Oh, then you're the guy."

"What guy?"

"The guy who hired my husband to go out into the woods with that militia bunch."

"I asked him to do me a favor along that line, yes."

"Then he became a hunted man and ended up getting shot a few times."

"He told you all about that, huh?"

"He eventually had to explain the wound in his shoulder."

"He said you'd not be happy with him."

"Yes. That's a mild way of putting it. He's now retired, Mr. Marshall. We've had some very frank conversations about him taking on government work."

The Constitutionalists

"I'm sorry, my dear, I hope this didn't result in any discord between the two of you. I apologize to you for asking him to participate in the mission. If he had declined it, I would have been fine with it."

"Well now you know. But I'll tell him you called. But please call him anytime…as a friend…not as an employer. Merry Christmas."

And so that's how Ben threw me under the bus. When I returned his call, he said, "It was apparent Adriana was quite miffed with me."

"Like I am with you, Ben. So, if I had declined the mission, you would have been fine with it?"

"Well, that's true. I didn't twist your arm, you know."

"Yeah, okay. But anyway, you called for some reason. Or did you just want my correct address as where to send my Christmas present?"

"I already gave you your Christmas present in the form of seven days pay. Anyhow, I wanted to give you an update on Albrecht. He's now gone full-blown terrorist if he wasn't there before. He just sent the president a threatening manifesto."

"What's the content of the manifesto?"

"Here's an excerpt. "You have allowed thousands of illegal immigrants in this country, many of whom are Islamic jihadists, the very terrorists I hunted down and killed for the

American government. You have betrayed all Americans and treason is punishable by death…your death."

"Threatening the president is automatically life without parole."

"Here's something else he wrote, plagiarizing Norwegian extremist Andrew Breivik nearly word for word. *"You and the liberal government's multiculturalism policy has weakened national identity and encouraged Islamic extremist expansion."*

"Hmm, as I remember from college, plagiarism is also punishable by death. Any clues where he is right now?"

"We're sure he's still in the Clarksburg area as that's where the letter was postmarked."

"Obviously, one of his people is putting him up. But the Bureau would have to have the full list of his militia members to start their search. There were close to 300 at one time. I'd first go after the big guy financing him."

"The Bureau did arrest Mr. J. Hoyt Nelson for aiding and abetting. His house was re-searched. No list of militia members was found in his personal papers. The same in Albrecht's cabin, or in his room at the compound and store office. You're right, though; he's boarding with one of his loyalists. Maybe we get lucky and somebody spots him. He's now on top of the America's Most Wanted list."

"He's also been right here in Greenbrier County. He perched his Jeep one night at the edge of my yard; then while

The Constitutionalists

Adriana and I were in New York over Thanksgiving, he tacked his militia flag to our door. He's called my phone twice, threatening to kill me, "any place, anytime," and I won't know when the bullet's coming."

"So, he's still after you, huh? You and now the president. At least you're in good company."

"Well I wouldn't go that far."

Chapter Thirty-Four

Our conversation continued another couple of minutes and then he said he had to go. "Adriana sounded like a nice lady. I told her I hoped I didn't cause you two any disharmony by asking you to take on the assignment."

"I'm a big boy, Ben. Like I said, I could have refused it."

"No you couldn't. I know you and you needed something to drag you away from that blasé, rocking chair retirement you chose."

"I beg your pardon; I stay active with a little golf and go bowling a couple times a month."

"Sorry to have taken you away from all that excitement. Anyhow, I'll keep you in the know about Albrecht? You do have a vested interest."

And so, former counterterrorist operative Kurt Albrecht had officially become a terrorist himself, although he had been one all along when he began planning the EMP attack. But now he had made his quest a personal one against the leader of the free world. If he actually intended to carry out his threat, he had the skill to do it. What he needed was opportunity. Even though American presidents in general are the most protected people on the earth, this one was known to get out into crowds, especially at campaign fund-raisers, shake hands and kiss babies. Government cameras, heavy lenses and gunsights would be zeroing in on every face in the crowd. However, true assassins don't advertise in manifestos their intent to take down leaders and other important targets. As a former covert operator, he knew that. In my opinion, his manifesto was nothing more than a meaningless threat on paper…a narcissistic gimmick to get his name out there in the same company with other domestic terrorists.

But as far as I was concerned, unless he still wanted to bring his war to my doorstep, I was done with him. Somehow, though, I knew I would still be on his annoyance list. He hadn't forgotten about me. Christmas Day we spent with Joey and his family. His girls, all grown up and married, brought to the old McGowan homestead their babies, which made me feel older than dirt. It seemed only months ago his daughters were eight and ten, flitting about excited about the gifts they had just opened. My sitting in the parlor listening to Burl Ives' singing Have a Holly, Jolly Christmas on the old Victrola and watching Joey, his wife and my Adriana prepare the holiday dinner brought back memories of Christmases past when Mom was tantalizing our olfactory senses with her ham, yeast rolls and pecan pie. And then there was that aroma of cinnamon simmering on the stove, that permeated throughout the entire house. Two days before, Joey and I had gone into the Greenbrier woods and cut down a lovely pine, now sitting in a corner of the parlor near the decorated fireplace where Lionel laid curled up on a rug. As I sat smiling in Joey's recliner, which used to hold our dad's derriere, nothing could ruin my Christmas. Except for a phone notification from my security company that our alarm at Wolf Laurel had gone off.

Col. Lee Martin

Of course, the first thing I thought about was Albrecht...a man with no family with which to celebrate Christmas, trying to ruin mine. Talking with the agent at the security company, I told her we were away from the house and to go ahead and summon the police. As dinner was not quite ready, I hustled to my SUV and drove the two miles to our house. The sheriff was already there.

Deputy Sheriff Bobby Jaworski was standing on our veranda waiting for me. "I would ordinarily wish you a Happy Christmas, Bruce, but as you can see, this is not a false alarm. Someone smashed the front door window and reached in to twist open the deadbolt. I went inside but was unable to determine if anything is missing."

"I'll be able to tell," I said. "We don't have any valuables out in the open. My wife keeps her jewelry in a large safe where I also keep most of my guns. I'll look around." I was 90 percent sure it was just another message from Albrecht that he was going to continue his threats, cause me apprehension, and otherwise get my goat with his surprisingly lame antics. He had nothing else to do that Christmas Day.

After doing a walkthrough of the house, I didn't readily see that anything had been taken or damaged. Considering the security alarm would have gone off, sending a shrill siren throughout the community, any burglar would likely not have spent more than 10 seconds inside.

"I'll make out a report, Bruce," Bobby said. "I didn't expect crime to be comin' to the mayor's house on Christmas. I'll help you secure the door so you can get back to your folks. Do you have any plywood out in your shop?"

The Constitutionalists

"I do, but thanks, Bobby; I'll take care of it. Sorry, you had to come out here on your holiday. Merry Christmas."

"And a Merry Christmas to you, Bruce."

Whoever had broken in was long gone. Of course, I knew who that someone had to be. When Deputy Bobby had departed, Albrecht could have continued to lurk close by and then rush me while I was securing material to repair the front door. But if he was the culprit, he probably wouldn't do that. He preferred to cause me trepidation as long as he could, like a cat plays with a bird before it eats it. He would get his satisfaction out of harassing me, and then in grandstand fashion, set me up for the kill. It was the psycho in him. Nonetheless, before I went to my woodshed to cut a piece of plywood, I went back to my Suburban for my pistol. I thought I could at least get through Christmas Day without having it on me.

I made one more pass through the house and then began securing the front door with the plywood. For quite some time, I had thought about replacing the vulnerable door with a metal one having no window glass. The next day, I'd be at the Home Depot when it opened.

When I returned to my brother's house, Adriana was noticeably unsettled. "Did someone actually break into the house?"

I nodded. "The door glass was broken, and deadbolt unlocked, but I didn't find anything taken. The alarm probably scared them off."

Col. Lee Martin

"Good grief. Crime doesn't even take a holiday. I guess they were looking for presents under a Christmas tree."

"Well, considering we didn't even put up a tree and brought our presents with us, I'm sure the burglars were disappointed. But let's forget about it and go back to having a joyous, old-fashioned family Christmas."

"Thank you, Clark Griswold."

We had only been home a few minutes when I heard Adriana's blood-curdling scream from the kitchen. When I hustled in, I found her standing at the open refrigerator door. "Look," she said.

There lying on a shelf was a large, dead rat.

"That son-of-a-bitch!" I bellowed.

"Who would do this?" she asked, almost in tears.

As she was already rattled, having found the rat, I didn't know if I should cause her any more angst by giving her my suspicion. "Whoever it was is sick in the head," I replied.

The rat in the fridge was all he did. It was all he needed to do to terrorize us and to make Adriana's blood run cold, especially. But it made mine boil. I knew then I had to somehow find the bastard. It wouldn't be easy, though; everybody from the FBI to the locals had been looking for him. Yet, he was able to pull a sick prank like this right under everyone's nose.

The Constitutionalists

After I disposed of the rat, we sat in our den nursing our glasses of Merlot and listening to Poulenc's Four Motet's for Christmastime, the melodic sweetness of which worked the opposite by placing us in a somber mood. Adriana couldn't get the violation of our house at Christmas out of her head. The rat was a metaphor. Albrecht had called me a dead rat for not only deceiving him and sabotaging his mission but for setting him up to be captured by the Feds. But I had sealed his fate by subsequently discovering the plans he had hidden that provided the proof the feds needed of his conspiracy against the government. Now, he had a two-fold objective…take out the president, which might be no more than thunder and smoke, and set me up for the kill, which would be a much easier and more gratifying task to accomplish. Payback was hell, and that's what he wanted me to be feeling.

Adriana was quite an astute woman, not to mention perceptive. As we sat with lights low, quietly whiling away what was left of our Christmas Day, she said, "You know who it was that broke into our house, don't you."

"I have an idea."

"It was the man you were sent to investigate…the leader of that militia, the one who had set you up to kill."

"Kurt Albrecht."

"It's all your fault, husband, dear. Because of you, he lost his militia group, his clout, his store business, his home, and his freedom. At least, that's what he believes. You infiltrated his little army, secured the evidence on him, and reported his conspiracy plans to the government. Now he wants revenge and is pulling monkey shit like this."

I had to laugh. No profanity ever came out of her mouth, mild as it was. But it took the refrigerated rat to bring it out of her. Any woman but my wife would be scared. But she was more pissed than scared.

"Yeah, I can't prove he did this, but I haven't heard of any burglaries happening around here. This is like a prank a bunch of teenagers would pull; however, the kids I know in this town would never do anything like this. But don't worry…Bobby said he and the other deputies will keep a lookout for any future activity."

"And so will I, along with the .357 you gave me," she added.

"Good for you, Madam Mayor."

I think it was nine-thirty when my daughter Caroline called. "Are you having a Merry Christmas, Dad?"

"It could have been merrier if you were here."

"I wanted to come up, but I was one of the lucky agents chosen for duty today."

FBI Special Agent Caroline McGowan had been transferred to the Atlanta field office only six months before, and although she had tenure over other agents, they had been promised time off at Christmas. It had happened to me a couple of times in my service with the Bureau, so I was understanding.

"How's Adriana?"

"Just a little tired these days. She's been going back and forth to her parents the past few weeks to be their caregiver. I'm sure I told you that her mother broke her hip. Then a pulmonary embolism developed from the surgery."

"That's awful. I hope she recovers well."

"Did you get our present?"

"I did. I love the jogging suit. But it didn't have to be an extravagant Ralph Lauren."

"Sure it did. Nothing's too good for my girl."

"And did you all get mine?"

"We picked it up at the gallery downtown. Speaking of extravagant…an original P. Buckley Moss?"

"You're my only dad."

"That's true. I was there when you were born."

"Uh…is there anything you want to tell me, Pop?"

"Like what?"

"Like something going on with some anarchist up in Clarksburg?"

"How do you know about that?"

"The FBI family is pretty close-knit as you will remember."

"Meaning?"

"I received a call from an agent I went through Quantico with."

"Okay."

"You told Marco Rivera that you had a daughter who's a special agent in Atlanta. It didn't register with him at the time that it was me. Then he remembered my last name was also McGowan and called me. After talking with him, I pulled up the matter on the Bureau's Uniform Crime Report and guess whose name is on the report as a government informant? And then it says you were also assaulted? I hope you weren't hurt. Are you still in some kind of danger?"

"You know me. Danger is my middle name."

"Except you are retired, Father dear. You're not supposed to have any danger in your life anymore. Why are you involved in this matter?"

"You know…I get a call from someone in the government asking me to help them out."

"You have to stop this, Dad. They have people in every division of law enforcement who can do this stuff. I'm sure Adriana is not happy with you."

The Constitutionalists

"You're correct about that."

"How were you assaulted?"

"Very rudely."

"Quit being frivolous. I'm serious."

"It wasn't anything austere…a couple of bumps on the head, chased through the woods by people with guns who wanted to kill me, catching a couple of their bullets…fun stuff like that."

"I'm going to end our conversation if you don't stop being so flippant."

"Caroline, I'm done with it all. I provided my report to the NSA and have had a sweet Christmas Day with Adriana and your Uncle Joey's family. Wish you were here."

"Alright. But promise me, from now on, you'll stay out of the crosshairs of bad guys."

"Right. Now go home and celebrate what's left of Christmas."

"Bye, Dad. I love you. Stay safe and well."

Chapter Thirty-Five

Ben Marshall was true to his word in keeping me up to date on Albrecht's threats against the government, specifically against the President. He sent me not only a copy of the original manifesto but also an addendum, one that included as targets the Vice President, Speaker of the House, and Secretary of State. On the 10th of January, he called to follow up.

"I assume you received my letter. I went ahead and sent you the information as his intentions are now out in the open. These latter threats on the VP and staff would be much easier to carry out, but they'll be receiving Secret Service protection along with the President."

"This is definitely not the same Kurt Albrecht that I knew years ago. I had a good discussion with a psychiatrist friend of mine a month or so ago. Without mentioning his name, I bounced some questions off him. From our discussion, I am wondering if the taking down of terrorists by every means, from sniper bullets to organized team raids, may have caused PTSD. He had also lost his wife which might have put him over. When I first saw him after all these years, it didn't take me long to realize that he was prone to mood swings where he could be calm and friendly one day and vehemently angry the next."

"Like someone having bipolar issues."

The Constitutionalists

"Yes, but he also has a list of personality disorders including Narcissistic and Antisocial, the latter meaning criminal, manipulative, and abusive. He can be like a time bomb, ready to explode at any time. When he thought I was coming in with him, he was beguiling…like old times…pals. I found that if you're on his team one hundred percent and feeding his ego, he can be very charismatic. But when he found out I was a government plant, out came the sociopathic behaviors."

"Making him a dangerous, unpredictable threat to anyone who stands in his way."

"He's proved that." I then told him about the calls and the dead rat.

"He actually did that? A rat?"

"I'm ninety percent sure it was him, although he hasn't called to take credit for it."

"That's nasty. Sounds like a schoolboy prank or something Alex Forrest would do."

"Who's Alex Forrest?" I asked.

"You know, the psycho role Glenn Close played in Fatal Attraction."

"Oh yeah. Wicked woman. I remembered you liked all those nutcase movies, such as The Shining and Silence of the Lambs. Says a lot about your personality."

He laughed. "Well, I need to be going," he said. "I have a feeling something is going to crack open soon. I hope it doesn't involve you. Be safe and stay away from the refrigerator."

"I would say give the President my best…but nah."

January was a cold month, as it is always expected to be in the hills of West Virginia; however, it was a dry cold. Not a flake of snow fell. However, snow generally doesn't fall when the temperature drops into the teens. And when it is that cold, I'm generally not jogging. The pound, pound, pounding of my feet on the frozen ground makes me feel like every bone in my body is about to crack. But I do run on our treadmill that sits in one of our old guest rooms converted into a home gym. Lionel sits and watches curiously, probably wondering why my running is not taking me anywhere.

There hadn't been a peep out of Albrecht for weeks, and I wondered if he had finally given up on his vendetta against me. He may have lost his EMP bomb and his potential of launching it over Washington, D.C., but I also wondered if he was serious about assassinating the President and his people. In threatening to do so, he had written himself a prescription for ninety-nine years in federal prison. However, although he had been quiet, I, having long since determined that he was now a wacko, expected he would at some point resurface to have it out with me, "anytime, any place," as he had threatened. I'm sure I was still first on his priority list.

However, as the last day of January, as Ben had predicted, something did crack open. It was a day Adriana was working at city hall with the council and contractors on a new road deal.

She was tied up in meetings the entire day. And it was the same day I received a frantic call from Gail Delancy.

At first, her voice was low, almost a whisper. "Bruce, he's in my house. I came home early and…*no*! Get Out, Kurt! Don't come near me! "

"Gail, are you alright?"

"He's…he's coming toward me. He's got a gun in his hand."

"Then call 911! Call the police!" I yelled.

But then I heard a commotion, like the phone being dropped. A moment later, Albrecht's voice came on the line. "Too late for that, Scorpion. Gail is in deep ca-ca. It's just she and me now."

"Albrecht, if you harm a hair on her head…"

"Hey, old boy, I know you had the hots for her. And no doubt she'd like to have your shoes under her bed. But this is your opportunity to shine. So come on, Bruce, it's only you who can save this damsel in distress. Remember I said this day was coming? It's your day to be a hero. But you have to get past me first. And don't call the police when you get off the line. I'll be watching. If I see a police unit outside, either unmarked or with flashing lights, Gail automatically dies. I only want to see that black Suburban pull up into the driveway. What you do from here will prove if you are a hero or a rat, like the Christmas present I left you. I'm going to give you until six to get here. That's two hours and twenty minutes. If you're not here by then or you send the police, your little nurse friend bites the bullet…literally."

"Listen, you psycho bastard…"

"Stop the name-calling. The clock has already started. Don't waste time threatening me. It's goodbye for now or goodbye, Gail." The phone was then silent.

If I called the FBI, maybe they could take him down without her dying. I wasn't so sure about the locals. They might go in with guns blazing. It had come down to being my life for hers. He had patiently waited for this moment. But I'd be damned if I surrendered to him. I first had to get there within the next couple of hours so that he wouldn't just go ahead and kill her. And he would do it, the psychotic prick that he was. It would be two former counterterrorist operatives in a final game of cunning, both of us using our well-honed skills to take the other down. But there would be no way I was just going to waltz my ass in Gail's front door.

I did make a call, however. I called for Adriana to tell her I was driving to Clarksburg. But she was tied up in a meeting, and the clerk said she didn't want to be interrupted. It was just as well that I wasn't able to talk with her. If I told her what I was going to do, she would not only beg me not to go, but she would call the police herself. I had to do this my way. I left my message with the mayor's assistant. I'd try to be back that night by ten or eleven.

Before I left the house, I placed my XDM in the paddle holster that lay inside my jeans against my body. I had less than two and a half hours to devise a plan that did not include pulling

The Constitutionalists

my SUV into her driveway. I had had a hell of a lot of experiences involving the element of surprise. Unfortunately, so did he.

If I left at four. Barring any construction or highway accidents, I should make it by six. But as I needed a few minutes to execute my plan at her house, I decided to leave at three forty-five.

All the way up the winding road to Clarksburg, I tried to remember the house's outside features, considering I had sat looking at it three nights in a row. But it had been dark, and the street was poorly lit. However, there was something about it I did remember…and it would serve as my entry point.

Since it was January, the daylight was long gone by the time I reached her street at five-fifty. Rather than pass by the house, which would have attracted a watchful eye, I parked my Suburban around the corner on the street before Jackson. Hustling through a couple of backyards, I found the rear of Gail's house. If Albrecht was true to his words, I had about seven minutes to get into the house. First, trying the back door off the small rear porch, I found it locked. I knew it would be. If I tried forcing the lock or breaking the window glass, the noise would be heard inside the house. So, then I went to that part of the outside I had studied those nights of surveillance. A basement door. Trying the door, I found it was also locked…or was it just stuck? It did seem to have some movement.

When my phone lit up and began to vibrate, I saw the same number pop up that had called my phone two-plus hours before…Gail's number.

"Yeah," I answered in a low voice.

"In five minutes, Gail dies. I hope your SUV is about to pull into the driveway."

I didn't respond and touched end on the phone.

Whether the door was stuck or locked only at the knob. I put my right shoulder into it. It dislodged. When it swung open, it made less noise than I expected. Using the flashlight on my phone, I worked my way around some boxes and old furniture to the stairs that went into the house. If the door to the inside was locked, there would be a problem. Thank goodness it wasn't. The door opened into a narrow hallway that led into the kitchen. The house was old, and the wooden floor creaked and popped under my feet.

I could hear voices coming from a room at the end of the hallway, which I surmised was the living room, so I headed toward it, gun in hand. Just when I was near the opening to the room, I heard Albrecht say, "Come on in, Scorpion. I've been expecting you."

I let out a puff of air. So much for the element of surprise. When I stepped inside the room, I saw that he was sitting on the couch with Gail beside him. He was holding a .45 automatic in his left hand aimed at her. It had a suppressor attached. And then I noticed that he no longer had much of a right hand. Two fingers were missing, and it had become what resembled a lobster claw. "Toss your gun in that sofa chair!" he barked.

I thought about putting a round between his eyes, but as his finger was on the trigger, my shot could cause him to squeeze it. So, I did as he demanded. "Now, the one in your boot. I know you carry one. Take it out with one finger and your thumb and toss it as well." I stalled for a moment, but he then placed the muzzle of his gun against Gail's temple as though he were about to shoot. So, I threw it onto the chair alongside the XDM.

"You look surprised, Bruce. Did I really expect you would park in Gail's driveway and walk through that door? That's why I left that basement door unlocked. You're predictable. And I saw the look on your face when you glanced at my mangled right hand. That's right, Bruce. I lost my fingers. Did I thank you for that?"

I then looked at Gail who surprisingly seemed rather tranquil, even buoyant. Had he drugged her?
But then she produced something that caused a fiery jolt of adrenaline to shoot through my arteries.
A pistol of her own…a .357 and pointed at me. She smiled. "Yes, Bruce. It's exactly what you're thinking. You got played. Kurt and I are an item, as you put it. We've been so ever since I joined the Constitutionalists."

Albrecht laughed. "Surprise, surprise."

Gail continued. "I played my role so believably, didn't I? The sweet, concerned nurse who helped patch you up and came on to you. If it's okay with you, I'll now humbly accept my Oscar."

I have to admit I was dumbstruck, but finally got the words out. "Bravo!" I then clapped. "Yeah, I gotta say, I'm totally shocked. So, which one of you will pull the trigger? And will it happen here in your house? Careful, you don't hit an artery and make me spurt all over this pretty, white rug I'm standing on, Gail."

Col. Lee Martin

"I really did like you, Bruce, and hoped, as did Kurt, that you'd come in with us." She laid her hand on Albrecht's leg and smiled at him. "No, I wouldn't have gone to bed with you, although you're a hell of a great-looking guy. And if it was your design to get inside my underwear, sorry about that."

"You think highly of yourself, Gail…more than you should. Why would I want to go to bed with you? You aren't even a fraction as attractive as the woman I have at home."

Albrecht then laughed, and Gail came down hard on his thigh with the butt of her gun. "Not funny, Kurt."

"So, answer my question," I said. "Do you whack me here or take me somewhere out in the woods?"

Albrecht shrugged. "Well, as you're standing on Gail's pretty, white rug, would you mind moving off of it over by the wall? Gail would appreciate you not changing its color to red."

I moved a few steps to the right until my shoulder touched the wall. Then Albrecht raised his pistol. I noticed his grip wasn't too steady. He obviously wasn't used to handling a gun with his left hand.

"Goodbye, Scorpion. Sorry, it has to end this way."

But as not two feet away from me was the wall switch, I quickly flipped it off and dove to the floor. Whether it was the sudden night blindness or his unsteady hand, the first of his rounds sizzled over my head into the wall behind me. I then groped for the sofa chair and, finding its cushion, latched onto my

XDM. When he fired errantly once again, the flash from the gun's muzzle pinpointed where he was. That's when I aimed for it, firing twice. I heard him cry out in pain.

But then a spray of quickly fired rounds from Gail's gun began whizzing by me, fortunately not finding their target. Like a flash, I scampered toward the door and flung it open. Bounding onto the porch, I then jumped down onto the grass below and rolled out of sight behind a large hedge. A couple of seconds behind me, Gail was quickly on the porch, firing two more shots into the night, her rounds zipping harmlessly through the branches.

It was then that a single, almost silent, round spit from the open window of a Toyota Land Cruiser parked on the opposite side of the street. Gail arched violently and reeled off the porch onto the sidewalk. Cautiously, I stepped out from the hedge and went to where she lay, her bright red blood slowly pooling beneath her. Gail's body jerked for only a moment, and then she was still.

Simultaneously, several men began exiting the Land Cruiser. The shooter, an FBI sniper, exited first, followed by three more SWAT agents. A familiar face was among them. He approached me.

"Thanks, Rod. I was hoping you guys would show up."

But suddenly, I was surprised by a noise on the porch behind me. Albrecht, who had taken two non-fatal rounds from my XD, stumbled through the door and, with his left hand shaking uncontrollably, fired his gun errantly in my direction. Fortunately for me, his bullet whizzed harmlessly over my head. However, before anyone from the SWAT element engaged him, my XD still in my hand, I quickly fired a round into his chest, sending him tumbling off the porch and down the steps onto Gail's legs. Amazingly, as he lay without moving, even with my bullet buried in his chest near the heart, I saw that he was still breathing.

Rodney Chapin then stepped onto the sidewalk and stood over him. "So, this is Kurt Albrecht, eh Bruce?"

"What's left of him."

But Albrecht, the die-hard that he was, still wasn't through. Sucking in a labored breath and then coughing out a spittle of blood, he managed to say, "You…you bastard. I should ha…have killed you when…when I had you…at the camp."

I heaved a sigh and shook my head. "Yeah. You had your chance, Kurt. But I think you enjoyed playing the cat-and-mouse game too much. Bad judgment on your part, old man. But in case you're wondering why you are lying here, coughing up your last breath, as I was driving in, I contacted my friends in the Clarksburg FBI office and set all this up. Yeah, I knew you'd be waiting for me and maybe you'd take me down. But these guys would see to it that you would end up just like you are now…a dying cockroach lying on your back, wondering when the end will come. But I'm sure you realize, you're only seconds away. Better get right with God."

Looking down at Gail, her eyes closed in death and blood oozing from between her breasts, I saw that the FBI sniper had fired a pinpoint shot. The bullet appeared to have struck her dead-on in the heart. I felt badly about her but was glad her death came quickly. She didn't suffer.

Chapin asked me, "Was this the woman he was holding hostage? If so, why was she shooting at you?" "She wasn't a hostage after all, Rod. She was in the militia and was this prick's girlfriend all along. She played me…and I don't play easily. I hate that she had to die but I don't feel as bad as I would have if she were a genuine hostage."

I then turned and looked back down at Albrecht. My initial rounds fired blindly inside the house had caught him in the gut and kneecap. His eyes were now starting to glaze over. Death was imminent. Gasping desperately for air, however, he finally sucked in a last painful breath and then spit it out with a groan. A slight smile formed on his lips as he only managed a whisper… "See you in hell, McGowan." His head then fell back onto the concrete.

Chapter Thirty-Six

Yes, I did feel badly about Gail. Even though she turned out to be a co-conspirator. And yes, I was totally shocked that she was in with Albrecht all along and had pulled one over on me. But I had liked her...not in a carnal way; she had a sweet personality, fake as it was. The Kurt Albrecht case was over. The Constitutionalist militia was history. Washington, D.C., and its big cheeses had nothing more to worry about. All that I had left to do was go home and face the music about charging out of the house to go save another woman. Okay, Gail was dead and turned out to be a bad girl, but that wasn't the point. The point was, she was another woman, and although one might think it was all about risking my life for hers, it wasn't. I had to take that opportunity to face off with Albrecht.

As I was driving home, I received a call from Ben Marshall. He had already heard. "You, sir, are amazing. That's why you're still in such great demand. The director filled me in on Albrecht's death and his agents having to also kill his female accomplice. You get better with age, my friend, except where it involves assessing women. Anyway, I can just see you at ninety-five going after some bad dude, cane in one hand and Glock in the other."

"Oh, come on, Ben. When I'm ninety-five, I'll be sitting on my front porch worried about falling out of my rocker and breaking a hip."

"Well, anyway, you've always been the government's go-to guy. Once again, you put your body and your life on the line. And this time, you nailed America's most wanted criminal. I have just advised the President of Albrecht's demise, and he has authorized a bonus check of $50,000. Does this change your opinion of him?"

"Not in the least but tell him thanks for me. I will need that money to appease my wife, who's going to be mad as hell. I ran off to save another woman's life."

"I'd like to meet that wife of yours. Bring her up to Washington, D.C. sometime."

"For a nice, non-business, vacation-type visit, I will."

"Your country owes you a huge debt that can never be repaid in money or accolades. But hey, a piece of advice, my friend: don't take any more phone calls from people like me."

"I believe the lovely Adriana will henceforth be screening all my calls."

He laughed. "Have a great life, Bruce."

"Thank you, sir. You as well."

It was 10:10 on my dash clock when I arrived home that night. I sat for a moment behind the wheel before turning the ignition off to think about the words that were waiting for me inside. No, I wasn't afraid of my wife because, at other times, when I did something contrary to her wishes, she would chastise me calmly, have her say, and then it would be over. But the eyes, those beautiful eyes of hers, would bore into me like carpenter bees for hours beyond our squabble. The eyes might say, 'I'm still angry at you.' But after they had closed for the night and reopened the next morning, they smiled and danced, reassuring me that all was forgiven. I was wishing it was morning.

When I went inside, I saw that she was sitting on the couch in the den waiting for me, Lionel at her feet. I could generally read her mood by looking at her face, but that night, I couldn't. It revealed no anger or disappointment, nor did I see any other emotion that would cause me any angst. But as I stood there close to the door, where I could run, if necessary, she said softly, "Come sit down." She patted the cushion beside her. I wished she had instead said something else like, "I'm really, really pissed at you;" then I would know what I was in for. But I dug out my gun and holster from my waistband, laid them on the coffee table, and sat obediently beside her on the couch.

She didn't say anything for a moment, but then took from the end table a glass of Merlot and handed it to me. "Glad you're back home safely," she said softly.

No, no. This wasn't my wife, the woman I had shared a third of my life with. And now I really was afraid.

I then asked her, "Do I need to explain my evening to you?"

"Not at all. I already know everything."

"You do? How?"

"I had the TV on a while ago. A special news bulletin on Channel 4. The FBI released their film to the media, and the networks jumped all over it. I'm proud of you for two reasons: you're a hero, and you didn't come home with bullet holes in you."

I knew there was a camera guy in the van who came out as soon as the melee was over, but I didn't know Rod Chapin and the FBI would readily release the footage.

"I had to do it, sweetheart. It was my opportunity to take this guy down and rid us of any further madness he may have planned against me…against us. Yeah, okay, I could have gotten hurt or worse, but I thought Albrecht was going to kill Gail Delancy…"

"Who turned out to be in cahoots with him all along. That agent, Rodney something, told the entire story. You swooped in like a knight on a white charger to rescue her. The media's calling you a hero. And I am married to that hero."

"Are you being satirical or flattering?"

She leaned into me and kissed me on the lips. "I'm singing the praises of the man I love. I am proud of you."

"You are?"

She then smiled, grabbed hold of my ear lobe and twisted it. "But don't you ever, ever, ever do anything like that again."

****

Col. Lee Martin

Yet another mission for the government was in the books. It took a few weeks, but National Security Advisor Ben Marshall finally came through with my paycheck. However, I had to face it; the adventures of action man Bruce McGowan had come to an end. I now realized, after hearing it from my lovely wife, that I was too old, too beat up, and too married to answer the call any longer…any calls. I was done. What next…if anything?

Maybe I could spend my waning days doing something purposeful, like writing my memoirs, revisiting all the exciting missions I had completed as an FBI Special Agent, counterterrorist operative, and government contractor? And then I thought, who would want to read them? I was not anyone important, like a movie actor, a politician, or a popular singer. I was not someone whose name was easily on the lips of the average person. No one knew about the dauntless and daring missions I had accomplished, saving America's ass and that of the President himself. No one knew it was I who had snuffed out scores of terrorist factions before they put their plans into action, like Jamaat ul-Fuqura and the world's number one terrorist who had taken the place of Osama bin Laden. No one knew it was I who located weapons of mass destruction in Yemen before they landed in the hands of a madman. Even though I had accomplished enough missions to match the triumphant exploits of a hundred men, I had always been tight-lipped about it…actually, sworn to secrecy. Anyway, most of my clandestine government undertakings had been classified as Top Secret. For the most part, no more than three people knew what I was doing, and one of them would be the President himself. Furthermore, I've never been a glory hound seeking praise and admiration for my service to the American people, boasting of my exciting Action Man feats.

The Constitutionalists

For all the above reasons, any writing of memoirs was not going to happen. All the accounts of my work in the counterterrorist arena had been compiled and written down by me in unofficial after-action reports sent to no one. Even Adriana didn't know they existed. They're locked away in my safe. They will be for my eyes only. Maybe one day, when I start forgetting who I am, I'll get them out to read and marvel at who I was.

* * * * *

About a month and a half after Albrecht's takedown, however, I felt something was happening to me. Maybe it was the weather. Still cold and bleak, I started losing my desire to go on morning runs, preferring instead to piddle around the house even though that certainly wasn't providing any real activity. As most days, I found myself listless, restless, and falling asleep in my recliner in front of the TV, watching the Hallmark Channel with Adriana; I felt myself spiraling into what my brain told me was apathetic complacency. I knew it was happening; I just didn't want to admit it. Adriana let it go for a few weeks, but then, one day, as I was finishing up a half-dozen pancakes that were drowning in syrup, I found her just staring at me across the breakfast table.

"Okay, Skip. What's going on?"

I looked back at her, swallowed a bite, and took a sip of my coffee. "I don't know what you mean?" I did of course.

"Go check yourself out in the mirror. Your eyes have bags under them, mainly because you're only getting two to three hours of sleep. You haven't shaved in two days. You don't talk much anymore, and I don't see that lively little twinkle in your eye. And...we haven't been intimate in a week. I'm not looking at the man I married."

"Well, thank you very much, dear wife," I replied sarcastically. "Then who the hell am I?" Actually, I was hoping she'd tell me.

"I'm sorry, Skip. I didn't mean to be denigrating, but frankly, you've turned into a human sloth."

I laid my fork down and gave her a laser-like stare. The comment wasn't like her. "I see." I then scooted my chair back from the table and said, "Excuse me."

As I began walking from the dining room, she called after me. "Skip, I..."

"Save it. If you've nothing nice to say to me this morning, don't say anything." With that, I went to the den, plopped in my recliner, and turned on the morning news. I then began thinking over what she said. Although she probably regretted her choice of words, I closed my eyes, kicked off my slippers, propped my bare feet up to eye level, and started thinking about just who the hell I was now. Big breakfast, retiring to my recliner to watch TV...maybe I had become a sloth...a ten toed sloth.

She didn't immediately go in to rescue me. She wasn't the rescuing type. I think she wanted to let me stew and think for a while; then, she'd come to have a calm and rational conversation about the aloof, indifferent man who lived in her house.

The Constitutionalists

We had had a few testy moments in our marriage. As always, it was about my taking off at every beck and call at the request of someone high up in the government, more recently National Security Advisers and further back, the Birdman, Lionel Byrd himself. It always involved danger and located in some place where I would be away from home for days and weeks. The time I was sent back to Vietnam to investigate the American military massacre of a village, the company commander became a presidential candidate. I was gone for more than two weeks. Probably fifty percent of the time I would return from missions beat up and even shot up. I had enough holes in me to begin whistling in a windstorm. But all of those times, I considered Adriana and her wishes for me to be out of the business. I actually respected and valued how she felt each time I left the house. She would worry and cry thinking there was a chance I may not return. Although she rarely knew what I was doing, she knew that somehow, I would be in danger.

After about five minutes, she did come to the den and took a seat opposite me on the couch, pulling her legs and feet up under her. I glanced at her, but obviously, it was my stupid pride that wouldn't allow me to open up a dialogue. Like most guys having just had a tiff, I waited for her to say something.

"Are you going to talk to me this morning?" she asked.

"Haven't we been talking?" I replied.

"Not with the kind of words and tone of voice we normally use. Can we talk about you and what's been going on with you the past month?"

"Okay. What's going on with me?" A loaded question if I ever asked one.

"You've just been moping around in a fog, mostly like you don't care about anything. You've always been motivated and energetic about something. Smiling, lively, flirtatious, the latter thing I miss the most. What is it, Skip? When am I going to get my husband back? I believe you're…"

"What? What am I?"

She paused a moment. "Depressed. You have all the symptoms."

"Now you're a psychologist?"

"That's not fair. I just know enough about the subject to recognize there is some clinical issue involved here. And I'm pretty sure what the catalyst is?"

"I'm all ears."

"You can't stand yourself when you're not involved in some kind of government mission…chasing down bad guys, doing covert stuff, anything that has the element of danger to it." I didn't immediately respond. How could I argue with the truth? I knew I missed it all. Even though I told myself every day the same thing she was telling me, I didn't dare admit it to her. It was that pride thing again. I think I also didn't want her to think about my life with her as her husband no longer contained any excitement. It did, of course, a different kind of excitement. My problem was self-worth. My life, to this point, been filled with purpose and contribution. But that didn't mean I didn't find purpose in our marriage. We had been happy together these 20 years. I couldn't imagine life without her. Why couldn't I get that through my thick head? This self-pity thing had really kicked me in the gut. The fact that I was no longer the 'man on a mission' I used to be was causing this depression thing she was talking about to fester in me like cancer. I almost wished she would have come over and slapped it out of me.

And then she said, "I prayed for you last night, Skip. I prayed that somehow, some way, your vigor, and happiness would be restored, that something would happen to restore within you that sense of worth you need. I don't mean something that involves going back into the contract business working cases for the government. You're approaching your seventh generation of life. You're at least in the October of your years. I know you realize that. But I want you to also know I'm praying for you."

I heard her, heard her to the point that, almost miraculously, it seemed that the anvil that had been crushing my chest had been lifted. My wife had humbled herself to me and to God to pray for me. To her, it was that serious. Tears were now glistening on her cheeks.

I then lifted myself from the recliner and walked to where she was sitting. While on my knees, I placed my arms around her waist and laid my scruffy face onto hers. "I can't tell you how sorry I am, sweetheart. I don't deserve you. I actually haven't deserved you all these years. Yes, I've been wallowing in self-pity and realize it's time for me to straighten my ass up. Forgive me, Adriana. And help me be a better me."

She began sobbing. "I will. You know I will."

I then stood, looked down at her, and smiled. "I think I'll go knock these whiskers off."

She dabbed at her eyes. "Good idea,"

Chapter Thirty-Seven

———•◇◇•———

The next morning, after lying in our bed longer than I normally did, I rose with a new resolve. Be the old me. Get back on the running trail, generate a new attitude, find something to monopolize my time…like cleaning out the storage shed, changing the oil in the Suburban and taking the lovely Adriana to lunch at that new French restaurant in town. And I did all those things. Now, what would I do in the afternoon? Whatever it was, I told myself, do it with snap and zip. And don't worry; be happy. I was determined not to fall back into that pit of funk. Depression was not my friend.

While I was pulling some weeds that had popped up around the early crocus and daffodils that had pushed through the soil on that fine sixty-degree afternoon, Adriana called from the veranda that I had a phone call on my cell. When I bounded up the steps, she had that look on her face. It wasn't as pained a look as she normally gave me when a 202 area code appeared on the phone's face, but it was close. She held the phone out to me. "It's your friend Ben Marshall." That's all she said. No repugnance, no lecture.

I took the phone. "No, no, and did I not make it clear…no?"

He laughed. "Hello, Bruce. Ms. Adriana was quite nice. Seemed happy to hear my voice."

"No, she wasn't. I'm sure in hearing your voice a shot of adrenaline shot through her arteries. I hope this is a 'hi, how ya doing' phone call. Like I'm sending you more money for the Clarksburg job."

"Ha, you wish. No, it's not another contract, Bruce. But something you might be interested in."

"I can't imagine."

"I was talking to the Vice President yesterday. You know, the guy who could be the next President?"

"Collins."

"He wants to talk with you. It will entail you and Adriana coming to Washington to meet with him."

"Uh huh. Sounds like another hotbed of a mission somewhere. I'm sure the word has gotten around that she will be putting the squelch on any more missions."

"Nothing like that, Bruce. No more missions for you, old boy."

"Then what on earth would he be talking about?"

"Something that both of you would be making a decision about."

"Alright, don't keep me in suspense."

The Constitutionalists

"Remember two presidents ago, you were offered the job as Director of CTT?"

"Okay. I didn't know anyone else knew about that. The Prez must have squealed."

"Vice President Collins wants to re-offer you the job...or something similar to the former job The State Department's counterterrorist headquarters will now be in Washington, D.C. The government would put you and Adriana up in a nice little apartment somewhere in the city, and you would direct a Zulu-type operation from there. Dream job, Bruce."

"As flattered as I am, I can't imagine Adriana will be on board with this...for a dozen reasons. By the way, how do you know about our old unit? This was a totally clandestine group that only three or so people in the upper echelon of government knew about."

"I was briefed in on the Zulu element about four years ago. The former President, the Vice President, and I, as the National Security Advisor, are the only ones still in the know. Not even the Secretary of State knows what the group was all about. Or that it even existed. He only knows that there was a covert element somewhere in the State Department that was profiling suspected subversives. When you guys hunted and took down terrorist elements, he thinks agencies of the justice department accomplished it. Each president up to this one wanted to keep it that way. But as you have been used to the old CTT, it's all about to change. The man who carved out plans for the revised unit is the Vice President."

"The VP, huh; does the dude in the White House not have a hand in this?"

"He does not. Again, the Chief MFIC on this is Collins, not the President. I won't go into the reasons why."

"I think I know the reasons, Ben. But I know you can't comment."

"Just let me set you and Adriana up with a meeting with Vice President Collins. You work on Adriana."

"That is if I decide to meet with him."

"Just do the meeting, Bruce. Hear what he has to say. This organization needs a guy like you. No, actually, it needs *you.*"

"Thanks for the call, Ben. Will get back to you tomorrow."

When I hit END on my phone, Adriana came alongside me. "Okay, where does he want you to go this time?"

"Sit down, my dear. It's not what you think. There's no assignment. He just wanted to talk."

"Uh huh. I think you're about to tell me you're breaking our agreement about you taking on assignments. What did he want?"

She sat down on the divan, and I sat beside her.

The Constitutionalists

"To tell me the Vice President has asked about me."

"To go on some kind of mission for him, I presume."

"Again, not a mission. He wants me to take a position in Washington, D.C."

She sighed. "A position? Of course, you can't do that."

"Unless you come to Washington, D.C. with me."

"I'm not understanding."

"He wants me to take over a covert counterterrorist team."

"The job you turned down years ago."

"Yes. But it's primarily a desk job managing the operation. No missions. No danger."

"Except that's what Mr. Byrd was doing when he was killed along with everyone else on your team. He was behind a desk."

"That was because one of our own betrayed us."

"Are you really thinking of doing this, Skip?"

"I don't know. Part of me says it will give me that sense of purpose I've been needing, but then again, I know I have to consider you. It would mean closing up Wolf Laurel for a time, although we could come home on weekends. And then you'd have to quit being the mayor of our fine town."

"My term as Mayor is up in two months and as you know, I'm not seeking re-election. Four years is enough."

"So, by that, you're saying you're not against me taking the position."

"This is so sudden, Skip. I don't think we can make a decision this soon after you getting this phone call."

"You're correct, my dear. We not only have to think hard about it, but we also have to think long."

"When does Ben plan to set up your interview with the VP?"

"I just told him I'd first need to talk with you and then let him know tomorrow if I'll speak to the Vice president about it…not that I would take the job."

She nodded. "Let's talk about this more after dinner. I can't think on an empty stomach."

"The way you eat…or don't eat…you always have an empty stomach."

"Let's just forego the Hallmark Channel tonight and take a look at all the pros and cons."

"I'm with you on that." *Anytime I can avoid slipping a Hallmark coma, it's a good night.*

The Constitutionalists

What was preying on my mind at the dinner table, however, was the fact that Adriana had not said no. Considering the emotional pit I had allowed myself to fall into, perhaps she was just temporarily trying to appease me. Give me just enough latitude to bring me out of my fog. But she wouldn't do that. She wouldn't play with my feelings. She wouldn't allow me to think I could take the position and then, when I had built myself up, pull the rug out from under me. But that which was stirring my emotions was…people were still valuing Bruce McGowan, especially the vice president who had gone from CIA Director to his current office. Maybe just the offer itself was enough…enough to give me that shot in the arm I needed.

I let most of the next morning go by before I called Ben back. I needed the time to digest what Adriana and I had decided the night before. Had we made the right decision? I dialed Ben's number on my cell. Surprisingly, he picked up immediately. Things must have been slow in Washington, D.C..

"Good morning, Bruce. I didn't know if I'd hear back from you."

"And yet, here I am."

"Your decision?"

"Thank the VP for me, but after conferring with Adriana, I decided…we decided not to go meet with him. When I retired years ago, I was content with accepting a few contractor jobs here and there to satisfy my yearning for a little action. It kept the blood flowing in my arteries. Maybe I've now gotten too used to being Adriana McGowan's full-time husband. That role is enough in itself to keep my motor running. There are younger people out there more up to date on counterterrorism than me. I'd have to be re-indoctrinated big time, and I'm not sure I have enough brain power to soak it all in anymore."

"Nonsense, Bruce. You have the kind of skills, abilities, and wisdom that a Johnny-come-lately in the business would take years to cultivate. The VP needs somebody in this position that can hit the ground running and never miss a beat."

"Yeah okay. Tell me a little more about Bart Collins. I know he came up through the CIA ranks to become the director and that he was a friend and cohort of my former boss, Lionel Byrd. It's all I remember about him."

"A genuine patriot, Bruce…someone who sees how our country has gotten off track and left itself dangerously exposed to international terrorism on many fronts."

"Mainly because of his boss's inability or lack of desire to keep this nation strong. I'm not a political guy, but he has done more to weaken the infrastructure of our country than any president before him, and I don't mean roads and bridges."

"You know I can't comment on that, Bruce. Just know that the VP is the kind of fierce warrior for truth and justice like we used to have."

"Don't forget 'the American way.'"

"You mean what was at one time 'the American way.'"

"I hear you, Ben. Again, tell the VP I appreciate his confidence in me, but I'll have to pass."

"Alright, Bruce, but don't be surprised if he calls you personally about this."

"He knows my number?"

"He knows everything about you."

I chuckled. "Sounds like my old prefector, Lionel. Of course, as you told me, he and Lionel Byrd were friends and collaborators." I then paused. "Sorry. Not taking the position, Ben."

"Okay, but the VP will not be happy. If you change your mind, call me."

"Yeah, So long, Ben."

Col. Lee Martin

Chapter Thirty-Eight

I didn't hear any more from Ben after that and assumed the VP had given up on trying to recruit me for the director job at CTT or whatever it was now called. As I didn't know anyone any longer on the current State Department team, I didn't know if it did have a new name. As I understood it, the entire counterterrorist division had been overhauled. Moreover, there were enough new sub-elements in the State Department I had no idea what now came under that umbrella.

A week after my conversation with Ben Marshall, I threw my clubs into the Suburban and set out for the cow pasture we call the local golf course. It had been months since I played golf, mainly because the temperature had not elevated above 40 degrees all winter. But it was now the last of March and fickle Greenbrier County can reach temps into the mid to upper 50s on any given day. For me, a light golf jacket would be all I needed at that temperature. Of course, a couple of my golf buddies might be bundled up like the Michelin Man. Today, the high was to be 55.

This was the day, March 31, that we kicked off our golf season with our annual March Madness tournament. The names of the participants and teams were even listed a few days before the tournament in the Mountain Messenger. Our team was made up of Deputy Bobby Jaworski, who could consistently hit a drive over 300 yards; Methodist Pastor Grant Shuster, who ⁱ ᵒn a wing and a prayer; mortician Joey McGowan, who d somewhere in the mid-80s, and his brother

The Constitutionalists

Bruce who was a fairly decent golfer himself. Well-publicized, the tournament brought in a solid sixteen teams from as far north as Marlinton and east Lexington, Virginia. But at $100 a pop, it was all for charity.

My team came in at 3rd, but I had accomplished something I had never done before. No, not a hole-in-one. However, I won a nice golf shirt and sleeve of balls for being closest to the pin. After a barbecue lunch and digesting a few words from Pastor Shuster about the kids whose medical maladies we were financially supporting, I traded fist bumps with my brother, Joey, and headed for the parking lot. He stayed a while longer for the cake and ice cream. I didn't, as I was turning over a new leaf…no sweets, junk food, or depression episodes.

I was just a dozen steps from my vehicle when two cars pulled up beside me. One was a black Charger, which appeared to have both red and blue lights, except not flashing, and a Lincoln SUV limo. Immediately, two men dressed in black suits stepped out of the Charger and were upon me before I took another step.

"What the hell?" I exclaimed. The only weapons I was packing were my golf clubs as I hadn't seen any need to shoot anyone out on the links.

A tall, beefy guy with a skin head and wearing sunglasses quickly approached me. "Mr. McGowan?"

"Yes. How do you know me?"

"I don't, but the gentleman in the limo does."

"I was immediately wondering who that could be. Obviously, an important dude."

The skinhead cleared it up for me. "Please step over to the SUV. Vice President Collins would like to speak with you."

And so, I knew what it was about. When Mohammed did not go to the mountain, the mountain came to me. But how did he know where I'd be?

The second Secret Service agent also approached me and began performing a body frisk. I said, "Got only weapons of self-destruction, and they're in the bag."

He smiled and nodded. "We must have the same weapons. Let's go to the car, sir." He then opened the driver's side rear door, and a voice from within said, "Come on in and have a seat, Bruce."

I recognized VP Collins immediately. Although I had not personally met him, his face had been all over the TV. "Mr. Vice President," I greeted. He held out his hand, and I shook it.

"Well, my friend. You wouldn't agree to come to Washington to talk, so you made me come here."

"And how did you know I'd be here, sir?"

'Contrary to popular believe, I can actually read. I read every newspaper every day...even your tiny Mountain Messenger. How did you shoot out there?"

"Not bad. An eighty-one."

The Constitutionalists

"Good. I'd give my right you know what for an eighty-one." He then took on a serious look.

"Bill," he addressed his driver, "would you mind stepping out for a few minutes?"

"Right, sir." He then opened the door and closed it behind him.

"Okay, my friend, let's get it on." The VP appeared to be about my size and age, looking a little older than he did on TV. His hair was silver, and his eyes were fierce. "I've thought long and hard as to who I want in the director job. Mr. Byrd and I spoke about you often, and I've read your history." He offered up a wry smile. "Yes, I know about most of the missions you and the Zulu team performed. Lionel didn't have a loose tongue, but he confided in me often. I know you have a lot of him in you."

I didn't respond. I just sat and listened.

"Is it possible that we can go to your residence at Wolf Laurel? I'd also like to meet your wife. Adriana, isn't it?"

"Yes. Appears you know quite a bit about the both of us. You've obviously done your homework. But, fine. I'll call her and tell her we're on the way. It would be too much of a surprise to come home with the Vice President."

"My wife doesn't like unexpected guests, either. Yes. Please do so. We can follow you."

Col. Lee Martin

I walked back to my car and after tossing the clubs into the rear compartment, I slid onto the driver's seat and took a deep breath. After touching the 1 digit on my cell and hearing the usual three rings, she picked up. "Hi, Babe."

"Hey, sweetheart, do you have anything planned this afternoon?"

"I don't guess so; why?"

"We're going to have a visitor."

"Okay. Who are you bringing home?"

"Remember the talk we had last week? You know…about the Washington position?"

"Of course."

"The Vice President was waiting for me at the golf course when I finished the match today."

"Tell me this is one of your practical jokes."

"I wouldn't make something like this up. Can you put on some coffee and pull out those peach crumb bars you made yesterday?"

I heard her groan. "Bruce McGowan, how could you? How could you bring the vice president into our house?"

"It was his idea. He wants to meet you."

"But I haven't cleaned and dusted the place. I…"

"Our house is never dirty, my dear. Just suck it up and get ready. We'll be there in fifteen minutes. It's no big deal. Remember, we entertained the President here a few years ago."

"Yes, and I remember his own agents were out to kill him. Our house got all shot up, and people died here."

"Not to worry. That won't happen today. I received good vibes from these Secret Service agents. Just ready yourself, sweetheart. Be there soon." I didn't give her a chance to continue protesting and hit END on my cell.

Upon leaving the country club I began leading the two black cars along 219, down Seven Bridges Road then a few hundred feet later pulled into our driveway. Adriana was waiting for us on the veranda, arms folded and smiling. That's my girl. She would deal with me later.

Vice President Collins immediately stepped out of the limo and bounded up the steps to greet her.

"Ah, what a lovely lady," he said, taking her hand and kissing it like the Frenchies do. "I'm Bart Collins. It is a pleasure to make your acquaintance."

"Adriana McGowan at your service, Mr. Vice President."

"You are so accommodating receiving me like this, considering I dropped in on you unannounced."

Col. Lee Martin

"Pleased to make your acquaintance, sir. Won't you come in?"

He smiled and nodded. I assumed I was welcome too, so I followed. The three Secret Service agents didn't follow but took their positions on the veranda, the back yard and as a rover.

"Please sit," Adriana said, gesturing her hand toward the couch in the den. "May I get you some coffee or maybe a soft drink or water?"

"Water would be fine, Mrs. McGowan."

"Please call me Adriana, sir."

"I will, and I prefer Bart."

"Oh, I can't do that, Mr. Vice President," she replied.

I chuckled under my breath. Can I call you Bart as well? I didn't say that of course.

Adriana added, "I'll get the water for you, sir. It's good ol' West Virginia mountain spring water. I hope you'll like my Peach Crumb bars. An old family recipe."

"Sounds delicious, my dear. On second thought, I believe I will have some coffee. It'll go better with the dessert bars."

"Coming right up," she replied.

When she departed for the kitchen, Collins opened up our dialogue. "You know, Bruce, I was genuinely impressed with you taking down that militia group and its kingpin a few weeks back. Tells me you still have it in you. This Albrecht fellow was a member of your CTT element, I believe."

"Yes, sir. At one time, he was one of the best we had; unfortunately, when he was let go, he went rogue. I'm convinced he was a patriot and had the soul and spirit of this country at heart. But he became anti-government and had plans to commit sabotage by blowing up the electronics and communications infrastructure there in Washington."

"Yes. The NSA provided a briefing about that to the executive office and the Justice Department. It could have been catastrophic. But I'm looking at the man who risked life and limb to stop it. That's why I need you to run a revised covert counterterrorist unit."

"How is it revised?"

"It's no longer called CTT. Officially, it's just CT, Counterterrorism and Countering Violent Extremism. On paper CT, which is under the State Department, is no longer covert. The revised State Department CT contains sub-units like Arms and International Security that come under the same umbrella along with Asian, European and Middle East Affairs. Nobody but you, the National Security Advisor and I will be privy that your element exists. The unit will be named Terminus. Either I or the NSA will ask you to employ personnel to perform Top Secret missions that will provide for dire consequences as to terrorist individuals or elements. Countries fostering terrorism, such as Syria, Iran, Yemen, and the like, will be fair game. Missions will be swift and punishing. No one, not even the CIA, FBI International, or the State Department's CT section,hg will know what the hell happened."

At that moment Adriana came back into the room with coffee and dessert bars. Collins rose and waited until she set the refreshments onto the coffee table. As she knew we were involved in serious dialogue, she excused herself graciously.

"It all sounds intriguing, Mr. Vice President, but you left POTUS and the Secretary of State out of the equation."

"I can't go into why, Bruce, but they are not in the equation. The Terminus aspect of this unit will only be executed covertly. I cannot discuss with you the political ramifications of the matter which most certainly come into play."

"It all sounds like what we have historically done in CTT with the exception of the bifurcation."

"Yes, very similar."

"Sir, aren't you taking a risk with me knowing of this Terminus when I told you I'm not taking the position?"

He glared at me sternly. "You wouldn't do anything with that knowledge, Bruce. I think I know you. Anyway, I'd hate for you to disappear."

"I beg your pardon, sir?"

The Constitutionalists

A grin broke out on his face. "Just messing with you, Bruce. I'm not worried about you for two reasons: first as to the Terminus aspect, you operated covertly for eight years under Lionel Byrd doing the same kind of thing. Secondly, you're going to take this job."

I glared back at him and didn't say a word for a few moments. Then, "Here's the thing. I have a really, really good marriage, Mr. Vice President. You can't imagine how great. As much as this opportunity intrigues me, my wife would have to be totally on board. Although when we talked about this last week, she didn't say no, I'm not sure how she really feels about closing this place up and moving to D.C."

"Do you mind if I speak to her about it?"

I thought the whole scenario was not only strange but hilarious. Who would have believed the Vice President of the United States had traveled four-and-a-half hours down to our house to beg my wife for me to take a job? "I don't mind at all, sir. Just don't get your expectations up."

I called to her in the kitchen. "Sweetheart, can you come here?"

"Of course. Be there in a moment." I then heard the rattling of dishes in the kitchen followed by her footsteps in the hallway on her way to the den. "Do you need more coffee?"

"No, dear lady," replied Collins. "I thought it important to speak with you. Please have a seat."

She obediently sat down in one of our sofa chairs and laid her hands in her lap. "How can I help you, sir."

"You're the town's mayor, aren't you, Adriana."

"Yes, for the time being. How did you know that?"

"I have to admit, I've done a good study on the both of you."

"The Vice President taking time to check up on me? I'm not sure if I'm supposed to feel flattered or frightened," she said.

"Oh, it's all good…I assure you, my dear."

"It's about the position you offered my husband, I assume."

He nodded. "Apparently you're not terribly enamored with the idea."

"Not terribly."

"Please allow me to tell you about what I propose. I already laid it out for Bruce. He will take over a section that falls under the State Department. It would be similar to the position Mr. Byrd had…pretty much an office job. He'll supervise a counterterrorist team. After gathering all the intel on alleged terrorist elements posing threats to the United States, he will dispatch individuals or teams to investigate and eradicate the terrorist threat. Adriana, your husband has the background and experience we need to lead this section. Admittedly, our national security has floundered lately, and Bruce is just the person to help us restore it."

"A question, Mr. Vice President."

He held up one finger. "Bart."

"Bart. Why is it that someone who is but a heartbeat from the Presidency is recruiting someone for this position? Why not the Secretary of State or one of his undersecretaries? Forgive me, but I'm just not sure how and why you're involved at your level."

Collins looked over at me then back to Adriana. "Well, well, Bruce. You are married to a very insightful lady. That is a good question. My dear, this organization I would consider to be one of the most important within the government. The security of the United States is always at stake. I was recently the Director of the CIA. You may have known that. I guess even though I am the VP, the fervency and zeal that came with the director job has never left me. Yes, okay, I still want to have my fingers in the pie. And I want to see people like Bruce occupying this very important desk. Excuse me…not like Bruce…Bruce himself."

"So, you want Bruce and me to ditch our retirement life, then pick up and move to Washington for him to take a position that a hundred other people could do."

"But not as well as Bruce could do it."

"And what kind of salary are you talking about, not to mention perks?"

He laughed. "You do get to the point, Adriana. I'm impressed. Maybe you could hire on in some government capacity yourself, Madam Mayor."

"No. I'm perfectly content with being Mr. McGowan's wife, wherever we live."

Collins leaned forward. "Did I detect in your response you could be amenable to living in that very nice condo in Georgetown at the government's expense?"

"Maybe, but that would be for Bruce to decide. I will be good with whatever he says."

Collins then looked at me for my answer.

"Can I have a moment in private with Adriana, Mr. Vice President?"

"Of course. I need to see what my agents are up to anyway." He then stood and walked from the room to the veranda.

I looked over at her and she shrugged. "You surprised me," I said. "I thought we had this settled. Do you want me to take the offer?"

"Skip, you've been moping around this place for weeks, and I've been worried about you. When the position was first offered, I saw something in your eyes I hadn't seen in quite a while. Eyes filled with hope and even euphoria. This is what you've needed. And as long as there is an assurance from Mr. Collins and whoever will be your boss that you will not personally take on missions, placing yourself in the kind of that always brought you home to me fed up, beat up and

The Constitutionalists

shot up, I will go to Washington with you. Now you go out there and tell him your decision."

I nodded. "Maybe we can make this work." I then kissed her.

When I opened the door to the veranda, Collins turned around, held out his hands and said, "And?"

"My sweet wife mentioned salary and perks to you, Mr. Vice President. May we talk?"

Col. Lee Martin

The McGowan Collection Series by Col. Lee Martin

Col. Lee Martin suggests you read them in this order:

> Wolf Laurel
> Provocation: Return of the Weatherman
> A Hateful Wind
> The Justice Club - (intro to a new character)
> Killing the Viper
> Saving Eagle One
> Blood Protocol-Avenging the Viper
> Red Kings Rising
> Sting of the Scorpion
> A Lure to a Kill

And these other Murder, Mystery Thrillers by Col. Lee Martin

> The Third Moon is Blue
> The Six Mile Inn
> Starbright
> The Valiant
> Ten Minutes till Midnight
> **Southern Psalms**
> **Palisades**
> Panther's Breath
> The Justice Club
> At the Devil's Tea Table
> Retrogame

Praises for Books in the McGowan Collection Series:

Wolf Laurel

The main character in this novel, Bruce McGowan, is truly a "John Wayne meets Clint Eastwood" cowboy. I love this character! This is a great read for anyone who enjoys reading about patriotic heroes, intrigue, espionage and covert action. Lee Martin is a true master of fantastic story telling and "suspension of disbelief". In fact, I would not doubt that some of the features in this tale hold quite a bit of truth. I could not put this book down and I have read all of the sequels since.

-JCL-

Lee Martin introduces us to Bruce McGowan in this first of three wonderfully intriguing books with McGowan as the protagonist. Once you meet McGowan, you won't stop reading until you've finished the third book (A Hateful Wind) and beg for a sequel!

-Andy Black, VA Beach P.D. (Ret)

Provocation: Return of the Weatherman

A good follow up to Wolf Laurel. I gave five stars because the story and characters were great.

-Kindle Reader, Anonymous-

Col. Lee Martin

A Hateful Wind

I love it! Always another twist coming up. Really excited to be meeting Lee Martin at a book signing in 11/5 in Eatonton, Ga.

-MUFTR-

I was thrilled to see a third novel in the Bruce McGowan series from Lee Martin. Andrew Black's review is spot on regarding the great imagery, accurate descriptions, and how Martin hooks you into the story and characters right away. I truly felt like I experienced post war Vietnam in this one. McGowan will always be my favorite fearless patriotic hero. This novel is full of action, intrigue, and suspense; A definite must read!

-J. Laurie-

Killing the Viper

I have read many of Lee Martin's novels. All have been great reads that never disappoint. Having known Lee Martin personally, I think I can see how some people believe Bruce McGowan is his alter ego. Having read "The Justice Club" before I started the "Wolf Laurel" series was by pure luck but a real treat. This was another great adventure in the life of Bruce Gowan and it was masterful the way he brought in a ˚er from a book he had written outside this series. I have

The Constitutionalists

already started the next book, "Saving Eagle One" and have the following book sitting here waiting. Thanks, Lee, for sharing your talent with me. I'm sure I am not the only one that feels this way. Looking forward to many more books from you. WELCOME HOME BROTHER

-Ernie F.-

Saving Eagle One

One of the better books I have read in a long time. Can't wait for Lee Martin's next installment of this trilogy.

-Rex A. Davis-

Sting of the Scorpion

A fast-paced action thriller with a twist. Great book, great series. Lee Martin's latest in his series with Protagonist, Bruce McGowan, leads you into the dark world of ISIS from the newly retired McGowan's home in West Virginia and by way of Scotland. Danger and action have a way of finding the former operative and in true McGowan form, he responds with his uncanny lack of tack, sarcastic wit and deadly combat skills to not only find the bad guys, but also make sure they pay for their crimes. It's a page-turner so saddle up.

-Cherie Heringer-

Col. Lee Martin

McGowan! He's the man! The one you want beside you when you're in trouble, the someone you want as a friend. I was introduced to Bruce McGowan in one of Lee Martin's early novels, "Wolf Laurel". Since then I have followed his exploits through Lee's later novels in the series. Lee is a great storyteller. His latest novel, "Sting of the Scorpion", follows Bruce as he weaves and twists his way through the plot line keeping the reader on his toes and wondering what is coming next. Lee's extensive research adds layers of atmosphere, drawing the reader into the story. This is a great book that takes you on a voyage through different countries and ends in an unexpected climax. I'm looking forward to the next McGowan adventure!

-Joe Romagnoli

Thank God and Bruce McGowan for making the United States and the world a safer place. Lee Martin's books never disappoint. I have read them all and enjoyed them all. Mr Martin is a very descriptive writer whose characters are well developed and believable. As a retired FBI agent I particularly enjoyed all the books in the Wolf Laurel series which feature as the protagonist a retired FBI agent and counterterrorism operative named Bruce McGowan. "The Sting of the Scorpion" was the last of the series thus far and as always was well researched, believable and very exciting. COL Lee Martin is a writer who is in the league of David Baldacci , Harland Cohen, and Lee Child.

-David M. Parker-

A Lure to a Kill

Excellent author. We really enjoy this author's work. Highly recommend starting at the beginning of his work and reading books from start to current.

-Eugene Hoover-

The McGowan Collection Series

Website: https://colonelleemartinbooks.com

Made in the USA
Columbia, SC
26 July 2025